Outworld Apocalypse

Dawn's End Book 3

Bonnie Ferrante

Outworld Apocolypse (Book 3 of Dawn's End)

ISBN 978-0-9921037-2-9

Other Books by Bonnie Ferrante

Nightfall - Dawn's End Book 1

Poisoned - Dawn's End Book 2

Desiccate

Bouquet (short stories)

Inhale (short stories)

Terror at White Otter Castle (novella)

Dedication

For Elvin, in memory

Chapter One - Inheritance

"Durward! Durward, come here!" Bedad shouted from the laboratory. He brushed his long curls, limp with steam, out of his eyes. "I've got it! I couldn't have done it without your last input."

Durward entered the room and rubbed his long, narrow nose. His golden hair was a mass of unruly half-curls and tangles. He always looked as though he had just crawled out of bed.

Bedad's spotlessly clean laboratory smelled of ammonia, sulfur dioxide, lemongrass, and lilyvern root. Magic bristled in the air. The room had no glass windows, only slotted openings for fresh air. On the counter, along one wall, rested a jumble of small coal-burning heaters, animal horns, vials, spoons, metal scales, tongs, gauze, knives, wooden containers, crystals of various colors, dishes, and silver stirrers. A long, wooden table, covered with flasks, beakers, and tubes holding various substances, sat in the center of the room.

"Look!" Bedad held up a vial containing green liquid with a trembling hand. "Now all we have to do is deliver it."

Bedad carefully placed the tube in a stand and offered his fist to Durward. Awkwardly, Durward bumped the fist with his own. This strange ritual was one of the ways Bedad felt connected to Anastacia the Bold from the Outworld. It was she who had taught Bedad the significance of the gesture.

Once the people of Dawn's End learned that Anastacia's mother, Nicole, had died, possibly as a result of spending time in their world, they became concerned for Anastacia's future. Durward, one of the companions who helped Anastacia save Dawn's End from destruction, immediately began searching for an antidote for the cell mutations that consuming food, water, or air in Dawn's End could trigger in Outworlders. Fortunately, time flowed faster in Dawn's End than in the Outworld, making it more likely Durward could complete his research for a cure before Anastacia fell ill.

When he became Durward's apprentice, Bedad made it his foremost life goal to help create a potion that would protect Anastacia from an early demise. She had not only saved his world, but she had risked her life to come to his individual aid. Her ready wit, warm personality, and quiet courage had left him awestruck. He would consider it his greatest life achievement if he could ensure her good health. He absorbed everything Durward taught him. Before long, the student had surpassed his teachers in skill.

Bedad ran his hand through his curls. "I'm so glad you were here when I finally completed it. Now, we just have to get it to her."

Durward scratched behind his ear, creating yet another blond cowlick.

"I know the perfect person to bring it to Anastacia" — he pointed at Bedad — "You."

"Me?" Bedad grinned as he scratched his scruffy facial hair.

Durward gestured toward the shelves of drying plants, bottles, and boxes. "Of course you should go. You've been going back and forth to the Outworld for years, collecting samples. You're more familiar with the Outworld than any of us."

"Yes, but . . . ."

Durward lifted his eyebrows. "I know you want to see Anastacia."

Bedad feigned interest in a bit of powder on the counter and didn't answer.

"Besides, your triple-crystal bracelet holds power three times longer than mine. It may take you a while to find her."

Dawn's End could only be reached by magic through invisible portals that faded and strengthened according to their own patterns. Opening a portal was difficult and exhausting, and one could accomplish the task only by using a crystal-powered panther bracelet.

Several such bracelets existed, each possessing almost limitless power in the magical world of Dawn's End. But, once the bracelets entered the Outworld, their power drained quickly. The longer the wearer spent in the Outworld, the more power drained from the bracelet. Eventually, a fully-powered, golden panther bracelet would turn copper-colored and become useless.

In most circumstances, once the bracelet's power had drained completely, the wearer would be unable to open a portal to return to Dawn's End. Since many of Dawn's End's sentient inhabitants were not human and could not blend into Outworld society, becoming trapped on the wrong side of the door posed an enormous risk. Even for humans like Bedad, the prospect of getting stuck in the Outworld was frightening. But Bedad was willing to take any risk to help Anastacia.

"I didn't want to see her before I completed the potion," Bedad said. "I couldn't look into her eyes knowing what she sacrificed for me."

Bedad bit his lip, remembering the cave, the boiling caldron, the screams, the blood—and Anastacia, steadfast and bold, refusing to surrender.

Durward corrected him. "For all of us."

"I was too ashamed to face Anastacia before," said Bedad. "But now I have good news." He raised his arms in the air and jumped around the room. "Good news! Good news."

He paused and grinned at Durward. "By the way, I'm not worried about my bracelet losing power and trapping me in the Outworld."

"Don't be so—"

"No, I made a spell that gives each of the three stones in the bracelet ten times the duration it already had." He rubbed his left eyebrow with his thumb. "I'm hoping that means I can stay outside of Dawn's End safely three hundred times longer than before."

"Three hundred times the duration." Durward's brow furrowed. "But that may work against you."

"How's that?"

"If you know the power will last for weeks, or months, you may be unaware when it is about to turn copper color. You'll forget to check it. The bracelet could become drained and trap you in Anastacia's world while you're distracted by other matters."

"I thought of that," said Bedad. "I cast a spell so that the bracelet will signal me with an increasing headache when it starts to weaken. The shorter the time left, the stronger the pain."

Durward nodded. "Good. Pain is hard to ignore. Still, I was worried when you went for short excursions to gather plants and chemicals. I'll be even more concerned when you are gone for a long period. As will your parents. The Outworld is a perilous place. The people are dangerous, and the environment as well." He bent closer to a jar of chartreuse leaves and squinted, trying to identify the contents.

"I know. But Ellsworth and Lissa know how important this is to me. To all of us." Bedad paused and slowly licked his lips. "We owe Anastacia. She took tremendous risks to save Dawn's End. I can't fail her."

Durward pointed at Bedad. "Don't fail yourself either. If you can't find her, or the potion doesn't seem to be working, come back. We'll try again."

"But Anastacia could already be sick," said Bedad. "She could already be—"

"She's not."

Bedad nodded, swallowing the lump in his throat. He forced the worry from his mind.

"Before I go, I want you to check my work."

He walked over to the wooden counter and picked up a pile of papers covered in words, numbers, and diagrams. "Please make sure I haven't made any mistakes." He held out the pages to Durward.

Durward clasped the younger man's upper arm. "Of course."

Durward's hand seemed surprisingly small. Bedad realized he had not only grown taller than his mentor, but filled out as well. He hoped his shoulders were strong enough to carry the hope of all Dawn's End—that the debt to Anastacia and her mother, Nicole, could be lessened.

Durward took the pile of papers, sat on a stool, and began to read. Bedad left the laboratory, knowing it was best for his mentor to work alone. He mustn't try to influence him in any way.

More than once over the course of the next few days, as Durward checked Bedad's calculations, light flashed from the lab, and the ground shook. Bedad had to steel himself not to run in to investigate. He was sure, pretty sure, the procedure he had used to create the potion was not hazardous. He chewed off two fingernails before he realized he had returned to the once-abandoned habit. Pacing back and forth outside the laboratory, he wore a trail of flattened grass.

Periodically, Durward would emerge for food or exercise. He gave Bedad an encouraging smile but said nothing. Bedad choked back his questions. Patience was a valued trait that he was struggling to cultivate.

On the fifth day, Durward emerged. His wild, golden hair was in need of a wash, and his hands were stained green and orange. He stretched and gave his scalp a thorough scratch.

Bedad stopped pacing and stared into his mentor's blue-gold eyes. He held his breath.

Durward's long face broke into a huge smile. He nodded.

Everything felt wrong. Trying to figure out why, Anastacia stared at the computer screen, until her eyes itched with fatigue. She had tossed and turned until well after midnight before finally giving up and switching on her laptop. Quietly, while her cousin, Julie, slept in the other bed, Anastacia set the computer on her lap, plugged in her earbuds, and went on the internet.

A comment Anastacia's stepfather had made about climate change transforming North America into a dustbowl had stuck in her mind and burrowed deep beneath its surface.

When she'd left Thunder Bay, in northern Ontario, she had seen barely any snow on the ground. Not how it should be in February. Now, here she was in Whistler, British Columbia, one of the ski capitals of the world. Without a great amount of manmade snow, the downhill skiing season would not have happened this year.

In the wintery days of her childhood, snow had been abundant. Her memories were not merely the result of a child's exaggerated perspective. Neighborhoods had often run out of places to put the snow before the spring melt. But, now, cross-country skiing was impossible. Summers had grown increasingly dry, and hot as well. Were these weather changes the result of global warming?

The laptop screen cast a weak light around the hotel room. Periodically, Anastacia heard voices in the hall and a room door open and shut. Everyone seemed to be having a great holiday, but she couldn't get rid of a sense of doom. Perhaps spending time with Julie had triggered uncomfortable memories of her hospitalization in Lucerne four years earlier during her visit to Switzerland for Julie's wedding.

After hours of clicking on links and reading articles about climate change, Anastacia's neck ached, and her legs felt numb from the weight of the computer. What she found online shocked and frightened her.

In 2005, Natural News had said, within the next hundred years, global warming would cause massive drought, covering over fifty percent of the earth's surface and threatening the lives of millions. She had discussed the news report with her stepfather.

"A hundred years is not so long," her stepfather had said. "Your grandchildren, maybe even your children, will still be alive."

Anastacia had put the disturbing discussion out of her mind. But seeing how little natural snow had fallen in Whistler this season had renewed her concern about climate change. In light of recent events, experts had reassessed their predictions about global warming; they now expected catastrophe to come more rapidly. According to the Drought Monitor, almost fifty million people currently lived under exceptional drought conditions, and many more were living through a moderate to extreme drought. Anastacia chewed anxiously on her lower lip as she examined the red, orange, and yellow map of the globe, shocked at the widespread disaster.

Wildfires had devastated the central United States in 2011 and 2012. In Texas alone, 3.6 million acres had burned. Anastacia tried to swallow the lump in her throat as she watched the videos—acres of blackened forest, beautiful homes ablaze, water bombers dropping chemicals onto fires so huge they made the aircrafts look like toys in the sky, and horizons engulfed in orange flames. The earth was so dry that some major cities experienced dust storms.

The United States had used 148 trillion gallons of fresh water in 2011, an unsustainable amount. Thirty-six states faced water shortages. Experts predicted California would run out of water by 2030, New Mexico by 2020. In spite of the preciousness of this essential and irreplaceable resource, almost half of the lakes and rivers were too polluted to drink from. Half. Anastacia's mouth dropped open at the thought.

Sixty years of little to no rainfall had triggered the starvation of millions in Kenya, Somalia, Sudan, and Ethiopia. Rates of civil war doubled in areas of drought. Anastacia had watched the water level of Lake Superior in Canada drop steadily for years, leaving boathouses meters away from the shore. When the Great Lakes could no longer supply enough water for both Canada and the United States, would there be war between the neighboring countries?

The most recent storms that struck the Eastern Seaboard, including Hurricane Irene, which devastated the North Carolina coast, had been among the fiercest and most damaging in decades. All over North America, cities faced extremes in weather — stronger winds, brutal storms, more hurricanes and tornadoes, increased flooding, heavy snowfall followed by early melting, and blisteringly hot summer days. During storms, trees and utility poles frequently fell on electrical lines, causing power outages in Thunder Bay. No tornadoes had hit urban Thunder Bay yet, but the strong recurring winds were dangerous enough.

Anastacia's stepfather finally agreed to install air-conditioning, but he did so begrudgingly.

"We're only contributing to the problem, you know," he said.

It seemed the same day they stopped using central heating they switched on the air conditioner. In the course of one dramatic spring day, the temperature varied thirty degrees Centigrade. Anastacia wore a sunhat in the afternoon and a woolen toque in the evening.

Anastacia knew damage to the environment was global. In China, eighty percent of the major rivers were now lifeless from pollution. She wondered if this was how the Chinese could make and sell boatloads of department store products so cheaply. She had heard that the Chinese government allowed manufacturers to dump tons of toxins into the environment in pursuit of profit. China wasn't the only country doing this; they just did it openly and without apology. Westerners eagerly bought the cheap items, ensuring the system continued.

After clicking on page after page of dire warnings and compiled environmental data, Anastacia's head buzzed with fear. What she read seemed like the premise for a science-fiction movie—no, a horror movie. But the situation was all too real. Each new fact hit her like a punch to the gut. Earth was heading for an apocalypse within her lifetime.

Unknown to everyone, even her family and closest friends, Anastacia had already helped avert the end of the world. When she was sixteen years old, she had found herself in Dawn's End, an obscure and secret place accessible only by magic. While there, she, with the help of Dawn's End companions, had fought off an oncoming apocalypse that nearly engulfed both worlds. But the dangers she had faced in Dawn's End paled in comparison to the intensive global disaster that now threatened to destroy her planet.

The inhabitants of Dawn's End included humans, talking beasts, races of people who were part human and part animal, and a wide variety of mythical creatures including faeries and lilyverns, who were part human and part plant. They all lived in harmony with nature and considered Outworlders—their term for people from Anastacia's world—to be foolish and self-destructive. In Dawn's End, half-bird people coexisted in peace with half-bear people. But, in Anastacia's world, humans could not coexist peacefully with one another, and now they were destroying their planet. Perhaps the residents of Dawn's End had been right to try to block all influence from the Outworld. She was amazed now that they had trusted her to come to their aid.

She suspected the major reason they trusted her was that her mother, Nicole, had once saved Dawn's End as well and had given birth to Anastacia there.

However, Nicole's early death from cancer aroused suspicion that her activities in Dawn's End may have caused deadly cell mutations. Anastacia did not know yet whether her journey beyond the door had poisoned her as well. She feared she could suffer the same fate as her mother.

After Durward left to return to his home on the edge of the unsettled forest where he lived with his wife, Misty, Bedad worked on creating enough of the antidote for Anastacia. He remembered her as a tall, fit woman with long, earth-colored hair and lovely, light brown skin. He estimated her body mass and created a single vial of potion. It was exhausting work, calling for repeated use of the panther bracelet in order to bind the ingredients that he had derived from two different worlds. The bracelet drew its power from the crystals, which, in turn, drew power from Dawn's End itself. However, even with the help of the bracelet, controlling and channeling that power was physically and emotionally draining. Bedad rested for a day between each step in making the potion.

When he was finally satisfied with his results, Bedad prepared for an extended stay in the Outworld.

"I have plenty of dried food for your trip," said Misty. "Help yourself. But you're not going looking like that, are you?"

Bedad walked over to the mirror. Days of black facial hair growth and his dirty, tangled curls confirmed his commitment to completing the cure. Redness ringed his aquamarine eyes.

"Anastacia won't care how I look, just that I've brought the antidote."

"Really?" said Misty. "After all this time, you want her to think you're still the grubby little boy she forced to scrub in the river?"

Bedad blushed. On his left temple, a scar showed white against his flushed skin. He studied his grimy face in the mirror; it was not the face of the skinny child whom Anastacia would remember. But the grime seemed familiar. "Yeah, all right. Bathing might be a good idea."

"Might be?" said Misty. "She couldn't even see your dimples under all that dirt. And a good night's sleep wouldn't hurt either."

After he bathed, Bedad went to bed early. The next morning, he prepared for his most important visit to the Outworld yet. He packed dried food, water, a compass, rain gear, and a change of clothing. He hid gold coins in various spots in his clothing and tucked a small bag of silver coins into his belt.

The beings of Dawn's End remembered Anastacia's mother, Nicole Newman, as a tragic hero. Bedad was determined to spare Anastacia the same fate.

Bedad hoped Anastacia still lived in Thunder Bay with her stepfather, Jamail, and her stepbrother, Ali. Anastacia had left her address with Durward, and Bedad had committed it to memory. He was determined to bring his potion to her as soon as possible. He had learned where he could trade his gold and silver coins for paper money and how to calculate the value. Once he had exchanged them, he should have enough currency to travel and survive in the Outworld for as long as necessary to get the antidote to Anastacia and make sure it worked and had no ill effects.

The door Anastacia's mother, Nicole, had used to enter Dawn's End was located by a pond near Centennial Park in the Northern Ontario city of Thunder Bay. Bedad had used this door to travel back and forth collecting plants from the Outworld when he was working on the antidote. Unfortunately, it was not presently operational. Bedad instead used a western door near the home of Josh the boatman on Long River to exit Dawn's End. He stepped through the portal into the Outworld, entering near an abandoned miner's shack on the Sibley Peninsula, about one hundred kilometers away from Thunder Bay. He had been fortunate to find another access point so close to Anastacia's home.

A small cottage community named Silver Islet occupied the point of the peninsula. In the second half of the nineteenth century, Silver Islet had been the site of the largest silver mine in the world. After the mine closed, the workers' homes, boarding houses, and offices had been sold to people in the region, who converted the buildings into camps. Now, three-quarters of the peninsula comprised Sleeping Giant Provincial Park: 244 square kilometers of trails, woods, ponds, lakes, streams, cliffs, gorges, and abundant wildlife available to the public. The park included campgrounds and beaches for summer fun and ski trails for the winter.

This February, however, little snow lay on the ground. The ski trails were muddy and unused.

Bedad made his way overland to the road between Grassy and Ravine Lakes. He had been careful to wear clothing that resembled that of the Outworlders and he looked like an ordinary northerner. He had been walking along the road for an hour when a pickup truck stopped beside him.

"Car trouble?" The bearded man behind the wheel adjusted his baseball cap.

"Yeah, I'm afraid so."

"Want a ride?"

"Yes, thanks." Bedad stood on the side of the road.

"Well, get in." The man motioned with his arm.

Bedad examined the side of the truck and then pulled on the handle. The door swung open. He stepped up on a metal shelf and climbed in, found a niche for his hand on the inside of the door, and pulled it shut. The man's brow furrowed as he watched Bedad's fumbling.

"I don't often ride in trucks."

The man pulled on the seatbelt and pressed the buckle into Bedad's hand. Bedad nodded and snapped it in place.

"So you're not from around here?" The driver shifted gears into drive, and the truck surged forward.

"No," Bedad said. "I've come a long way. I'm going to Thunder Bay."

"You're a bit off the trail then, pal. But, no worries, I'll get you there."

The driver pushed a button, and music filled the vehicle. Bedad listened carefully as a woman sang a song about confessing her love and yearning for her lover's arms. Thankfully, the driver didn't ask any questions, just drummed the steering wheel as the songs changed.

Bedad asked the driver to drop him off at a small hotel in the Current River area near Anastacia's home. His room held several marvels. He pressed down on the coiled mattress, amazed by its comfort. A large, black frame held prominence in the room, but, instead of holding a picture, the middle of the frame was black as well. A small box with changing, glowing numbers, its purpose a mystery, sat on a little chest by the bed. But it was the shower, with temperature control, that left him in awe. Perhaps importing some of these positive innovations from the Outworld to Dawn's End wouldn't hurt.

After scrubbing himself under the bountiful shower, he

bounced up and down on the end of the bed, giggling. The mattress squeaked loudly, and the headboard gently thumped the wall. Finally, someone in the next room pounded on the wall and shouted, "Get it done already, and go to sleep."

Unsure what "it" meant, but understanding the angry tone, Bedad quietly crawled between the sheets.

In the morning, he read through the fat book beside the bed and deciphered the telephone. He received Anastacia's number from information and dialed, his heart thudding loudly.

Anastacia's stepfather, Jamail, answered.

"Hello."

Bedad cleared his throat. "Good morning, sir. I am searching for Anastacia Newman."

"Anastacia isn't here. Can I take your number and have her call you back?"

"Oh, I'd rather talk to her in person." Bedad ran his fingers nervously through his thick curls.

"Are you a friend of hers?" asked Jamail.

"My name is Bedad Ellsworthson. I met her in . . . Lucerne. I promised to visit sometime."

"Oh. She'll be sorry she missed you. She's gone skiing for the week in Whistler with her cousin."

"Julie?" asked Bedad.

Bedad remembered that Anastacia had flown to Lucerne, Switzerland, to attend her cousin's wedding. She had almost missed it by accidentally entering Dawn's End.

"Yes, that's right," Jamail said.

"Perhaps I could visit her there. Is Whistler nearby?"

"No. It's in British Columbia, over three thousand kilometers away."

Chapter Two - Unexpected Visitor

Who could be banging on Anastacia's hotel door at six in the morning? After only three hours of sleep, her head felt hot and heavy. A vision of uniformed officers with bad news hammered her thoughts. Had something happened to her stepfather? She whipped open the door, dreading what she would see.

A tall man in a brown parka smiled at her, his aquamarine eyes sparkling above a tightly wound scarf.

"I have something you might be interested in—" He reached into a suede bag.

"Good God, not at this hour." Anastacia started to shut the door.

"Anastacia, look."

She paused. How did he know her name?

The man set the bag on the hallway carpet and pushed up his sleeve.

Anastacia's mouth dropped open at the sight of a triple-stoned, gold panther bracelet on his wrist.

"What is it?" Julie mumbled groggily from her bed.

"I got it. Nothing to worry about. Go back to sleep." Anastacia stepped into the hall.

"I had a devil of a time getting here." The man pulled his sleeve back down over the bracelet. "I rode on two terrifying monsters—a Greyhound bus and a passenger train. We went through these amazing mountains!"

Anastacia stared. He was about six feet two inches tall, slightly taller than she was. She looked up at him.

"You haven't changed at all, but I guess I have. It's the time difference. Don't you recognize me?" The stranger peeled off the scarf and pulled down his hood. "I'm Bedad."

Anastacia gasped. "Look at you! Taller than I am. And your voice. You were a little boy the last time I saw you."

He chuckled. "I told you, time passes more quickly in Dawn's End than it does here. It's the time difference between our worlds. I've aged more than you."

"I'll say! What are you doing here? Never mind. Wait here." She raised her hands in a double-stop gesture. "I'm just going to get dressed. Don't go anywhere."

She retreated into the room, scrambled into her clothes, and then stepped back into the hall. He was still there, leaning against the opposite wall.

"Let's go down to the lobby," she said. "The continental breakfast will be out. We can talk."

She led him down the hall and into an area with tables and chairs. An elderly man with wispy, white hair sat reading the paper as he drank his coffee and ate a bran muffin. A middle-aged man in a business suit was typing into his cell phone. The only other person around was the clerk who watched the front desk and kept the breakfast area clean and tidy.

Bedad pulled off his toque and parka as he entered. Anastacia led him to a small table in the farthest corner by the windows. He set down his winter clothes, reached into his packsack to remove a small pouch, which he attached to his belt, and then followed Anastacia to the breakfast bar. She poured a coffee and set a carrot muffin and a banana on a plate. Bedad started to copy her.

"Wait," said Anastacia. "Have you ever had coffee?"

"No."

"Try this instead." She filled his cup with hot chocolate and scooped in a teaspoon of marshmallows.

Back at their table, Anastacia sipped her coffee, staring at him in wonder.

"Why are you here?" she asked.

"The lilyvern blends held the key all along." He took a deep whiff of the hot chocolate.

"Blends?" Anastacia whispered. "Key? What are you talking about?"

Bedad ran his hand through his dark curls. "I'm getting ahead of myself. I've brought you a present."

He reached into his bag and pulled out a small box. He opened the box and unfolded a white cloth, revealing a vial.

"What is it?" Anastacia puckered her face in bewilderment.

"The antidote."

He sat the vial on the wooden table between them.

"I have been gathering vegetation from your world for quite some time, blending them with plants and chemicals from Dawn's End, trying to find exactly the right balance. At first, Durward came with me, but, once he realized I knew what I was doing, he let me go alone."

"Why didn't you come and say hello?" She studied Bedad, puzzled by his failure to visit her when he had been traveling so frequently to the Outworld.

Bedad slipped his spoon into his cup and stirred, his gaze pinned on the dissolving marshmallows. "I couldn't take the time. I had to get everything before the bracelet's power drained, or else I would have been trapped in your world—"

"Oh, God! You'll be trapped here when your bracelet stops working." Anastacia leapt to her feet. "How long did it take to find me?"

"It's all right," said Bedad. "I figured out a way to make the bracelet's power last here. I have plenty of time. Don't worry."

"Wow, that's some trick. How did you extend the bracelet's energy?" Anastacia sat back down and took a sip of her coffee, trying to calm herself.

"It wasn't easy. I wanted to be sure I could find you and administer this."

Anastacia looked at the vial. "What exactly is it?"

"A mixture of science and magic. If Dawn's End caused your mother's cancer, this should stop the same thing from happening to you. My antidote should counteract any negative effects from your last visit to Dawn's End. If any of your cells have mutated from eating our food, drinking our water, or breathing our air, this antidote will return them to normal. If nothing has changed, it should prevent any mutations from occurring in the future."

"Thank you," said Anastacia. She blinked back tears of relief. "I have to admit, I've been pretty nervous. Nobody my age gets as many checkups as I do. I've been vigilant about watching for signs of cancer."

"I'm sorry you went through that," Bedad said somberly.

Anastacia gave a crooked smile. "After so much time passed, I thought maybe Durward had given up researching."

"He didn't, but he did pass it on to me when he realized I had exceeded him in skill." Bedad grinned, revealing his dimples, and shrugged. "I know, that sounds arrogant, but it's true."

Anastacia laughed. "So, are you leaving right after I drink the antidote?"

"No, I want to monitor your condition," said Bedad. "Make sure there are no side-effects."

"You mean like sprouting flowers out of the top of my head like the lilyverns have?"

Bedad's eyes widened. "Do you think I would take such risks with you? Nothing that terrible. "

"So my hands won't turn green?" She picked up the vial and stared at the contents. The blue-green liquid gleamed. "I won't start growing roots?"

"Stop it!" Bedad's spoon clattered on the table. "I just want to be sure you don't get sick to your stomach or have headaches."

Anastacia set the vial down, reached out, and put her hand over his. "Relax. I'm just teasing. I know you wouldn't take chances like that."

Bedad sighed. "Sorry, I've been kind of driven. I don't have much of a sense of humor these days. "

"I can tell." She patted his hand and then released it. "We'll have to see if we can get that back."

When Bedad smiled, Anastacia realized she was looking into the face of a man, not a boy, and a handsome one at that.

"You grew up while my back was turned," she said. "How old

are you?"

"How old are you?" He picked up the banana and eyed it curiously.

"Twenty."

"I don't really know how old I am because I've spent so much time traveling back and forth between Dawn's End and here. I'm in my mid-twenties, I guess."

"Older than me now! That can't be right. You should be sixteen. It's been four years since I left Dawn's End."

She peeled the top half of her banana. Bedad watched and then copied her.

"Do I look sixteen?" he asked.

Anastacia studied his healthy, clear skin, bow-shaped lips, and strong chin. He had a face women would notice. No trace of the thin child he had once been remained in this tall, broad-shouldered man.

"No, you look about twenty-five. That's freaky. I have this picture in my mind of you as a skinny, grubby twelve-year-old."

"Hey, I wasn't always grubby." He took a bite of the banana. "Mmm."

Anastacia laughed. "Not after we insisted you have a good scrub and change your clothes, anyway. You weren't keen on getting cleaned up."

He pouted. "That river water was *cold*."

They laughed.

While Bedad enjoyed the rest of the banana, Anastacia asked

about Durward, Bedad's mentor; Lissa and Ellsworth, his parents; and others she had met in Dawn's End.

"It sounds like things are going well," she said. "I thought they would. But I never would have thought you would grow up to be some kind of super wizard."

Bedad shrugged. "I guess not. People *here* are pretty unpredictable too."

"What do you mean?" Anastacia watched him wipe a dribble of chocolate from his chin.

"I felt doubly pressured to gather plants from your world, seeing how quickly many are becoming endangered or extinct. Humanity is fast-tracking to self-destruction and bringing hundreds, maybe thousands, of species with it."

"Yeah," said Anastacia. "I read an article that said about a quarter of the plants and animals in existence now will be extinct by the time I'm old enough to retire. It didn't mention how many already are. I was up half the night reading some rather frightening statistics and predictions. Changes are happening quicker than we expected."

"Because of the increasing carbon-monoxide levels?" Bedad sipped his hot chocolate and licked his lips.

"That and a whole lot of other damaging behavior. Did you know Earth has had five mass extinctions?"

Bedad shook his head, slipped the spoon into the cup, and stirred, listening attentively.

Anastacia slumped back in her chair. "Yeah, well, I'm a little worried I might be around for the sixth."

Bedad pointed at her with his spoon. "If you know what caused the other ones, maybe you can stop it."

"The first one was about four hundred million years ago. Sea levels dropped when glaciers formed and then rose again when they melted. We don't know what caused the second one, about three and a half million years ago."

"And the others?"

"In the Triassic extinction, there were massive floods. Erupting volcanoes. Lava pouring into the Atlantic Ocean. That's what caused global warming."

"It doesn't sound like any of those were preventable."

"No." Anastacia picked up her coffee cup with both hands, holding the comforting warmth against her skin. "Not the last one either. We think an asteroid or volcanoes caused the end of the dinosaurs."

Bedad tipped his head. "You can't do anything about volcanoes *or* asteroids. Can you?"

"No, but we don't need to rush global warming either." Anastacia set the cup down. "We're making it happen quicker. I think we're screwing up a lot of stuff. There's been all sorts of strange weather all over the globe — floods, droughts, hurricanes, tornadoes, you name it."

Bedad nodded. "I noticed during my visits. I've been using different portals around your world."

"Even in Thunder Bay, every year, the wind gets worse, the storms get wilder, no tornadoes downtown yet, but we can't count on the seasons to behave the way they used to. That's why I came to Whistler to ski. Did you see how little snow there was at home, in February?"

"I don't know what's normal, but there were a lot of bare patches."

"It should be at least up to here." Anastacia held out her hand at about thigh level.

"Oh, then it is bad."

She dropped her hand. "Mother Earth is getting testy, and I think we're causing a lot of the problems."

"Why don't you stop?"

"Darn good question there, Bedad. Darn good question." Anastacia frowned, but then she looked into Bedad's eyes and grinned.

"What?" he said.

"I figured I probably wouldn't make it to old age, so I wouldn't get to see the next end of the world as we know it. But now"—she pointed at the box—"with this vial you brought, all bets are off. So, how did you manage this?"

As she finished her breakfast, Anastacia listened as Bedad narrated the story of how he had created the antidote with Durward's assistance.

Julie joined them at 7:00 a.m. in the breakfast area. Anastacia told Julie she had met Bedad in Lucerne before her inexplicable "accident." Four years earlier, Anastacia had flown to Switzerland to attend Julie's wedding and disappeared. Due to amnesia, she was unable to explain where she had been or what happened. In actuality, Anastacia had spent the time she was missing in Dawn's End.

Since they were leaving the ski resort the next day, Julie agreed to let Bedad sleep on a cot in their hotel room.

Fortunately, Julie didn't inquire much about Bedad, perhaps because she was afraid of upsetting Anastacia, who did not like to talk about her experience in Lucerne.

"You don't look like cousins," said Bedad. "Except you have the same blue eyes."

"My mother had them too," said Anastacia. "But she didn't really look like either of us."

Julie had long, blonde hair, and her skin was like peaches and cream. Except for her slightly large nose, she looked like a model for Swiss yogurt. Anastacia looked like a typical African-English-Canadian, which was how she had viewed herself until her trip to Dawn's End changed everything she thought she knew about her origins. There she discovered that her father, Alaric Morrel, was actually a panther man—part human, part panther—from an important family and that she had been born in Dawn's End. She still liked her African-Canadian friends, but she felt dishonest pretending to be one of them when they talked about the slavery of their ancestors or fighting for civil rights. She had a different heritage, one she could never explain to others. The truth was too fantastic for Anastacia to tell anyone, even Julie with whom she was so close.

The next day, Julie returned to Lucerne and Anastacia to Ontario. Anastacia brought Bedad with her on her trip home to Thunder Bay. His mouth hung open the entire first hour of the plane flight.

"Such powerful magic," he muttered. "Sitting in a chair *in the sky*. Eating snacks. Going to the washroom. Watching this . . . this television. I am deeply humbled."

When they arrived in Thunder Bay, Anastacia convinced her stepfather that Bedad was just a friend visiting from Lucerne and asked if he could crash in her brother's old room for a few weeks. Jamail agreed.

In a private moment, Jamail pulled Anastacia aside to talk about Bedad. "I see the way he watches you, wistful and yearning at the same time. You may think of him as a friend, but I have a feeling he wishes it was more."

"No, Dad, he's just worried about me."

Jamail rubbed his chin with his index finger. "Why would he be worried about you?"

Anastacia paused. She should not have said that. Her stepfather did not know about Dawn's End or about what had really happened to her during her lost time in Lucerne. He knew she had some concern about developing cancer, since her mother had. He did not know, however, that she worried her journey in Dawn's End might have mutated her cells.

"Oh, you know. I guess he thinks I need a big brother to watch over me since Ali is so far away."

"Hmm. He does not look at you with the expression of an older brother. He's a polite and caring young man. Don't dismiss the possibility that he could be just what your heart needs."

"Dad! Please."

Jamail lifted one hand in an "I surrender" motion, but the expression in his eyes was hopeful.

When her stepbrother, Ali, phoned from Minneapolis, he scolded Anastacia for causing their father concern.

"You brought a boy home. He'll be imagining all sorts of things."

"He already has."

"He worries that he doesn't know how to raise a daughter, especially in a culture he wasn't born to," said Ali. "I don't think he'll ever get used to the way young people paw at each other over here."

Anastacia snorted.

"You weren't born to it either, and I bet you and Lucinda hold hands on the subway, maybe even steal a kiss now and then," Anastacia said, referring to the Iraqi ban on public displays of affection.

"You think you're so funny," said Ali. "Just don't make his worries justified."

"Not with Bedad." She laughed. "He's like a little brother. You should hear him cheering at my hockey games."

"Just behave yourself. And I'll tell you right now, if he is like a little brother . . . younger siblings can be very unpredictable."

Chapter Three - The Flood

Spring arrived early in March, bringing flooding along the banks of the Kaministiquia River. Anastacia joined the volunteers sandbagging around Fort William Historical Park in an effort to minimize damage. When the torrential rain fell, the Neebing River in the south end of the city overflowed onto sidewalks and streets and around the trunks of trees. Churning, brown river water submerged Anastacia's favorite bike path; the tops of poles she used to ride under now barely showed. Tree branches lodged against the side of the Edward Street Bridge, as the water rose up to mere inches below the pavement. The Neebing-McIntyre floodway, a man-made construct, was filled to capacity, but water still went where it did not belong.

On the south side of the city, the basements of many buildings filled with runoff. Ontario Hydro shut off the power as the danger of electrocution rose. In the east end, the lowest and the oldest part of Thunder Bay, a third of the homes suffered similarly. As if that wasn't bad enough, the sewage plant's pumps became submerged and stopped working. Sewage backed up through the pipes and into hundreds of structures. The city council declared a state of emergency. The flooding damaged thousands of dwellings. Thunder Bay became a certified disaster area.

Emergency responders could not keep up with the cries for help. Roads and gravel driveways washed out. The rising water trapped one rural family; their driveway washed away, leaving their home sitting on an island. Washouts turned local roads into a confusing maze. A police officer, rushing to assist an eighty-year-old man in distress, felt the pavement give way as his vehicle suddenly sank.

When the rain stopped, restoration companies ran out of pumps, trying to keep up with demand. Those homeowners with sewage in their basements had to leave their doors and windows wide open. Looters took advantage of the unoccupied buildings. Devious entrepreneurs bought dozens of pumps and sold them for triple the price on the internet.

Anastacia's home, recently installed with a sump pump, upgraded weeping tile, longer downspouts, and landscaping, stayed dry. Stories she heard of other people's suffering brought tears to her eyes. The cashier at the grocery store, a painter, lost all the artwork she had prepared for her first gallery showing. A collector who worked at her bank couldn't save his comic book collection, a lifetime investment that included first editions of Spiderman and The Punisher. Two dogs in crates drowned because their master was working and did not know his basement was flooding. A young parent who had fallen asleep in front of the television heard her baby cry and rushed downstairs to the nursery. Water had reached the level of the crib, and the mattress was floating two inches above its proper place, with the baby on top.

Not all the stories were gloomy. Media companies joined together to launch a fundraiser. Three times the funds expected poured in from citizens. The Red Cross, the Salvation Army, and local churches and volunteer groups stepped in to provide food, shelter, and clothing for those who could not return to their homes. Volunteers from other cities arrived by bus and truck. Command posts sprouted up in community centers, the Confederation College, and Lakehead University.

As cleanup began, Anastacia realized how fortunate she had been. Numerous neighbors dumped piles of furniture, toys, appliances, musical instruments, sheetrock, wallboard, and carpeting curbside. The city arranged free pickup of all flood victims' refuse. As horrible as Thunder Bay's situation was, other spots around the world succumbed to worse flooding.

As March progressed, rapid changes in temperature, combined with increased winds, created perfect conditions for hail in the Thunder Bay region. Hailstorms became so frequent that roofers could not keep up with repairs. Plastic tarps draped over houses waiting for more permanent solutions. Steel and canvas garages sold out as people tried to protect their cars, but pitted hoods and roofs and cracked windshields still occurred regularly. A new "car quilt" was invented and sold out immediately. The Thunder Bay Community Auditorium parking lot was a sea of thickly blanketed cars and trucks. Since storms occurred so frequently now, no one wanted to leave a vehicle unprotected for even a couple hours to watch a performance. The quilt did not live up to expectations.

Anastacia's stepfather subscribed to the Emergency Management Ontario site and bought a pump. "Just in case," he said. He also tripled the size of his vegetable garden.

Bedad contributed to the yard work, proving himself both diligent and willing to learn. He and Anastacia helped Jamail build frames enclosing the garden. As they fastened the last beams, Anastacia felt a tingle in the air. She looked up and saw black storm clouds rolling in. The temperature dropped precipitously. Four crows landed in the trees behind the yard and cawed loudly to each other.

"Won't glass just break under the hail?" asked Bedad as he tightened the last screw.

"I'm going to cover it in Plexiglas." Jamail gathered up the box of screws. "It doesn't break easily. It'll be ridiculously expensive, but a single hailstorm will destroy anything I plant. I'm going to replace the shattered windows in the greenhouse with the same thing." He shook the frame in several spots to check its strength.

"You must love vegetables," said Bedad as Anastacia took his screwdriver and returned it to the shed.

Bedad and Jamail followed Anastacia as they continued their conversation.

"The price of food is rising and will probably keep on rising," Jamail said. "Planting a vegetable garden makes good economic sense. I think the Plexiglas is a good investment. It will pay for itself in a couple of summers. Besides, food is a precious commodity. You can never have too much."

"Have you looked in our pantry?" asked Anastacia as she emerged from the shed. "You can't even step inside. Dad has enough food there for an army."

"What are all the barrels for?" Bedad examined a row along the side of the house.

"Collecting rain," she said.

"Really? With all the rain and hail you're worried about water?"

Jamail nodded as he picked up the hammers and level. "Lake Superior is the lowest it has been in eighty-five years, and it just keeps dropping. I Googled it. Summers are hotter and drier every year."

"It's awful," Anastacia said in agreement.

The wind picked up, whipping Anastacia's black hair into her face. She pulled off her scrunchy and remade her ponytail.

"But we're luckier than most," she said. "The Canadian Shield is the most stable place on the planet. At least we don't get earthquakes here."

Bedad looked up as the wind increased. "What does it signify when your sky is green?"

"What does this mean, green?" asked Jamail as he locked the shed door.

Bedad pointed. Threaded through the ominous billowing black clouds was a gleam of phosphorescent, olive green, which widened as they watched. Anastacia hoped her stepfather interpreted the words "your sky" to mean the sky in the western hemisphere.

"Nothing good, that is for certain," said Jamail. "We had better head to the basement."

A bolt of lightning jumped from one cloud to another, followed almost instantly by a deafening clap of thunder.

"Yikes." Anastacia held the door as Jamail and Bedad rushed inside. "That's right in the crease."

After the storm passed, Anastacia called Julie. Julie had become the sister Anastacia never had. Their emails and phone calls were long and chatty. So far, Switzerland had escaped flooding. Instead, they needed rain.

"I never thought we'd spend so much time talking about the weather," said Julie. "It's not as if we can do anything about it."

"That's true," said Anastacia. "I feel powerless."

Anastacia had to be careful what she revealed. Obviously, she could never mention her struggle in Dawn's End. Julie would think Anastacia's memories were a delusion, the result of some unknown trauma she had suffered in Lucerne.

Julie talked about life as half of a young married couple, her job, cooking, and movies. Anastacia discussed sports, her stepdad and stepbrother, her friends, and her dismal love life. She had dated a few times, but she found most guys either boring or irritating. The man she wanted to date, Max Marshall, worked as the program director of Empowerment Ventures Center, a non-profit organization for low-income children where Anastacia volunteered on the weekends. Max was different from the other men she knew in several ways.

First, she found him physically and emotionally appealing. Second, he had never asked her out, or even flirted, in spite of the signals she sent. Frustrated with her inability to attract his attention in a girl-guy kind of way, Anastacia mined her cousin for tips. Anastacia had always been more at home on the hockey rink than in the dating field. Julie thought Max might feel the age difference was too much.

"So, I'm twenty, and he's twenty-five. That's nothing. Girls mature faster." Anastacia flopped onto her bed, the telephone pressed against her ear.

"That's when you're adolescents," Julie said. "Boys catch up. Most do, anyway. Perhaps he isn't looking for a relationship. Or maybe he plays for the other team."

"No, definitely not," said Anastacia. "He's straight. Maybe it's because he's several inches shorter than me. Maybe my size and strength, and my kick-ass skills on the ice, intimidate him."

"Well, that's dumb," said Julie. "Almost everybody is several inches shorter than you. A lot of men find athletic women attractive. Besides, you could be an international model with your height and beauty."

"Aw, you are so good for my ego," Anastacia said. "But I've got the body of a steak-eating hockey player, not a lettuce-eating model. I guess I'm just not his type."

"His loss," said Julie.

Anastacia decided she should concentrate on keeping Bedad occupied and let things unfold naturally with Max. She wondered why Bedad was still hanging around. She felt perfectly fine—no side-effects from the antidote. She hoped Max wouldn't get the wrong idea about Bedad living with her. She wanted the luscious Max Marshall to know she was interested and available, but she couldn't exactly hide Bedad in the basement.

Dating was so complicated. She was used to relating to boys, and then men, on the ice. Since she was one of the star players, Anastacia's teammates expected her to lead them to victory. As a child, she participated in a mixed minor hockey team. By adolescence, she was the only female on an otherwise all-male team, on par with the best players. No one could outskate or outshoot her; her speed and power were legendary. But now she played on a mixed team again, just for fun. After her last visit to Dawn's End, she had lost interest in competition. It didn't feel like a true contest when she knew she was more than human—the daughter of a panther man. Her biological father had given her extraordinary strength, speed, and stamina. If she could teach the panther people to skate, no team on earth would be able to get near them.

As well, her life and death experiences in Dawn's End made the angst over goals seem trivial. She no longer followed every game in the NHL. The words "Wanna go?" bored her silly. She would shout in frustration at the television when two players tore off their gloves and went at it. "Just play already!" Life was too short for such nonsense. When you had to fight for your life, punching someone over a puck seemed stupid.

She still loved the game of hockey, though, especially playing it herself. But she also felt she had an unfair advantage over the other players, given her true ancestry. Sometimes, to be fair, she let the puck slip past. She longed to feel truly challenged by her opponents.

Bedad loved watching her play. She was glad he attended all her games since she felt a little uncomfortable leaving him alone as much as she did. On the weekdays, she had university classes; she was a student in the Master's program in Environmental Studies in Nature-Based Recreation and Tourism at Lakehead University. She also spent several evenings and Sundays working at Primal Connection, a wilderness supply store. And, every Saturday, she volunteered at Empowerment Ventures Center, where Max worked, helping the children experience sports, crafts, and other activities. However, Bedad had discovered the lure of the internet, the call of the outdoors, the pleasures of playing with Stumpy (Anastacia's black and white cat with half a tail), and the joy of helping Jamail with his home projects. He seemed content.

One evening, when they were playing crib, Anastacia invited Bedad to join her at Empowerment Ventures.

"I think you know enough about the Outworld to fit in now. Just remember to watch what you say," Anastacia said.

"I will."

"I can't really bring you to hang out with me at the store while I'm working," she said. "The boss, Franz Hahn, goes ballistic if we socialize on the job. But coming to the center and helping out with the kids shouldn't be a problem."

"What could I do there?"

"Help out with whatever we're doing. Arts, crafts, sports, games. You have to provide a criminal background check, though. I don't know how we can do that since you don't exist here."

Bedad examined his hands. "I look pretty real to me." Anastacia explained what a criminal background check with a vulnerable persons component meant. She showed him hers.

Bedad nodded. "I can do this."

"It takes six to ten weeks."

"I'll have one tomorrow."

"But—"

"Trust me." He took Anastacia's criminal background check out of her hands and walked away, studying it.

Anastacia proudly showed Bedad around the Empowerment Ventures Center. Several teenagers were practicing boxing in the downstairs room, which smelled like wet socks and adolescent sweat. In the kitchen, younger children braided friendship bracelets with multicolored beads and strings. Two children shared a book in the quiet room while a pretty, petite, thirty-two-year-old brunette helped two others with homework. Anastacia introduced her as Sally. Although she was confident and engaged with the children, she had difficulty making eye contact with Bedad.

"Why wouldn't she look at me?" Bedad whispered as he and Anastacia headed for the games room.

"Trust me, when you're not looking, she is," replied Anastacia. "She is a little insecure with guys like you. You *are* intimidating.

"But she doesn't know I'm a wizard." He checked that his panther bracelet was well hidden under his sleeve.

"Not that." Anastacia chuckled. "You're all grown up now, and you've become quite the hottie."

"Hottie?"

She gestured toward his puzzled face. "Attractive. Good looking."

Bedad smiled. "Do *you* think so?"

Anastacia shrugged. "I admit it. But don't get too full of yourself. You're not my type, kiddo."

The smack of a ping-pong ball greeted them as they entered the room. A gangly teenager was playing against a stocky man in his mid-twenties.

"What's your type?"

"*He's* my type. Max Marshall. Ginger-licious." Anastacia nodded toward the man.

Max was shorter than Anastacia, but his snug T-shirt revealed well-developed biceps and triceps encircled by Celtic tattoos. His hair was autumn brown, trimmed above the ears with a hint of sideburns. His thin, pencil moustache, brett beard, and arched eyebrows were a slightly darker auburn than his hair. His skin was peaches and cream, and his eyes were steel-blue.

Bedad muttered. "I'm not a kiddo. I'm older than you."

The teenager slammed home a shot. The ball hit the edge of the table and flew over Max's left shoulder.

"Good one!" shouted Max as he set his paddle down. He high-fived the teenager.

"Don't people fist-bump here?" Bedad asked.

Anastacia ignored him as she approached Max.

"He's got your number," she said.

"That's the problem with teaching these kids all my tricks," said Max. "Then they turn around and beat me."

As the teenager headed over to watch two other teens play an air hockey game, he waved. "Hi Anastacia!"

She waved back. Max lifted the front of his T-shirt and wiped the sweat from his forehead. Anastacia glanced at his formidable six-pack and swallowed.

"Who's your friend?" asked Max.

"This is Bedad Ellsworthson," she replied.

"Max Marshall," he said as he shook Bedad's hand. "Soft hands. Not an athlete like Anastacia then."

"No, I'm a . . . scientist. In a laboratory."

Anastacia had told Bedad to keep it simple and not offer information about where he was from or how they had met.

"Cool," said Max. "Maybe you can help some of the kids with their science homework."

"I . . . uh . . . . "

"Bedad's English might not be up to that," said Anastacia. "It's his second language."

"He doesn't even have an accent," said Max. "Where—"

"Anasasha!"

A four-year-old boy entered the room. His hair was brown

and unruly, his eyes mahogany and slightly upturned, his nose wide, and his skin lighter than Anastacia's, but darker than Bedad's. He raced over and gave her a high five. She messed his already unruly hair even more.

"This little bundle of fun is Rupert Papis," she said.

The child grabbed her hand and dragged her toward the door.

"I guess I'm going this way." Anastacia tilted her head.

"We've lost her now." Max laughed and then went to watch the air hockey game.

Bedad followed Anastacia and Rupert down the hall and into the kitchen, which was filled with a collection of mismatched tables and chairs gathered from donations and yard sales.

"We need help," said Rupert. "We're making fruit salad."

"You bet," said Anastacia. She turned on the tap, soaped up her hands from a pump dispenser, and washed.

"Your turn," she said to Rupert, as she slid a step stool over to the sink. "Then Bedad."

"Are you Bedad?" Rupert slid his hands under the water.

Bedad nodded.

"I never heard that name before."

"Oh, well, you're the first Rupert I've ever met." Bedad gave him a warm smile.

"Cool," said Rupert as he scrubbed. "Can you peel the bananas?"

"Yes, Anastacia taught me how," said Bedad.

Rupert's little face scrunched up as he looked at Anastacia in puzzlement.

"They don't have bananas where Bedad comes from," Anastacia said. "He's visiting from far away."

Rupert nodded and dried his hands. "Okay, Bedad, you peel. I cut. I'm not 'lowed to use a sharp knife so I can only cut the bananas."

The table was set by Chester Otter, a ten-year-old Anishinaabe, a First Nations tribe also known as Ojibwa. Kyle Brewbaker, an eleven-year-old with shiny, brown hair cut straight across his forehead and a pale complexion, peeled oranges with a plastic tool. Sally, Bedad, and Anastacia cut the rest of the fruit while Petal Hoang, a pretty nine-year-old Asian girl in a ruffled, dirty, pink-and-white dress, spread cheese slices on bread.

When the table was ready, children and teens wandered in, grabbed sandwiches and a bowl of fruit, and found chairs.

"This reminds me of eating at home," said Bedad.

"How many children do Lissa and Ellsworth have now?" Anastacia said.

"Still living at home or coming and going?" Bedad laughed.

"That many, eh?"

Bedad nodded. "This is nice. Sometimes I find your house too quiet."

"My stepbrother, Ali, lives in Minneapolis now, with his fiancée, Lucinda," said Anastacia. "I miss him, but he comes to visit when he can. I really like his fiancée. She's actually taught him to relax a little."

"Are you coming to shoot arrows with us?" Rupert asked as he perched beside Bedad.

"Yes," Bedad said. "But I'm not very good. I'm much better with a sword."

"A sword!" said Chester. "Can I see it?"

"He doesn't have it with him," Anastacia said. "It's illegal to carry a sword around."

"That means it's against the law," Chester said to Rupert.

"I knew that!" said Rupert.

Anastacia bit down on her sandwich to keep from smiling.

"Anasasha's really good with a bow and arrow," Rupert said.

"Oh? Have you seen her?" asked Bedad.

"No, but she said so." The little boy nodded knowingly.

"Ah, then it must be true." Bedad examined a slice of banana on his fork, smiled, and then popped it into his mouth. He chewed and made an appreciative sound.

"Anastacia's a good athlete," Chester said. He scratched his black hair, messing his Clooney front flip.

"I believe it," said Bedad.

"Me too," said Rupert. "I'm a good att-leet."

"No you're not." Chester frowned. "I beat you all the time."

"Am too!" Rupert glared back at him.

"Actually, you are both very good athletes for your age," Anastacia said.

"I'm four," said Rupert, holding four fingers up for Bedad.

"How old are you?"

"I'm not sure," said Bedad.

Rupert laughed loudly. "You're silly."

"Maybe he's adopted and doesn't know his birthday," said Chester.

"I *am* adopted," said Bedad as Anastacia shot him a warning look. "I think I'm twenty-five."

"That's the same age as my mom," said Chester.

"Imagine that." Bedad as finished the last of his sandwich. "This is good, but I think I'd like something else."

He reached out and pulled an egg out from behind Rupert's ear.

"How did you do that?" Rupert asked.

"He's a magician," said Chester. "But you're supposed to pull out a quarter. My dad can do that."

"Can you eat a quarter?" asked Bedad. He tapped the egg on the side of the table and started to peel it.

"Can I have one?" asked Chester.

"You already have one." Bedad pulled another egg out from Chester's shirt-sleeve.

"Hey! How did you—"

"Me too!" said Petal.

Then Kyle asked. Soon everyone at the table was cracking and peeling eggs.

"That's bloody impressive," said Max as he counted all the

eggs. "Where did you hide two dozen boiled eggs?"

Bedad winked at Anastacia.

Chapter Four - Thunderbird

Before signing in on Sunday morning at Primal Connection, Anastacia made a purchase of her own. Her stepfather had given her a list of emergency supplies to buy. He had recently acquired a back-up generator for the furnace in case of a power outage. Hailstorms had brought down power lines, and Environment Canada was predicting ice storms ahead. Now that the pantry was full, Jamail was stacking food supplies in the basement. After all he went through in Iraq, Anastacia didn't dare tell him she thought his preparations were extreme.

Anastacia purchased a disaster kit containing four eight-hour emergency candles, two twelve-hour light sticks, a first-aid kit, four disposable hand warmers, one bottle of water purification tablets, two emergency ponchos, two thirty-six hour survival candles in a can, two emergency blankets, two six-hour camp heat cookers, and two headlights. She also bought one large deflated ten-liter plastic bag for water, useful only if you knew ahead of time that the water would be shut off. Next, she selected one rechargeable, crank-handle radio/flashlight and a top of the line Swiss army knife. They already had some of the items, but Jamail had reminded her life was unpredictable. These precautions might be overkill, but, if they helped her stepfather feel secure, it was worth it.

She added a wickedly sharp hunting knife to the pile; it felt perfect in her hand.

Their neighbor, Mr. Ferguson, who had taught her to hunt with a bow and arrow, owned one just like it. The knife could be used to gut and clean an animal, as well as for defense.

She asked her boss, Franz Hahn, if she could store the items in his office until her father came to pick them up. Last year,

Franz had completely refurnished the room; the suite was handcrafted from imported cherry wood with genuine leather chairs. Behind his desk, he had hung a stunning Norval Morrisseau painting, *Mother Earth*. Franz bragged his father had purchased the Woodlands School of Canadian Art painting with a forty-eight ounce bottle of whiskey when the artist, also known as Copper Thunderbird, was going through a difficult time, possibly as a result of the two years he spent in a residential school. Anastacia felt a mixture of feelings every time she looked at it—shame, anger, awe, sadness, respect, mystery, and gratitude. Some of those feelings centered on the artist, some on the painting, and some on how Franz, a non-aboriginal, had obtained the artwork.

Franz kept a family photo on his desk. In the picture, Franz's hair, a light brown tastefully threaded with gray and balding into a widow's peak, emphasized his high forehead and his long face. A dimpled chin and grape-blue eyes completed his look. Tammy, his younger wife, an ultra-thin blond with perfect makeup and professionally styled hair, linked her arm through his. Their two blond children, eight-year-old Rocky and five-year-old Oprah, mimicked their poise, confidence, and brand-name style.

Franz's grandfather came to Canada after World War II with a number of questionable antiques and jewelry. He loved the space and wilderness around what was then Port Arthur and Fort William. Something of an expert in guns, he started a hunter's store. Upon his retirement, he passed his successful business on to his son, Franz's father, who added new items to the store's goods, expanding the clientele to yuppies and fitness buffs. Nine years earlier, Franz's father had died of a heart attack at age sixty-three, leaving the business to his forty-one-year-old son, who had since doubled the store's size and inventory.

Just as Anastacia stacked the last box in the corner of the

office, Franz entered.

"Expecting an earthquake?" He gave her a perfect, white-toothed smile.

"No," said Anastacia. "But Dad wants to get all this stuff in place in case the next hailstorm takes out our power."

"The wind is getting wilder," said Franz as he shut the door.

"Dad bought a generator, too, but it will take a while for the electrician to hook it up." Anastasia wiped her dusty hands on her jeans. "I don't think he's the only one worried about power outages. Actually, all the tradespeople are pretty swamped these days."

"You know" — Franz straightened his silk tie — "if you ever get in trouble, you can always crash at my cottage. It has a fireplace and a generator."

Anastacia suppressed a smile at the word "cottage." Everyone said "camp" in the north, but, even though Franz was born and bred here, he liked to sound like he was from somewhere "better."

"Thanks, Mr. Hahn," she said. "But I'm sure my Dad will manage. He knows how to take care of us."

Anastacia moved toward the exit. Franz stepped between her and the door.

"I know he survived some awful things in the Middle East." Wearing a sympathetic expression, Franz placed his hand on Anastacia's arm.

Anastacia didn't move. She had heard rumors about her boss.

He squeezed her arm. "But you have to remember. He couldn't save his wife and children. If things get dangerous, you need someone who can protect you. Someone strong, with money and influence."

He leaned toward her. Anastacia could feel his breath on her chin. He smelled of cinnamon gum.

"Someone like me. I could provide a lot for you, Stacy. I could take care of you." He stroked her cheek with the back of his knuckles.

Anastacia slammed her hand on top of his and flung it away. He looked shocked when, instead of stepping back, she stepped forward, her nose to his forehead.

"You have nothing I need," she stated. "And I can take damn good care of myself. In fact, if you had any idea what I am capable of, you would crawl under your big, posh desk and piss your fancy pants."

Franz stepped back and wiped his lips.

"Really, Stacy, you don't need to be so vulgar."

"You'd best keep your distance, Mr. Hahn, if you want to keep that expensive smile." She jerked open the door. "And my name is Anastacia. *You* don't get to call me anything else."

Face paling, Franz flinched. Her temper now under control, Anastacia resisted slamming the door and instead shut it with a firm click. She heard him muttering as she left.

"Stupid bitch. She'll be sorry."

She suspected he would be pulling out the bottle of Johnnie Walker he kept in his desk drawer.

When Anastacia's stepfather arrived, she helped him load the boxes of equipment into the back of his pickup truck. Jamail looked surprised when she hopped into the cab beside him.

"Don't you have a few more hours to work?" he asked.

"Nope," said Anastacia. "I quit."

She didn't tell Mr. Hahn, didn't even leave a note. If he made a fuss, so would she. Game over. She had drawn on every ounce of her self-control to refrain from committing "unsportsmanlike conduct" all over his ugly ass. She was never going back.

After Anastacia carried the boxes to the basement, she made tea for herself and her stepfather. Bedad joined them. The kitchen was mostly white — farmhouse-style table and chairs, cabinets with pinewood handles, gold-flecked counters, and white appliances. A pattern of large, white tiles with small, black, diamond-shaped tiles at the corners covered the floor. To one side of the kitchen lay the garage, and the living room was behind the opposite wall. The living room opened onto the dining area, which in turn opened onto the kitchen, like a backwards letter C. The space was bright, simple, and clean looking.

"Would you like to tell me what's going on?" Jamail asked.

Anastacia took a deep breath. "Nothing I can't handle, Dad." She poured three mugs of Earl Grey.

"I have no doubt of that," Jamail replied. "But I thought you might want to talk about it."

"My boss hit on me." She stirred a half-teaspoon of sugar into her tea.

"Ah," said Jamail as he reached for the milk. "And you set him straight."

"Damn straight."

Bedad looked back and forth from Anastacia to her stepfather, his face wrinkled in confusion.

"Do you want to press charges? I'll go down to the police station with you," said Jamail.

Anastacia blew on her tea and considered. "No, it's over."

"Will *he* be pressing charges?" asked her stepfather. "Depending on how straight you set him?"

Anastacia snorted. "No blood. No broken bones. Probably not even a bruise."

Jamail nodded. "Still, do you want to pursue this?"

"He's not worth my time."

"What does 'hit on me' mean?" asked Bedad.

Anastacia explained.

Bedad set down his mug so quickly that tea spilled over the top and onto the table. "What? You told me he was married, with a family."

"He is." Anastacia shrugged. "I guess it doesn't mean much to a slime-ball like that. He always did give me the creeps."

"I'll confront him and make him apologize." Bedad pushed back his chair and stood. "He cannot treat you like this."

"Sit down, Bedad," said Anastacia. "I can certainly take care of myself."

Bedad's face reddened as he pressed his lips tightly together. His fists opened and closed.

"You should probably sit down and drink your tea," said

Jamail. "If Anastacia wants to handle it her own way, it's best to let her. She doesn't like anyone stepping on her toes."

Bedad looked from one to the other, nodded curtly, and sat down. "Very well."

After he finished his tea, Jamail went to the basement to organize the emergency supplies. Anastacia rinsed the mugs and loaded them in the dishwasher.

"What if he had a knife?" asked Bedad.

"Who? Franz?"

"What if he was going to kill you if you didn't do what he wanted?" Bedad drummed the table with his fingertips.

"In his office with a store full of people?" Anastacia leaned against the dishwasher and crossed her arms.

"I worry about you." Bedad sighed.

"Well, you can stop worrying," she said. "You gave me the antidote. There have been no side effects. I'm going to live to be a hundred."

"Not if one of these crazy Outworlders attacks you."

"*I'm* a crazy Outworlder."

"No, Anastacia. You're not. You were born in Dawn's End, and you carry the blood of a great family. It is my duty to keep you safe."

"Unless you are going to follow me around twenty-four, seven, that's impossible." Anastacia wet a dishrag and wiped the table. "Besides, shit happens. People die. You have to accept it."

Bedad frowned. "No, I don't. I'll be returning home for a

while. I need to let everyone know that I found you and that you're well. I won't be able to protect you personally. But there is another way."

Anastacia hung the rag over the sink. "What way?"

"Do you still have your panther bracelet?"

"Of course."

"I think I can reactivate it." Bedad said. "Perhaps not to the same level of power it had in Dawn's End, but enough that no one could ever force you to . . . you know."

"Really? Hot damn. Do it. That would be awesome!"

"I want you to wear it at all times, but it is not to be used lightly," said Bedad.

"I know, I know. Unknown side-effects. Don't use it frivolously. 'With great power comes great responsibility.' Yadda yadda yadda."

"I don't know yadda yadda yadda, but if that means you will swear to use it only in emergencies, I will do what I can to activate your panther bracelet."

"I'll get it," said Anastacia. She rushed to her room before he could change his mind.

Chapter Five - Harmony

Even though the Outworld was an exciting place to explore and Bedad wanted nothing more than to spend time with Anastacia, he was glad to return to Dawn's End. On the other side of the portal, he stood for a few moments, simply breathing in the pure air. He had promised Durward and the others he would keep them apprised of his progress. He would tell them he had found Anastasia alive and well and administered the antidote. Perhaps her genetic inheritance from her father, Alaric Morrel, the panther man, had provided her with immunity and she had not needed the antidote after all. Regardless, Anastacia was well, without a sign of illness. Bedad was happy to be bringing good news. In his pack, he carried photographs Anastacia had given him to share with family and friends. The people of Dawn's End would celebrate tonight.

He rented a boat from Josh the river-man, who ferried both passengers and cargo up and down Long River, but also loaned vessels to those he knew personally and trusted. Bedad rowed south, passing the mountains where Anastacia's mother and father had traveled, seeking the magical key that enabled them to save Dawn's End from the encroaching darkness so many years ago. Though he could not see them from the river, he knew he passed Asa the Healer's cottage on the left, the Meeting Place, and the door to Lucerne, Switzerland in the Outworld. Swallows flitted from tree to tree, and the scent of flowers hung in the warm summer air. News spread fast in Dawn's End, a place where birds could carry messages faster than Bedad could run. He traveled quickly, wanting to surprise Durward with news of Anastacia's good health.

His mentor's home was on the bank of Long River. Bedad

pulled Josh's boat up on shore and walked through the well-kept herb garden to the house.

Durward and his wife, Misty, were ecstatic to see him. Misty was sister to Bedad's adoptive mother, Lissa. Since Misty and Lissa had an ancestor who was a panther person, both had grayish skin and gray hair, almond-shaped gray eyes, pug noses, and small, gleaming, white teeth. Misty was tall and lean, with a long neck that reminded Bedad of a swan. She wore her hair in a simple, short cut. Lissa was shorter and curvier, with thick, curly, gray hair. She blamed her plumpness on her incessant baking for her large family. Bedad loved them both dearly.

Durward shared stories of the progress in Dawn's End while Bedad had been away. Farmers had built an irrigation system to help in drier periods. Several communities had renamed their villages in honor of the Esteemed Nicole, Alaric Morrel, and their daughter, Anastacia the Bold. A new school had been finished at Bedad's village, now named Blue Jay, in honor of Morrel's faithful companion during his adventures with Anastacia's mother, Nicole. New road signs had been erected at crossroads, connecting people and aiding travelers. Every community showed progress and success. The evils Anastacia and her companions had fought against were losing their grip, and villages were returning to happier days. The leaders of Dawn's End had passed more laws to prevent contamination from the outside.

"How did you like the Outworld?" Durward asked. The three of them sat outside on a wooden bench and leaned against the front wall of Misty and Durward's cottage. Dusk was falling, and stars were slowly blinking into view.

"It frightens me."

"Then it must be dreadful," said Misty. "It takes a lot to

frighten you."

"Is it the violence and greed?" asked Durward. "Outworlders seem ruled by their lusts."

"The people do not understand their connection to each other and how their selfish behavior creates a world no one wants. But just as bad is what they have done to the earth."

Bedad went on to explain about rivers bursting into flames from pollution, communities unable to drink their tainted water, mass extinctions of plant and animal species, dying coral reefs, ocean acidification and loss of oxygen, overpopulation, and the Pacific Trash Vortex. He explained how irreplaceable farmland was being transformed into desert or paved over, about ozone depletion, overfishing, enormous landfills, acid rain, and deforestation. He spoke about PCPs, medical waste, toxic heavy metals, pesticides, herbicides, DDT, E-waste, the Alberta tar sands, nuclear waste, and dioxins. He explained sick-building syndrome, the rise in allergies, cities with air quality warnings, the poor quality of food sold to consumers, and wars over food and water.

"In addition, the earth herself seems to be fighting for survival. Wild weather is increasing dramatically, as well as volcanic eruptions and earthquakes. Perhaps the earth feels her only hope is to destroy the humans who are destroying everything else."

When he finished, Misty and Durward remained silent. The three of them sat, watching the stars unfold, listening to crickets, and feeling the fresh breeze on their faces. Misty surreptitiously wiped her eyes.

Finally, Durward cleared his throat and stood. "You have to bring her back here. No one should have to live like that."

Bedad nodded. Misty patted his shoulder and followed her

husband indoors. Bedad sat outside until the last star had opened her clear, bright eye.

The next day, Bedad returned the boat to Josh and trekked overland toward his own village of Harmony. He passed the faerieland valley on his left, and, on his right, a panther village now named Newman's Refuge after Anastacia's mother. His heart blossomed at how well Dawn's End was recovering from its last crisis.

He rested at the panther village, now named Alaric Place, where Anastacia had been born. Her father's family welcomed news of her, and Bedad did not repeat the litany of horrors he had shared with Misty and Durward. He handed out a few photographs and listened to their excited reactions with a bittersweet smile.

As he traveled the next day, he considered how things had changed. Life was improving in Dawn's End even though some of the new laws enacted to restrict outside influence were a bit strict and the proposed punishments extreme. Although Anastacia and others had saved Dawn's End from disaster, the inhabitants remained nervous about the risk of contamination from the Outworld. Village Councils had either destroyed or locked away all books, photographs, and other objects from the Outworld. Anyone caught with these subversive materials faced severe punishment. No one could use the portals without permission from his or her Village Council. Fortunately, with Durward and Misty's support, Bedad had quickly convinced the Council that his trips to gather medicinal plants would benefit everyone. Bedad suspected the pendulum had swung too far in reaction, but he believed things would eventually settle in the rational middle.

As he headed to Harmony, he tried to imagine how he could persuade Anastacia to return with him. Because of the antidote, she would be safe in Dawn's End. But she was stubbornly independent. She had spent most of her life in the Outworld and viewed it as home. Her only strong memories of Dawn's End were recent ones, from the last crisis, and, therefore, negative. If she could remember her earlier time here with her parents, Nicole and Morrel, she might be more positive. Perhaps his adoptive parents, Lissa and Ellsworth, would have some ideas.

As Bedad sat with his family around the wooden kitchen table, he was careful not to say anything upsetting in front of his seven adopted brothers and sisters. They peppered Bedad with questions about Anastacia and her world.

"Does she like dancing? What is the music like in the Outworld? Can she play an instrument? What's her favorite food? Does she like to draw? How far can she throw a ball? What does her room look like?"

Bedad would barely finish answering one question, before another would pop up. Several times he had to respond, "I don't know."

Telling them he hoped to convince Anastacia to return to Dawn's End would be foolish. If he failed, everyone would be disappointed. Although he did not believe in luck, he had an odd wish not to jinx himself by speaking his desire out loud. He wanted to bring Anastacia home for her own good. But not only that.

Bring her here, to his world, where he was the expert. Give her time to get to know him as an adult. And then . . . he felt himself blushing at the realization. He wanted to stroke her beautiful face, to taste her ample lips, to pull her strong, feminine body tightly against his. He hoped his desires didn't show in his words.

His family pinned Anastacia's picture to the wall over the fireplace.

"She's pretty," said one of the younger boys.

Bedad gazed into her blue eyes. "She's stunning."

He studied her light brown skin, elegant nose, and full lips. She conducted herself exactly the way a woman of noble heritage should. She never backed down, she spoke her mind, and she stood up for herself and others.

One of his sisters prompted him to speak further about Anastacia the Bold. "Tell us what she's like. What do people notice most about her when they meet her?"

Bedad related stories about Anastacia's love of sports, her studies at the university, her volunteer work, her sense of humor, and her ready smile. "I also hear she's a good hunter, although I haven't seen her hunt myself."

Bedad didn't tell his siblings about Anastacia's job at the wilderness supply store or why she had quit. Those details would only create confusion and concern, especially for young children. Instead, he finished by telling them about Stumpy, Anastacia's cat with half a tail.

"Stumpy is a sad name for a cat," said one of the boys. "Can't you fix his tail?"

Bedad scratched his lengthening whiskers. "I never thought of that. I probably could."

"Do it!" his little sister said. "It will make her and the cat happy."

"All right." Bedad laughed. "I will."

He spent the next five days in his laboratory. Lissa sent food in to him each day on a tray and shook her head when one of the children carried the meal back mostly uneaten. Finally, she marched into the laboratory.

Bedad's usually tidy workspace was chaotic. The table was covered with dirty apparatus, crushed herbs, and chemical spills.

She crossed her arms and frowned. "Really, Bedad, you're exhausting yourself over a cat's tail. That's beyond sensible."

He waved his hand in the air dismissively. "Oh, I solved that the first morning. I can get the tail to regenerate easily."

Lissa smiled, her chubby cheeks dimpling. "Good for you. What are you up to then?"

"I was thinking. If I could fix the cat, maybe I could fix other things as well." He went on to explain several of the problems the Outworld was facing.

"It sounds to me like most of those difficulties are caused by too many people wanting too many things they don't really need," she said. "You can't fix that."

Bedad pressed his lips tightly together and nodded. "I just want to give them more time. Maybe then they can learn to live in harmony with the earth and with each other. If I could repair what they've done to the water system, that would make the biggest difference."

Lissa pushed back a gray curl that was falling into her eyes. "What do you mean?"

"I want to find an effective way to remove heavy metals, toxins, oil spills, parasites, and other impurities from large bodies of water."

"That's a monumental job for one person," said Lissa. "Even someone as special as you."

"Yes," said Bedad, "I know. The hardest part is to purify the water, but not completely. Life doesn't blossom in sterile water. But I have to try."

Lissa gave him a gentle hug. "All right then, but first eat everything on this tray, or I'm going to get Ellsworth to lock you out of the laboratory." She gave him a warning look. "You know I will."

Bedad smiled. He and Lissa both knew Ellsworth could never find a way to keep Bedad out of any place he wished to enter. But they also knew Bedad would never defy his adoptive parents, whose love, patience, and generosity had healed the invisible scars of his childhood.

Bedad kissed Lissa's round cheek. "Yes, Mother." He sat on a stool and reached for a slice of cheese. "I also wouldn't say no to a cookie or two."

Chapter Six - Hunting

"When will we get to do archery again?" Kyle Brewbaker asked.

Anastacia was helping him practice dribbling a basketball.

"I don't know," she said. "Why?"

"I wanna get as good as you."

Anastacia smiled. "Probably not for a while. Now, focus on switching hands. You need to strengthen your left hand. That's it. Keep working on it."

She patted Kyle's shoulder and went on to Rupert who was throwing a red air ball against the wall and then chasing it when it bounced wildly beyond his reach.

"Would you like to play catch with me?" asked Anastacia.

"Yeah!" Rupert picked up the ball and stood in front of Anastacia.

"Back up a little," she said.

Rupert took two steps back and then threw the ball to Anastacia's left. She snatched it out of the air with one hand and pulled it into her body. "Good try. What do you look at when you throw the ball, Rupert?"

He looked up at the ceiling with his large, brown eyes and then shrugged.

"Put one foot forward like this." She demonstrated.

He copied her.

"The other one. Because you're right-handed, you put your left foot forward."

Rupert hopped into place. Out of the corner of her eye, she saw Kyle kick the ball against the wall and walk away, his arms crossed and his lip curled into a snarl.

"Now watch how I pull my arm back," she said to Rupert. "I'm looking right at you when I throw. See?" She gently lobbed the ball underhand.

Rupert caught it and then cheered.

"Great job. Now, throw it like that to me."

They practiced until seven-year-old Gabriel Wolozinski came in. "Lunch time!" he shouted.

Everyone put away the equipment and filed into the kitchen.

As he ate, Gabriel slurped his soup through the space in his front teeth.

"That's cool," said Rupert. "How'dya do that?"

Gabriel grinned, showing spaces where his upper lateral teeth were missing.

"I still have all my baby teeth," said Rupert.

"Another couple of years," said Anastacia. "Don't be in a hurry to grow up."

"Why not?" Rupert looked at her curiously. A tiny, ring-shaped noodle was stuck to his face below his left nostril. "Being big is good."

"Being little is good, too." Anastacia passed him a napkin. "You only get to be four years old once in your whole life. Then it's gone forever. And if you spent it trying to act like a grownup, then you missed all the fun of being four."

"Oh—"

Gabriel interrupted. "Like getting eggs from the Easter Bunny. Grownups don't get that."

"That's true," Anastacia said. "But we do get to make and eat good food for Easter dinner."

"We had kielbasa, pierogi, chocolate maurka, and babka for Easter dinner," Gabriel said, "and lots of candy eggs to find."

"Me, too," said Chester. "Not the weird stuff, the eggs."

"I like pierogies," said Petal. Her glossy, black hair was pulled on top of her head and fastened with a glittery clip. Her little fingernails were painted gold, and artificial diamonds sparkled in her stud earrings. "Even though my mother says they're fattening," she added.

"I like poggies, too," said Rupert. "They're great."

"Pie-ro-gies are great." Petal enunciated each syllable.

"Yeah, I said I like them."

"Chocolate eggs are better." Chester smiled, showing his crooked front teeth, which looked as though someone had pressed hard in the middle, turning them inward.

"I got grapes," said Rupert.

"What do you mean?" asked Anastacia.

"Auntie Faith said the Easter Bunny didn't know I was living with her, so he didn't bring eggs. She told me to go in my room, and she hid grapes for me. That was fun."

Chester and Petal looked at Anastacia, as if wondering what she would say.

Rupert continued. "She said, 'Maybe he'll find you next year.' Do you think so?"

Anastacia nodded. "Maybe."

"I hope so," said Rupert. "I wanted to write him a letter, but Auntie Faith doesn't know where he lives. Do you?" He absently scratched his sparse eyebrow with his pudgy, little fingers.

Anastacia shook her head. "I think it's a secret. But you know what? I bought too many candy eggs for me to eat, so how about I bring you some?"

"Yay!" said Rupert.

"How come you live with your Aunt?" asked Gabriel.

"My dad left when I was one," said Rupert. "I don't 'member him but that's okay 'cos Auntie says he's white trash."

"Where's your mom?" asked Gabriel.

"Mom went to Toronto. When I was three."

"Why?"

"For work. She's coming back though."

"Where does she work?" asked Petal.

Rupert shrugged his small shoulders. "We don't know. Auntie Faith said maybe her letters got lost."

"But she could telephone," said Gabriel.

"Auntie Faith said maybe she doesn't have a phone."

"But—"

"Who wants more juice?" Anastacia felt a sudden urge to

scoop Rupert up and take him home. She wondered if he even remembered what his mother looked like.

The littlest children cleared the table. The teens did the dishes and cleaned up. Anastacia was adding to the list of needed supplies when Franz Hahn walked into the kitchen with Max.

"Hi everyone," said Max. "This is Mr. Hahn. He's donating some supplies for our outings. We're finally going to have some of our own snowshoes and skis."

"Cool," said one of the older boys.

"Thanks, Mr. Hahn," said another.

Anastacia gritted her teeth and started sweeping the floor. She did not look at Franz. Max caught her eye, and his thin, auburn eyebrows pulled inward toward the bridge of his nose.

"He could use some help unloading the stuff and putting it in the storage room." Max looked at Anastacia pointedly.

She turned away, dumped the contents of the dustpan into the trash, wiped her hands on her jeans, and headed for the washroom. Scowling, Franz leaned over to Max, whispered, and nodded his head in her direction. She felt her face flush as she left the room. What could he be saying to Max?

For the next half hour, Anastacia avoided Max, trying to decide how to approach this awkward situation. Franz must not have access to any of the teenage girls who came to the Empowerment Ventures Center. How low would he stoop to get his thrills? Why would he donate to the Center?

She finally approached Max just as he finished setting two older boys up in the boxing ring.

"I have to talk to you."

"Sure, but I have to keep an eye on the kids." His steel-blue eyes never left the ring. He took supervision seriously.

"It's about Franz Hahn."

Anastacia studied Max's face—the slightly prominent forehead set off by arched, auburn eyebrows, the simple haircut. She wondered if he used hair product on his adorable, rust-colored mustache and beard. Would his facial hair be soft or scruffy to the touch?

"He asked me if you were always so unfriendly," said Max.

Her stomach clenched. What if Franz had turned Max against her? She chewed the inside of her left cheek. How should she say this? Straight out, the way she always did.

"He's a pig, Max."

Max glanced at her with a startled expression. "Go on."

He focused back on the boys. "Tom, arms up. You're leaving yourself wide open."

"I quit my job at his shop because he made a pass at me," said Anastacia. "He's married with two kids."

"Hmm."

"My dad wanted me to charge him with sexual harassment, but I didn't want the stigma. I can take care of myself."

"I'm sure you can." Max's voice was dismissive. "I have to coach now."

"Oh, okay."

Anastacia bit her lip. If only he had smiled at her. He would be able to tell she was being honest if he just looked her in the face. But he had set his square jaw and raised his sexy, crooked nose in a determined expression. Anastacia did not know what else to say. Usually, she hated when guys treated her like she needed help, but she would have appreciated a little sympathy or compassion in this situation. She nodded and left.

During the afternoon, she worked with some of the older kids on floor hockey skills. After they finished, she spent some time reorganizing the equipment.

Sally poked her pert, little nose around the door. "Have you seen Max?"

Anastacia shook her head.

"I have some papers he needs to sign, and I want to talk to him about giving Petal piano lessons. I think she is ready." Sally's voice was high with excitement. "I just demonstrated how to do the C scale, and she took to it immediately. I just had to show her the fingering once for each hand. She can already do both hands simultaneously, smooth as pink frosting. That's amazing."

"That's nice." Anastacia mumbled as she rinsed the protective goggles from floor hockey in a sterilizing solution.

Sally pushed back her frizzy, shoulder-length, brown hair. Her sweet smile broadened. "I've never taught a kid with such strong natural talent. Petal's mother is a single mom, so lessons might be out of her price range. We'll have to convince her Petal needs this. She can't possibly say no."

Anastacia dropped a pair of goggles in the sink and looked at Sally. "Of course, she can. It's not up to us to decide what's right for other people's children."

Sally raised her thin, penciled eyebrows in protest. "But Petal could be gifted. What right does her mother have to deny

Petal this opportunity?"

"The right of a mother to decide what's best for her own child," said Anastacia. "Mothers have reasons for what they do that other people may not know or understand."

"She might be worried about paying for tests and all that. But there aren't that many, especially at the beginning," Sally continued. "I'm sure she could manage the fee if she knew ahead of time."

"She'd have to start charging more," said Anastacia.

Sally's smile faltered. "What do you mean?"

"Nothing, never mind. I'm in a shitty mood."

Anastacia realized Sally did not know how Petal's mother made her living or what she spent most of her money on. The scars on her arms told a lot. Seeing her standing on Cumberland Street at one in the morning, in a miniskirt, in fifteen-below-zero weather, told the rest.

"I'm sure Petal's mother would be thrilled if you gave her little girl free piano lessons," said Anastacia.

Sally smiled again. "So I just have to check with Max before I give her the permission papers."

"Like I said, I don't know where he is. Last I saw him he was coaching boxing."

Anastacia did not see Max before she left. All the way home on the bus she wondered what lies Franz had told Max about her and whether they would ruin her chances with him. Surely Max wouldn't believe any bull from Franz. Sweet Max, yummy Max, with his solid, stocky body and his autumn hair. How would it feel to kiss that cute, sparse, reddish beard and moustache? And feel his front left chipped tooth on her tongue? A tingle fluttered over her body as she thought about his tight buns and his wiry six-pack. Rumor was he had a huge tattoo on his back of a snarling wolf, but she had never seen it. She wanted to. Wanted to run her hands all over it.

She probably never would. Depending on what lies Franz had told, Max might even tell her not to come back to Empowerment Ventures. Franz had a lot of clout in this city. As the bus pulled up to her stop, Anastacia sighed. Nothing could be done about it anyway. She had told Max the truth. He could choose to believe it or not.

Once she was upstairs in her bedroom, she emailed Julie, pouring her heart out and cursing herself for not charging Franz with sexual harassment when he came onto her. But it had only been one incident and he had only touched her face, yadda, yadda, yadda. Even if Julie didn't have an answer, venting about the situation was a great relief.

As she looked around her room, she wondered what Max would think of it. Her proudest possessions were a Thunder Bay flag autographed by all three Staal brothers; her MVP award for the final winning game of the season in which she had scored a hat trick; a shelf filled with basketball, soccer, and hockey competition trophies; a photo she took SCUBA diving a wreck by Neys Provincial Park; and a photograph of herself with her mother at the Winter Olympics in Vancouver. He'd be impressed, but would he find her lifestyle attractive or intimidating?

Sometimes, she hated being six feet tall and faster and stronger than most men. Her full physical power had developed after her return from Dawn's End. She was suddenly able to lift more than her body weight, to run and skate almost twice as fast as before, and to jump like an Olympic track and field medalist. Competitive sports began to bore her once she realized she was guaranteed to win most things she attempted. Since nobody liked a glory hog, she had to hold herself back in team sports. When she competed in single sports, she always felt she cheated the second-place winner of her rightful place. So, instead, she skied, hiked, dove, and shot arrows into very far away, red targets. Now, she only competed against herself or wild animals.

Hunting felt right. Anastacia's neighbor, Mr. Ferguson, who had taken his three sons hunting and fishing the moment they were old enough to sit quietly and follow his rules, had heard about her archery skills.

"Shooting at a target is fun, I'm sure." He scratched his thick beard. "But if you want to really test yourself, you ought to try a moving target."

"What do you mean?"

"Hunting, unless you're squeamish." He raised his bushy eyebrows.

"I doubt it," said Anastacia. "I'm not the squeamish type."

Mr. Ferguson laughed without dropping the ever-present toothpick between his teeth. He had substituted toothpicks for cigarettes the day his first son was born. "I've noticed. If Jamail says it's all right, I'll teach you how to hunt. You might want to start with a rifle first, though. Bow hunting takes a lot of strength and skill."

"No rifle." Anastacia shook her head. "If I kill an animal, do we split the meat?"

"Only if you help butcher it, too. Can you handle blood?"

"Ha. Have you seen me play hockey?"

Mr. Ferguson slapped her on the back with his large, heavy hand. "You're my kinda people, kid."

Hunting had been more challenging, and more rewarding, than she expected. Practicing with a target seemed as easy and natural to her as breathing. Twang, thud, twang, thud, twang, thud. Most people shot one arrow at a time, checking each for accuracy. Anastacia preferred to empty her quiver, shooting with a precise rhythm that left observers speechless.

Hunting, however, was where her instincts came alive. Mr. Ferguson, and his sons, treated her like one of the guys. She loved the hours spent riding in the pick-up truck, hunkering down by a worn spot near a stream, listening for changes in the forest sounds, anticipating a glimpse of prey. The first time she brought down a deer with an arrow, she shouted for joy.

"I guess there's no chance of us getting a second one now." Mr. Ferguson crossed his arms and flipped his toothpick up and down between his lips.

Anastacia clamped her hand over her mouth, mortified.

"Sometimes two or three travel together," he said. "Did ya think of that?"

"No. Sorry."

"No point in whispering now."

Mr. Ferguson taught her how to track partridge, rabbit, deer, and moose. Sometimes they stalked an animal, walking silently upwind. This method was called still-hunting, even though they were moving, which, Anastacia thought, didn't make much sense grammatically.

Mr. Ferguson was deeply impressed by her stealth. "Even though you're a big girl, you walk as silently as a cat. My boys sound like bulldozers compared to you."

"You're pretty quiet, too," she said. He was an enormous man, taller than Anastacia, with the girth of a grizzly. He had to order specially made boots for his enormous feet. They left huge zigzag prints behind.

Anastacia favored still-hunting over stand-hunting, where they waited in a blind on the ground or in a tree for an animal to approach. Some of Mr. Ferguson's friends attracted bears with stale donuts, but she preferred to find a frequently used path and stake it out without bait.

Flushing out a hiding animal was the most exciting of all. When a panicked partridge took to the air or a deer fled past, she had only fleeting seconds to aim, ensure the way was clear of fellow hunters, and fire before the animal was obscured by the bush.

In his garage, Mr. Ferguson directed the butchery and gave her a fair portion of the meat. Sawing into the animal's belly had been grisly but exciting. Julie thought hunting was barbaric, but the role of predator felt natural to Anastacia.

Did Max hunt? Would he think it strange that she took so much joy in the pursuit of quarry? At least she didn't mount partridge feathers and rabbit skins on her bedroom wall like some people did. Just posters, flags, and trophies.

Stumpy came running over for a chin scratch. Anastacia sighed as she signed out of her email account. She shut her laptop and knelt beside him.

"Hello, my baby." She rubbed his neck and scratched under his ear just the way he liked. "Aren't you a pretty boy?"

Stumpy purred and arched his body.

Anastacia stroked down his back to his tail and along the shaft.

"What the . . . ?" she exclaimed when she discovered the tail did not end in a stump but went on and on to a lovely, tufted end.

He twisted, as only a cat can, and tiptoed away, his new tail forming a long, cocky, question mark. How was that possible? She knew only one person who could even attempt such a thing.

"Bedad!" she shouted. "What the hell did you do to my cat?"

Chapter Seven - Where Has All the Water Gone?

After the early flood, the sun never stopped shining. It was the driest spring on record in Thunder Bay. Water levels were low to begin with from the lack of melting snow. The fire season started early and with a vengeance. Red as blood, the sun smoldered in a dismal, gray sky. The arid, smoky air irritated Anastacia's nose and caught in her throat like a dry cinder. Evacuees from the north and east filled high school gymnasiums, recreation centers, and church basements in Thunder Bay, Wawa, Sudbury, Sioux Lookout, Kapuskasing, Matachewan, and Greenstone.

The Ministry of Natural Resources imposed fire bans all across the province. Water bombers and fire fighters were stretched beyond their ability to cope. The Ministry warned people to stay out of the woods, closed campgrounds, and discouraged travel. A spark from a backfiring car could start a raging forest fire.

Patients suffering from asthma, emphysema, and allergies clogged the emergency room at the Thunder Bay Regional Medical Center. Hospital gridlock lasted for weeks. Even the hallways were filled to capacity.

Out west, the prairies dried into a dust bowl to rival conditions during the Great Depression. The price of wheat soared.

Quebec, New Brunswick, and British Columbia fought rampant forest fires. Rare old growth went up like year-old hay. Ancient totem poles on Anthony Island burned to ash, an irreplaceable heritage lost forever.

The western United States suffered its worst drought in eight hundred years. Arizona and New Mexico rationed water.

Several droughts blossomed into wildfires. California burned again, as did Minnesota, Oklahoma, Maryland, and Texas. The price of beef soared.

Jamail's water barrels were far from full. He had shoveled every bit of snow into them in addition to collecting the infrequent rain runoff from the roof. Anastacia wondered if, after all their efforts, they would have a garden at all. The ever-resilient rhubarb sprouted, but the leaves were undersized and lacked their usual glossy vibrancy.

Saving water became a city-wide imperative. Anastacia and her stepfather each showered only once a week. They plugged the tub and then bailed and added the water to the rain barrels, careful to use non-phosphate soaps and shampoos. They both sponge-bathed on the days in between. Jamail poured any water used to wash fruit and vegetables or for cooking around the raspberry canes and apple tree. They used half a cup of water to brush their teeth. Before washing their clothes, they wore them at least twice. People shared water saving tips through social media.

Still the water level in Lake Superior and the other Great Lakes dropped. Small streams and ponds in the area dried up. The Kaministiquia River, which had flooded its banks earlier, became a muddy trickle. Anastacia found dead birds, squirrels, and a woodchuck in the back yard, driven to search unsuccessfully for water, or killed by heat exhaustion. Spider webs threaded the birdbath. Dead leaves and dust collected in the dry bowl. Anastacia felt guilty for leaving it empty.

The price of food climbed. Restaurants closed. Children of middle-income families learned to eat everything on their plate or go hungry. Elders and the very young required extra care in the feverish temperatures.

Anastacia and Bedad helped Jamail in his garden. They

removed the Plexiglas covers, previously installed to prevent hail damage. Jamail worried more now about the intensified heat from the covers than the threat of hailstorms. Along with last autumn's leaves, he mixed twice as much compost as usual into his garden soil in an effort to slow drainage. Jamail planted drought-resistant cow beans, corn, mustard greens, purlane, spinach, and Swiss chard. He omitted the vegetables that hog space, such as broccoli and cauliflower, and instead set tomatoes, squash, peppers, eggplant closely together.

To diminish evaporation, Jamail layered mulch around and between the plants. To prevent water from draining away, he positioned the soil so that the plants sat in a depression. Even so, the usually robust vegetables were small and slow to mature.

"What other tips you got?" asked Mr. Ferguson. Since Jamail had grown up in one of the driest countries in the world, the whole neighborhood was turning to him for advice on how to garden in the extreme weather.

Everyone let their lawns turn brown and tried to grow something edible instead to offset the increasing expense of groceries. Food banks ran out of supplies. The Sally Ann sandwich truck was hard pressed to help the homeless. Vagrants and drunks died in the streets from the heat.

Anastacia was hand-watering the vegetables when she heard something crash through the woods behind her house. A deer? Deer had been wandering in and around the city for years. This close to Centennial Park and Boulevard Lake, the long-legged, graceful creatures were familiar sights and frequent garden pests. Now that food had grown even more precious, gardeners sought more and more elaborate deterrents.

This time, though, the intruder was not a deer. On gangly but powerful legs, a massive bull moose emerged from the trees. Taller than Anastacia, it lurched across the dead grass behind their property. The dewlap hanging under its chin swayed left and then right. It was dying, of thirst or starvation, or both.

The moose looked at her with bulging, desperate eyes. Its rack was small, three points only. Its brown fur was matted, dusty, and shabby. Awkwardly, it staggered into the yard and headed for the garden. Anastacia realized it would destroy all the struggling young plants.

"No!" She set down the watering can and waved her arms. The moose kept coming, a determined, dogged expression on its long, melancholy face.

Although Anastacia was six feet tall, the moose was almost a foot taller and, even though its ribs showed, five or six times her weight. The leaf rake was lying against the deck. Anastacia raced for it, picked it up, and intercepted the moose. She smacked the rake across its face. The moose tossed its head and bellowed but kept staggering forward across the burnt grass. She slammed the moose with the rake again. It lowered its head and tried to butt her. Nimble as a cat, she dropped, rolled out of the way, and sprang back to her feet. The moose turned away and took the last few steps to the garden.

"No bloody way!" Anastacia took a deep breath and pushed up her sleeve, accessing the panther bracelet. "Leave!"

The moose shuddered as light poured from her bracelet into its emaciated body.

"Leave!"

The moose lurched backwards on its legs as it stretched its head forward, trying to reach a pepper shoot. It shuddered, moaned, stumbled back a few more steps, and then collapsed, first to its knees and then onto its side, legs out stiffly. Slowly, Anastacia lifted her hand off the bracelet and lowered her arm. The moose quivered; its dewlap flapped. It tried to lift its head, snorted loudly, and then released a long sigh. Anastacia approached cautiously, poked its head and its bony butt with the rake. Nothing. She watched for breathing. Nothing.

"Shit."

Anastacia picked up the rake. She hadn't meant to kill it. A wave of nausea swept over her. She turned away from the moose and vomited.

That was weird. She could usually handle stuff like that. Hunting was far more grisly.

Hunting! Meat! Even though the moose was skinny, its meat shouldn't be wasted.

She dropped the rake and stumbled through the front gate and down the street, fighting nausea the whole way. She pounded on Mr. Ferguson's door. He had the supplies and equipment for butchering a large animal.

Her legs felt as weak as the moose's. She held the door frame, waiting. Luckily, Mr. Ferguson was home. He opened the door, barefoot in green shorts and a T-shirt that said, "I love deer . . . . with a full-bodied beer."

Anastacia tried not to stare at his huge, bare feet. Hobbit's feet on a giant.

"Mr. Ferguson, you got room in your freezer?"

He nodded and took his toothpick from his mouth. "What's this about?"

"A whole lotta meat for free. How'd you like to split a bull moose fifty-fifty? All you have to do is help me butcher it."

"Sounds like a good deal, but, unless it was killed on your front step, it could spoil before we get there." He scratched his heavy beard. "Can't afford gas for my trucks."

"It's just as close," said Anastacia. "Grab your stuff, and let's go."

Later that night, after they cleaned up the mess and stocked the freezers, two countries on the other side of the world upped the stakes for everyone on the planet. Bedad had gone to bed. Jamail turned on the evening news and stood riveted to the spot as the anchorman announced the biggest insanity humanity had ever committed. The whole world watched the reports of the nuclear bombings in India and Pakistan.

Anastacia sat on the couch, holding her stepfather's hand, as the casualty estimates were announced. She couldn't stop trembling, even when she wrapped Jamail and herself in a heavy, knitted blanket.

Bombay, India: estimated 480, 000 deaths and 700,000 injured. Faisalabad, Pakistan: estimated 340,000 deaths and 500,000 injured. Calcutta, India: estimated 360,000 deaths and 600,000 injured. Islamabad, Pakistan: estimated 155,000 deaths and 200,000 injured. Madras, India, estimated 370,000 deaths and 620,000 injured. On and on it went. Photos of mushroom clouds on the horizon filled the screen.

Border guards stopped refugees pouring out of both nations. No country was prepared to take on this many homeless, impoverished people, never mind those who would die, now or later, from radiation sickness. No one rushed in to ground zero to help the wounded and dying.

The unthinkable had happened. Madness had been released upon the world. Everyone, everywhere, sat glued to televisions and computers, waiting to see if any other country would get caught up in the carnage.

"I can't believe this," said Anastacia, tears pouring down her cheeks. "It's crazy. Why would anyone do this?"

Her stepfather squeezed her hand. "War is the greatest insanity of all. It can never be rationalized."

Chapter Eight- The Giant Sleeps

Anastacia brought enough moose burgers to Empowerment Ventures to feed everyone. She needed to do something good, even if it was only a small act of kindness in a world filled with huge acts of violence. The people in Pakistan and India were beyond her help, but here she could do something.

The children and teens in the center talked constantly about the war. Neither country had invaded the other with ground troops after the initial blasts. Die of radiation poisoning at home or on your enemy's land — neither made much sense. Every government held emergency meetings to condemn the attacks, but carefully resisted choosing sides. So far, no other governments had intervened. The United Nations called an emergency meeting. Every political leader came out against the use of the bombs, although some hinted as to who they thought ultimately responsible for the horrors.

Max drew the children around him. "We know you might be scared by what happened last night. The pictures on the news are disturbing. But please remember that India and Pakistan are far, far away from here. No one is going to drop bombs on Canada. We're safe."

Max smiled at Anastacia. "And today we have many things to be grateful for. We have some new friends who have come to share their traditions with us. Anastacia has brought enough moose meat for a feast."

Then Max whispered to her, "This is a great distraction from the catastrophe we've been watching on television."

Although the meat was tough and stringy, Anastacia knew it was a lucky gift. She did not tell Bedad she had used the bracelet but said that the moose had expired from thirst instead. He was too distracted by the news of the nuclear explosions, fallout, and mounting casualties to doubt her. What horrified him most was discussion of ash falling from the sky.

"I guess that's what's left of the buildings, and cars, and stuff," he said.

"And the people." Anastacia's voice was choked with emotion.

"By the Crystal," whispered Bedad. "What can we do?"

"Nothing," said Anastacia. "It's too late for them. But at least I'm going to make the kids at the center have a good day."

Loud, excited voices filled the air as the smell of sizzling, wild burger filled the kitchen. Max thumped her on the back and acted as though nothing had changed between them. Her heart did a small flip-flop when he said, "With the soaring price of meat, this will be the best meal many of us have had in a while. Thank you, Anastacia."

"Hooway for Anasasha," shouted Rupert.

Several people clapped.

She had brought enough moose meat to feed their guests as well. A tall Anishinaabe young woman in a white jingle dress and five First Nations men—one in his late twenties, two in their late thirties, one in his forties, and an elder in his fifties—had come to the center to share their traditions with the children.

"I like your dress," Petal said to the young woman, as she admired the rows of cone-shaped silver bells, the colorful ribbons, and the tassels on the hem.

"Thank you," the Anishinaabe woman replied and then smiled shyly.

Daniel Moonwind, the elder, had long hair threaded with gray that hung in a braid down his back. Behind gold-wire glasses, his crinkled eyes were so narrow Anastacia could not clearly discern the color. His teeth were crooked and dappled with gray fillings. The tips of his ears curled over, giving his face an elfish look. His skin was weathered and scarred. Around his head, he wore a wide leather band, decorated with white fox fur, and, in spite of the heat, he had on a collared shirt with a vest embroidered with cultural symbols.

Anastacia's bracelet tingled when Daniel Moonwind shook her hand. His eyes narrowed even further, and he held her hand a little longer, studying her face.

Because it was too hot and noisy outside, everyone went into the cooler basement gymnasium. The smell of grubby children and unwashed adolescents filled the room. Daniel Moonwind purified the space with a smoky smudge of sage and tobacco before beginning. The children sat at one end and watched quietly, listening as he sent his low, strange prayers to the Seven Directions. Then the drummers set up in the middle, and the audience formed two concentric circles around them. The Elder took the lead.

"The drum is the heartbeat of Mother Earth," said Daniel Moonwind, his voice strong and engaging. "There are some groups that believe only *First Nations* people should touch the drum. There are some who believe only First Nations *men* should touch the drum."

Anastacia sat up straighter, all her senses alert. Before her trip to Dawn's End, she had considered herself a woman of color. She still did, even though she no longer identified with African-Canadians. Heritage, race, and traditions interested her as well as prejudice, racism, and exclusion. Above race and nationality, she was always, first and last, a woman, even if she could probably kick Pavel Datsyuk's butt on the ice.

Would the First Nations people deny her as an equal?

"I am not one of them," continued Daniel.

Anastacia smiled and relaxed.

"However, sacred things should be touched with respect and reverence, so we ask that you do not finger it out of curiosity."

Daniel explained how the drum was handmade in the traditional style. "The skin is moose hide which I stretched over a log. Then I scraped away the hair with a *naanzhii'iganaatig* tool. When the Europeans brought wooden washtubs and barrels, my people used them as frames to stretch the rawhide. But I have gone back further, to the old, old days. I cut, burned, scraped, and hollowed a section of tree trunk, then wrapped the birch wood around it to make the drum frame. The oldest ways have the most power."

The children listened, wide-eyed.

"These represent the four directions and are made from white ash saplings." He touched each of the legs attached to the frame. They held the drum off the floor but also arched high above it. "We decorated them with feathers, bits of fur, animal claws, tiny shells, and silver disks that I hand — hammered. The Anishinaabek have a long tradition of working with silver." He pointed to the blue and red velveteen skirt encircling the drum. "These patterns are made from porcupine quills. We didn't use any plastic or glass beads. Each of the drummers worked on it as well."

Anastacia remembered her uncle was a dancer. Her mother had said he danced to a drum. Anastacia thought she meant an African drum, but now she knew it was something else. She wanted to learn about that. Something about her own heritage.

Daniel continued. "We are going to drum for healing, healing of the earth, its animals, and its people. Join us by focusing on bringing peace to the world before man destroys Mother Earth and her gifts."

Anastacia thought of the moose dying in her backyard. Mr. Ferguson had taken the hide. She wished it could somehow become transformed into a drum like this one.

Each drummer held one *baaba'akokowaan* or drumstick. It bent gradually toward the small end, which was wrapped in a piece of buckskin. The drummers sat at the four directions.

When the music began, the young Anishinaabe woman moved in short, shuffling steps, her dress jingling. The drumming filled the room and seemed to echo Anastacia's heartbeat. She found herself breathing in rhythm. Moving her arms in a "join me" motion, the woman invited all the children to rise and dance with her.

"I love pow wows," said Chester as he jumped up.

Rupert followed. Petal, dressed in a short, denim skirt, watched for a few seconds and then joined in, adding her own MTV steps. Gabriel waited until all the adults had started dancing and then cautiously followed Max's moves.

Anastacia removed her hoodie and dropped it on the floor beside Kyle, one of the few children who did not participate. The strange language rising and falling in simple sounds and the persistent booms of the drum carried her away. She wished she had been able to dance outside, to remove her sandals and connect the soles of her feet to Mother Earth. The power would flow through her into the soil and back again. The rhythm changed to a faster pace, and the Anishinaabe woman moved in half-circles and zigzags.

Anastacia, usually more at home on the hockey rink than the

dance floor, felt uplifted, alive, and invigorated. Her feet pounded to the beat as her body turned and bobbed. The sweet smell of sage lingered in the air. Sweat trickled down her back and chest, soaking her T-shirt. Her mind filled with the image of her father, Alaric Morrel, dark, bearded, and panther-like. She remembered him, so tall, smiling down at her, picking her up, and dancing around a white room. His chest was warm, and his hands were large and strong. She remembered the tickle of his facial hair on her cheek and his musky, masculine smell. His voice was deep and happy. She felt loved and secure. Never before had she envisioned him so clearly. The music stopped. The children clapped and cheered.

"That was awesome," said Gabriel as he pumped the air.

The children shuffled back to their spots.

Anastacia nodded, disoriented.

After the children had settled, Daniel Moonwind told the story of Nanabijou, the Sleeping Giant. When viewed from Thunder Bay, the shape of the Sibley Peninsula looks like a profile of a giant Anishinaabe warrior lying on his back with his arms folded on his chest. Anastacia had heard, and read, the story several times, but, when the elder told it, he spoke as though he had seen it unfold with his own eyes.

"Once the Anishinaabek wore striking silver jewelry mined from what is now the Silver Islet off Sibley Peninsula on Lake Superior. This was a gift from Nanabijou, the Spirit of the Deep Water, for their devotion. As long as the secret location was never given to the white man, the silver would be theirs. When their enemies, the Sioux, tried to force the location from Anishinaabek men they had captured, no one would divulge the secret. So, a Sioux warrior disguised himself as a traveling Anishinaabe and learned the location by trickery. He took several pieces of silver to show his chief. However, on his way home, the Sioux warrior met two white men who plied him with liquor and convinced him to show the whereabouts of the silver mine. A terrifying storm arose while they journeyed to the site, drowning the men. When it ended, the entrance to the mine was blocked with the giant stone, sleeping figure of Nanabijou. Plants and trees grew over his body, but, if you look closely, you can still see him lying on his back. Some say the land formation of the Sibley Peninsula is the Spirit of the Deep Water himself. Some people believe the Great Spirit sleeps until his people will need him the most. Then he will awaken and lead them to a new, happy life."

"I saw him in the harbor," said Gabriel. "My dad read about it, and we went to see him from Marina Park. I didn't know his whole story before."

"It is a very old story, well known to my people," said Daniel.

Gabriel continued. "Maybe the Sleeping Giant could help everybody. Maybe he could help Pakistan and India."

Daniel smiled. "Everyone who loves and respects Mother Earth, Father Sky, and the Great Water Spirit can learn from the story of Nanabijou. Whenever we want what another has, whenever our motives are filled with greed, we bring destruction."

"I'm going to tell my parents about this," said Gabriel. "They don't know the Sleeping Giant can wake up."

His family had arrived in Canada two years ago, able to speak only Polish. His father had been a lawyer but now drove a taxi. His mother had developed transverse myelitis last year and was confined to a wheelchair.

"I hope he comes soon," said Rupert. "My auntie was crying watching TV."

Everyone moved to the kitchen to make bracelets of deer hide. They sliced a wide strip of leather twice lengthwise in the middle, leaving the ends closed. Then they braided and twisted the leather through the slit.

"Now poke a hole in each end," said the young woman, "and tie it together with a leather string."

Sally dodged about the room, helping everyone with their tangles and confusion, but Anastacia could not get her strip of deer hide to work.

"I'm hopeless," she sighed, dropping the snarled mess onto the table. "I'm not the crafty type. I'll never be able to make a bracelet."

"Perhaps you already have the only bracelet you need," said Daniel quietly. "*Menidoowendaagozid.*"

Anastacia jerked in her seat and stared at the elder. He gave her a small smile as he passed a paint pen to Rupert.

After the drum group left and everyone began to clean up, Anastacia picked her hooded sweater up off the kitchen floor. An odd-shaped piece of fabric remained behind on the linoleum. Puzzled, she picked up and examined her hoodie. A chunk had been cut from the back. She saw several other long cuts as well.

"Who did this?" she asked.

Everyone froze, staring.

"Not me," said Gabriel. "That's bad."

"Why would someone want to wreck my clothes?"

She looked up. Kyle stared at her, his eyes bright with tears. He turned and ran out of the room.

Max gave Anastacia a puzzled look, and then he followed the boy. Everyone finished cleaning up in silence, except for Petal.

"Why would Kyle do that?" Petal said as she fastened lids on the paint pens and returned them to the carton.

"We don't know that he did," said Anastacia.

"My mom says clothes are expensive. That's why we buy ours at the Sally Ann."

"Kyle's a jerk," said Chester.

"Don't say that," Anastacia said. "We don't know what happened or why. Let's just finish cleaning up."

Sally started to sing *There are No Fleas on Me*. Soon, everyone was involved and laughing, the song moving faster and faster.

That evening, Anastacia told Bedad about her strange day.

"Kyle apologized afterward," she said. "But he couldn't explain why he cut up my sweatshirt. I thought he liked me."

"That may be why he did it," said Bedad.

"What do you mean?"

"You said he sat through all the dances."

Anastacia nodded.

"Perhaps he felt left out. Angry."

Anastacia sighed. "I guess. Who knows what happened this morning or last night? I'm pretty sure both his parents are alcoholics — don't repeat that. He was probably feeling frustrated and lonely. I'll bet the news was on at home, but no one was explaining it to him or reassuring him. Me up there, oblivious to his feelings, might have made him feel worse."

"Maybe he felt safer taking his anger and fear out on you rather than his parents."

"Hmm."

She told Bedad about Daniel Moonwind, how she had felt a tingle from her bracelet when he shook her hand and his strange comment after the dance.

"He sounds like a Shaman," said Bedad. "Do you have them in the Outworld?"

"I think so. Not many anymore, though. Man, this was one weird day."

Then she told Bedad what she had remembered about dancing with her father in Dawn's End when she was a toddler. "It was as clear as yesterday," she said. "I could feel his heavy beard against my cheek. How is that possible?"

"The heart remembers what the mind forgets," he replied.

Chapter Nine - Toxic

The news constantly broadcast the effects of the nuclear bombs dropped in India and Pakistan. Nepal, Burma, Bangladesh, Bhutan, Bahrain, Afghanistan, Tajikistan, and southern China experienced nuclear fallout, and the impact wouldn't stop there. High up in the atmosphere, winds carried the toxic mixture across Asia. Rain brought radioactive poison to earth far away from the initial blasts. Experts, who appeared on television and radio, speculated that contaminated rainwater or underground streams would carry it even further. Scientists explained that these events would dramatically escalate global warming and increase the incidence and scale of drought conditions throughout the world.

School closed six weeks earlier than normal. With the water shortage and the intense heat, the schools could not provide a proper level of comfort. Most of the children's homes were no better, so Max decided to give the club a face-lift. He opted to start summer hours, which allowed the children to spend more time at Empowerment Ventures.

Bedad knew Anastacia was attracted to Max Marshall. He couldn't blame her. The guy was fit, fun, tough, and generous. Everyone at Empowerment Ventures loved him. However, until Bedad volunteered to help paint the gymnasium one Sunday, he did not realize that Anastacia had a rival. Sally Phillips became tongue-tied and wide-eyed every time Max spoke to her.

Bedad's head pounded from the smell of urethane oil-based paint. It felt as though spikes where being driven up his sinuses and into his brain. His throat felt scratchy and swollen. The other three who were painting, even petite Sally, seemed to be taking the fumes in stride. He could not understand how they adapted to such a chemical-heavy environment.

The floor was covered with thick plastic tarp, and the vinyl baseboards were edged with green tape. They used two stepladders, one taller than the other. As the taller members of the team, Anastacia and Bedad were assigned the highest areas of the walls. Sally did the lowest, while Max did everything in between.

When Anastacia and Bedad went to the storage room at the same time to get more white paint, she whispered in his ear. "I'm so relieved. I thought Franz had turned Max against me."

A short while later, Bedad watched her joking with Max. Sally watched as well, with a wistful expression.

"So, Anastacia tells me you give the kids piano lessons," Bedad said to Sally.

Sally nodded from her position kneeling on the floor. "Yes, I was hoping we might have a little recital some time."

"How's Petal doing?" asked Anastacia.

"Great," said Sally. "She's very distractible for the first few minutes, but, once she gets into it, she's wonderful. Luckily, her foster mother has a piano so she can practice every day."

"Foster mother?" Bedad asked.

"Oh." Sally looked worriedly at Max. "Should I not have said that?"

"It's okay," Max said. "Petal talks about it with everyone. Besides, I don't want her to think it's some big shameful secret."

"What happened?" asked Bedad.

"Her mother is up on charges," answered Sally.

"Okay," said Max. "*That's* something we don't need to share."

Sally's cheeks turned red as she ducked her head.

"Bedad, that's not to be discussed with other people," Max said. "All right?"

"Got it," said Bedad. He looked back at Sally. "I guess Petal's lucky you were able to give her this. I'm sure she could use something enjoyable and challenging to take her mind off other things."

Sally smiled gratefully at Bedad. Max looked at the two of them.

"Sorry if that sounded harsh, Sally," Max said.

"It's okay," she replied. "I guess I just think of Bedad as one of us now. I'm sure he wouldn't gossip."

Bedad laughed. "If there is one thing I can do well, it's keep a secret."

Anastacia laughed, a little too loudly.

Sally looked at Max, who said, "Probably best not to ask."

Sally beamed at him, her brown eyes sparkling. A tendril of damp hair fell over her cheek. Max reached out and tucked it behind her ear. Bedad glanced at Anastacia, who rubbed her roller back and forth in the paint tray with grim determination.

Bedad cleared his throat. "So, why did Petal's mother have her if she wasn't able to take care of her?"

Max turned and frowned. "Well, we could ask that of a lot of people."

"So, why don't you?"

"What do you mean?" Max dipped his roller into the second tray.

"Why are people here not made accountable?"

"Is it different in Switzerland?" asked Sally.

"Switzerland?" Bedad rubbed his eyes with his fingertips.

"Where you're from," Anastacia said, giving him a warning look.

"Oh, yeah, right." Bedad shrugged. "I read about this group that calls themselves *Seven Billion*. They say people should be forced to use birth control. One child per family."

"Tell that to a daughter left to die because her parents wanted a boy," said Anastacia.

"What?" Bedad rubbed his eyes again. His chest was starting to hurt. He felt sick to his stomach.

"The *Seven Billion* group," said Sally. "Aren't they the ones who set fire to sperm donor clinics?"

"Yeah," said Max. "Pretty radical if you ask me."

"I think they have the right idea," said Bedad as he set his roller in the tray and stepped back. "They're just going about it the wrong way. But Outworlders need to stop breeding beyond all reason."

"Outworlders?" Max stared at Bedad who was now swaying on his feet.

"You people. You destroyers of the earth—"

Anastacia's voice rose. "Bedad, I think you—"

Bedad felt his eyes roll back in his head. His legs crumpled, and he fell flat onto the plastic, paint-splattered tarp.

Chapter Ten - Dry as Dust

Max insisted on taking Bedad to the Emergency Room. Anastacia didn't know how to stop him. Bedad did not have a medical card or any other proof of identity. When the intake nurse asked him about allergies, Bedad told her how the paint fumes made him feel.

"I also haven't been sleeping well. My chest often hurts."

"Lying down in a quiet room with an air purifier might be all you need," she said. "This heat and smog have been hard on everyone. But if you want to wait the eight or nine hours it will take to see a doctor, you can. In the meantime, you'll have to get someone to locate your medical card."

Anastacia and Max took Bedad home. Max believed her story that Bedad must have been disoriented by the paint fumes when he started raving about "Outworlders." He obviously had a chemical sensitivity, something that was becoming more common in an increasingly toxic environment.

"Feel better, buddy," said Max as he helped Anastacia set Bedad down on a kitchen chair.

"I'll give him a couple of aspirin and put him to bed in my brother's room," she said. "Normally, I'd open the windows, but the smoke outside seems to be getting worse."

"Maybe that set me off," said Bedad.

"Yeah, could be," said Max. "A lot of people are suffering from it."

"Sorry I didn't finish painting," said Bedad.

Max waved his arm. "Don't worry. Sally and I can finish it

up."

Bedad caught Anastacia's wince out of the corner of his eye.

"You can return to the Center," he told Anastacia. "I'll be fine on my own."

"No," Anastacia and Max said at the same time.

"I'll stay with you," Anastacia added.

She walked Max to the door and then brought Bedad a glass of water and a painkiller.

"This will help with the headache."

She set the air purifier on high and checked to make sure the windows were tightly sealed.

Bedad had trouble falling asleep but, finally, he drifted off. When he woke a few hours later, his stomach had settled, and his chest had relaxed. The pain in his head was much fainter.

With a sudden fear, he sat up and examined the bracelet. Had his headache been a warning signal that the bracelet's power was beginning to drain or simply an effect of the poisonous environment? The bracelet still had power. He sighed and fell back against the pillow.

As he lay in bed in Ali's old bedroom, Bedad listened to the faint sounds of the radio coming from the kitchen below. He heard the usual broadcasts updating the disaster in Asia, followed by announcements of wildfires and increasing skirmishes over water. The environmental crisis seemed to be intensifying.

Finally, the music came back on. Anastacia had turned the dial to Magic 99.9. She had explained to him that, despite the name, the radio station wasn't run by wizards.

Bedad had read one of Anastacia's books, *The Tipping Point* by Malcolm Gladwell. Gladwell hadn't discussed environmental problems, but his theory seemed to fit when Pakistan and India went to war. Since humanity had crossed that line, everything else seemed pale in comparison. Every news broadcast focused on nuclear escalation. The additional dust in the atmosphere had given global warming a push, and, now, the planet was like a juggler keeping too many balls in the air. One by one, they began to fall. The world had tipped into chaos.

In Africa, new wars broke out over water. The state of Texas became a dust bowl, devoid of life. Experts expected world wheat harvests to fall by fifty to sixty percent. Rice production was also at an all-time low. Water levels severely curtailed shipping on the Rhine, Danube, Mississippi, Rio Grande, Ganges, Yangtze, La Plata, St. Lawrence, and Nile. The Suez Canal and the Panama Canal closed. Civil wars rose in Africa and Asia, causing more environmental destruction. European countries fought over shared rivers and lakes. Even the United States and Canada threatened each other over the use of the Great Lakes.

Thankfully, Jamail had listened to his instincts and kept the large freezer packed full of food. He had hired an electrician to hook up the generator so it would keep running whenever the power went out. Jamail also had a huge supply — Anastacia said a dangerous supply — of stored fuel. He stocked the pantry to overflowing with cereal, grain, and cans of food, and a storage room in the basement was equally crowded. He started to store tanks of water as well.

The bleak news continued. Millions of dead fish washed ashore, both inland and along the seashores, due to temperature changes and drops in oxygen levels. Icebergs, broken away from Greenland and Antarctica, choked the Atlantic, making what little shipping that still continued even more dangerous. As fresh water levels fell, the sea level rose. Scientists did not offer much hope. The prevalent attitude seemed to be "We told you so."

Blackouts rolled throughout Europe due to low river levels. The Hoover Dam's hydroelectric turbines stopped once Lake Mead dropped below one thousand feet. Several cities initiated mandatory power outages.

Bedad heard Anastacia's voice from downstairs.

"Dad, Julie, hasn't answered any of my emails this week," she said. "I wish I knew better what was happening in Lucerne. I've been reading whatever posts I can access about Switzerland, and it doesn't look good."

Bedad could not hear Jamail's response. His head began to throb again. Were these people suicidal? What would it take to make them stop? He rolled over on his side, placed the extra pillow over his ear, and went back to sleep.

Chapter Eleven - Water, Water Everywhere

After a few days' rest, Bedad admitted he had pushed himself too hard. Over grilled cheese sandwiches and tomato soup, he explained to Anastacia what had caused his collapse. He had been working nights in the garage, while everyone else slept, experimenting with his water purification project.

"If you could do that, it would save millions of lives," said Anastacia.

"Would it?" said Bedad. "If I purify it, somehow, won't people just contaminate it again?"

Anastacia swirled her spoon around the soup. "Probably."

"What happens when the water runs out?" Bedad asked.

"Things are getting dire," Anastacia said. "But what can we do? Just cope the best we can."

Bedad frowned.

"We don't use our car anymore," said Anastacia. "Gasoline is worth more than gold. I bike and walk. All our budget is going toward groceries. We go to bed when it's dark and get up when it's light."

"We already do those things in Dawn's End," said Bedad. "It's not such a bad way to live."

"Well, I would give my left foot to be able to turn on the air conditioner," said Anastacia. "The house is suffocating with heat. Nobody can sleep upstairs anymore. I could cook biscuits up there."

"The basement isn't too bad," said Bedad.

The stairways to the upper-level bedrooms and bath and to the basement were located in the entry hall. The basement had a family room, laundry room, and storage.

"Yeah, we're lucky we have one," Anastacia said. "I haven't been much for watching television or even spending time on the computer, but I want to be able to watch the news. I've never been more conscious of how much we depend upon electricity. I hate these stupid brown-outs."

"I saw those gigantic lights at Subway Park are turned off," said Bedad.

Anastacia waved her hand dismissively. "It's too hot for baseball anyway, even after the sun goes down. No one has the interest or energy right now for sports. They've also switched off the expressway lights, but that's okay too. There are almost no cars on it anyway. I gotta say, though, it creeps me out when they switch off the city street lights after a couple of hours. And it's so weird seeing all the dark office buildings, banks, shops, and grocery stores."

Bedad nodded. "Your father said there have been more break and enter incidents. The police are having difficulty keeping up."

Anastacia sighed. "That doesn't surprise me. Make sure our doors stay locked all the time. I wish we could count on the security system, but since it's run by electricity . . . ."

Bedad smiled. "One thing you don't have to worry about is any harm coming to us while I'm here."

"Yeah, thanks," she said. "I'm not concerned about me. I worry about all my friends who don't have panther bracelets and wizards for friends. What about all the kids who come to the Center? Who is going to protect them?"

Fewer children came to Empowerment Ventures now that meals were small and infrequent. The basement was dark and stuffy, the ground level rooms hot and uncomfortable. No one wanted to exercise, and even board games seemed to require too much energy.

Anastacia noticed fewer and fewer Anishinaabek people on the street. At first, she thought they had wisely found a way to keep cool indoors. But, when she heard other people describe families walking in single file, their property on the backs, through rural areas, Anastacia realized they were leaving the city. Perhaps they felt they could better manage in the bush, or with family on reservations, since food prices in the city were astronomical. Weather was cooler in the north, so they might find more animals to hunt. But Anastacia remembered the dying moose and wondered if the First Nations people would find enough food.

"Auntie Faith says we have to wait for Mom here," said Rupert one Saturday at the club as they practiced tying his shoes. "If we go north, she might not be able to find us."

Anastacia nodded but thought it unlikely. If Rupert had not heard from his mother in all this time, she doubted he ever would. Toronto had swallowed her up, one way or another.

"My Auntie Charity died before I was born." Rupert struggled to form a loop in his black laces. "Both my uncles died in a fire. Mom is all Auntie has left."

"Your aunts' names are Faith and Charity?" asked Anastacia.

Rupert nodded and then stuck his tongue between his lips with concentration as he pushed one loop under another.

"Then your Mom's name must be Hope," said Anastacia.

"Yep," said Rupert. "You're smart." He tugged the bow into

place and threw his arms into the air. "Ta da!"

Anastacia gave his shoulder a small hug. If this little guy wasn't going to give up on Hope, neither was she.

Ironically, although the temperature rose and the droughts spread, some areas experienced the worst floods in their history. In those areas, every able person was drafted to work on sandbagging. Nova Scotia, Prince Edward Island, and New Brunswick experienced unprecedented flooding. Charlottetown, the cradle of Canada's Confederation, flooded with seawater. The government declared those areas subject to the Emergency Measures Act. Ocean water submerged the Nile Delta, most of Bangladesh, and New Orleans. Governments spoke of creating dykes based on the technology of the Dutch, but such huge endeavors seemed a long way off.

Scientists explained that flooding caused by severe rainstorms and extreme snow falls had increased by seven percent from 1999 to 2011. A British meteorologist related a study of England and Wales on rainfall. The autumn of 2000 had been the wettest in more than 230 years of record keeping. He predicted this autumn would be worse.

A representative of the Panel on Climate Change, who had predicted that sea level would rise another eighteen to fifty-nine centimeters in this century, revised his estimate upward. "Everything is happening much faster than we expected," he said, "partly due to the nuclear war between Pakistan and India, but mostly due to our lack of effort to change."

The latest talking heads discussed the melting ice caps. For years, the temperatures in the Arctic had risen twice as fast as elsewhere. The Ward Hunt Ice Shelf, the single biggest chunk of ice in the Arctic, which had been around for over three thousand years, had cracked in the year 2000. By 2002, it had split all the way through and began breaking into pieces. Now, those pieces were disintegrating swiftly. The disappearance of Minke whales, Emperor penguins, and polar bears was imminent. Eels became rarer than diamonds.

The ice caps on the Andes and Himalayas melted, causing massive flooding below. Overflowing rivers in Asia and Northern Europe dumped unprecedented fresh water into the Arctic Ocean disrupting the circulation patterns. The North Atlantic no longer received warm water. As a result, the average temperature in Europe dropped five degrees Celsius. Heavy rains struck Canada, Alaska, Northern Europe, Northern Asia and South-East Asia. Those areas that had been suffering drought sustained the most damage as the packed hard soil tore away in chunks.

November storms on Lake Superior had always been legendary, but this was May, usually the time when people began to enjoy the marina. Nonetheless, the rumble of thunder was constant. Lightning strikes brought down trees, set two houses on fire, charcoaled a pickup truck, and started several nearby forest fires.

Jamail's rain barrels overflowed. His garden vegetables were in danger of drowning. With Anastasia and Bedad's assistance, Jamail potted and brought indoors as many plants as possible. The bombarding rain and thrashing wind, punctuated by thunder, made hearing one another a challenge. Through the torrential downpour, Jamail used a combination of hand signals, pantomimes, and shouted explanations to demonstrate what needed to be done. They transplanted the remaining plants to newly created earth mounds and banked them with stones, bricks, and wood against erosion. Jamail reattached the Plexiglas shields to prevent the pounding precipitation from crushing the plants.

As Anastacia worked, rain soaked her face and ran under her poncho. Her pants were soaked to the skin, and water trickled into her boots. The periodic flashes of lightning and crashes of thunder made her flinch. Thunder Bay was one of the lucky areas. Pictures on the net and television showed areas completely deprived of power. People sitting on their rooftops waiting for rescue. A family struggling through waist-high water, the parents carrying their Labrador Retriever between them, the teenage daughter's arm hooking through the father's. Cars floating away. A man carrying a heavy trunk on his head, cushioning the weight with layers of white cloth. The tops of trees protruding from the water. A few swollen ditches and backed-up basements were nothing in comparison to what was happening in other places. Anastacia really couldn't complain . . . until the storage room in their basement suddenly flooded, resulting in the destruction of hundreds of dollars' worth of packaged food. Luckily, Jamail's pump prevented a total loss of all their food stores.

Anastacia helped Jamail remove everything from the room and spread it out upstairs on tarps to dry. Jamail discovered a leak had formed in a small crack below one of the basement windows. The cereal boxes were ruined. Labels had come off several cans, so it would be like playing *Deal or No Deal* when it came time to use them. They would have no idea if they were opening a can of soup, chopped tomatoes, or sliced olives. They wiped packaged food dry, but anything like noodles that wasn't encased in plastic was also ruined. All in all, they lost a quarter of their food supplies.

Bedad worked unceasingly at Anastacia's side. His face was wan and ghostly under his hood. He looked much older than when he had knocked on her door three months ago. She wondered if her mind was merely adjusting to seeing him as an adult or if the strain he had been under was taking a physical toll. Twice, she saw him stumble. His movements were slow and deliberate, like those of a geriatric patient afraid of falling.

If the foreign environment of Dawn's End made Outworlders ill over time, did her world make those from Dawn's End ill? Was Bedad poisoning himself by being here? He was a full child of Dawn's End; he did not have mixed blood like she did. Did he have an antidote for himself?

Chapter Twelve - Cemeteries

As soon as he felt well enough to travel, Bedad decided to return to Dawn's End. He promised to check in on Anastacia at a later date. At home, he could regain his health, and, when he felt well enough, continue his experiments on water purification. He would use the door on the Sibley Peninsula at the head of the Sleeping Giant to return home.

"I'd lend you my bike," Anastacia said, "but I use it all the time, and they are sold out everywhere. No one can afford gas these days."

"It seems much closer when you look out over the harbor and see Nanabijou, the Sleeping Giant, lying there," said Bedad.

"It probably is if you go by water," said Anastacia. "But I don't have a boat, and I wouldn't trust Lake Superior these days anyway. Too many storms. I'll just have to use some of the gas Dad stored to drive you."

"But you need that for the generator."

"We can spare enough to get you to Silver Islet."

Anastacia switched the windshield wipers to high. Highway 17 was eerily quiet. The road was cracked alongside embankments, the guardrails tipping in all directions. Flooding had taken giant bites out of the pavement; at several points, small washouts reduced the highway to one lane.

The road on the Sibley Peninsula was in worse shape. Erosion threatened to engulf the narrow, winding pavement completely, making driving a challenge. About halfway in from the highway, they came to a massive washout. The asphalt had completely collapsed, and a muddy creek was running where cars had previously driven.

"I'll walk from here," said Bedad.

"How far to the door?" asked Anastacia.

"It's close. I'll be fine." Bedad pulled his yellow, waterproof poncho over his head before stepping out of the car. Rain pelted down. He opened the back door and grabbed his bag, tucking it under his poncho.

"I'm going to go with you," said Anastacia as she removed her key from her ignition.

"No, you're not," replied Bedad. He slammed the back door, walked around the rear of the car, and stood beside her door.

Anastacia rolled down her window. "You still don't look so great. What if you faint again?"

"I promise I'm fine," said Bedad. "If you leave the car here, there could be washouts behind you. You could be stranded."

"I could walk back to Thunder Bay if I had to. I'm in better shape than you are."

"No doubt." Bedad smiled. "So let me go home and get out of this rain." He held up his fist for a bump.

Anastacia chuckled and bumped it. "I wish you could let me know you were safe once you get there. I hate not knowing. First Julie, now you."

Bedad stepped back from the window. He tucked his bag under his armpit and placed his hand over the panther bracelet. He ran toward the washout.

Anastacia sat bolt upright, watching.

Light surged around him. He sailed over the washout and landed safely on the other side. He turned and gave a small bow.

Anastacia stuck her head out the window, oblivious to the rain, and shouted. "Ha. I could have done it without the bracelet."

Bedad turned away, without hearing her, and started walking. It would take an hour to get to the door. He had thought it best not to share that information with Anastacia.

After seemingly endless days of rain and thunder, Dawn's End welcomed Bedad like a peaceful paradise. The sun shone, and the wood snipes were singing. Green leaves whispered in the trees, and the grass grew tall and healthy. The air was as pure as a baby's smile.

Bedad knocked on Josh's door. He hoped to get a boat to rent for a quick visit to Durward and Misty's. Receiving no answer, he decided to walk straight home.

When he passed by the crossroads to Newman's Refuge, he stopped short. The village's small cemetery had tripled in size and could now be seen from the road. The sight of row after row of small, wooden markers made his chest clench. What had happened? A war? No, things in Dawn's End had been improving when he had left. The evils imported from the Outworld were under control, and communities were rediscovering their original values. Had something harmed the village? Tainted food? He had planned on staying there overnight but decided he should talk to his adoptive parents, Ellsworth and Lissa, before making contact with anyone else.

On the second day, he passed through the edge of Alaric Place, the village where Anastacia had been born. No one was moving about, and the cemetery here was also choked with new graves. He looked around and then walked through the closest row. Many of the gravesites bore flowers, but what made Bedad's stomach turn was the number of toys. Miniature wagons, dolls, carved animals, and balls of all kinds sat in front of the simple wooden markers. The short, newly dug graves meant they were mostly for children.

The wind lifted, and a curly-haired rag doll with brown-button eyes flopped over, knocking an animal-skin ball aside. It rolled off the mound toward Bedad. He leapt back as though contact was poison.

Poison! Perhaps something had poisoned the water. But why so many children? And why both villages? It had to be a disease that affected panther people. Was it only panther people? What about other mixed races? What about full humans? What about home? What about his family?

His heart leapt painfully. He hadn't seen a living soul since his arrival, panther person or otherwise. He jogged out of the graveyard and down the road. If only he could run like Anastacia.

He sprinted until his breath caught in his chest. Gasping, he rubbed a stitch in his side and forced himself to keep moving. What if his family was sick? Or dying? He should have been here, in Dawn's End, when this catastrophe had struck. He tucked his bag under one arm and called on the power of the bracelet. Power flooded through his body, enough to help him keep going at a quicker pace. He felt no nausea.

When he arrived at his destination, dusk was settling over Harmony. In the falling light, he could see that the cemetery here had expanded, just like those at the other villages. His heart pounding in his throat, he ran up the steps to his family home and flung open the door. Lissa and Ellsworth were sitting at the table. Lissa's usually cheerful face was drawn and tired, her tight, gray curls mussed and in need of a wash.

She rocked a baby cradle with one hand. A fussy squalling rose from the bed. Ellsworth's dark-skinned face was somber. His usually neat, tight, skinny, black dreadlocks were askew.

Bedad looked around the room for toys, jackets, little shoes, but the only evidence of children was the cradle. This child must be a new addition to the family; he had not seen a baby the last time he visited.

"You're safe, thank the stars." Ellsworth jumped up and hugged Bedad.

Stumbling, Lissa wiped her tears, as she joined the hug. "We thought we had lost you, too."

"What do you mean?" said Bedad. "Where are the kids?"

Ellsworth and Lissa exchanged a sorrowful look. Lissa picked up the now howling baby and patted his back. Her expression begged Bedad not to make her say it.

"No, no," whispered Bedad. "All of them?"

Ellsworth nodded, as Bedad's eyes filled with tears.

"I saw the cemeteries." Bedad collapsed into a chair. When he finally gained control of his sobbing, he asked, "What happened?"

"A virus," said Ellsworth. "One we've never seen before."

"It took children mostly," whispered Lissa.

"Lissa was ill for a while." Ellsworth squeezed her arm as she stood rocking the baby. "I thought I was going to lose her, too."

"Whose baby it that?"

"Ours now," said Lissa. "He's the only one left from his

family."

Bedad pressed his hands to his face, his elbows on the table. "I should have been here. I might have been able to stop it."

"Or, you might have died," said Ellsworth. "Durward and Kaie, the wizard, did everything they could, as well as Hulda the Witch and Asa the Healer. Hulda didn't survive."

"Kaie? She was serving a life-sentence for the misuse of magic."

"We needed every able hand. After the deaths slowed, Kaie was granted a full pardon for her efforts and courage."

Bedad knew these three women possessed impressive skills. If they had been overwhelmed, the situation must have been horrific. "Durward and Misty?"

"Both alive," said Ellsworth. "We think the disease took fewer than half the adults, about seventy percent of the teens, and almost every child under the age of ten."

"This baby is a miracle," said Lissa. "That's what we call him. Miracle. We don't know his name. We found him with his family on the road into town. People were fleeing their villages, thinking they could escape the plague."

"But all they did was spread it faster," said Ellsworth.

"Is anyone still sick?" asked Bedad. "Is there anyone I can help?"

"Yes," said Lissa. "Durward and Kaie are working on something to make people immune using blood from those who were ill but survived. They took some blood from me. You're welcome to do the same if it will help."

"Of course," said Bedad. "I'll start right away."

As he unlocked his laboratory door, Bedad tried to force away a relentless thought. Had this disease been brought in accidentally from the Outworld by one of the panther people? Was it slowly working its way through the population a bit at a time, mutating as it went? Had Anastacia or her mother brought it? Or had Bedad brought it in himself, going back and forth to the Outworld trying to concoct an antidote for Anastacia? In saving her, had he condemned much of Dawn's End to death?

Chapter Thirteen - Off the Road

By the middle of June, the rain stopped. Numerous roads were washed out, thousands of basements were flooded, but Thunder Bay had been lucky. The city heaved a sigh of relief and began cleanup and repairs again.

Far more bicycles crowded the road than cars. Cyclists choked the bike lanes and paths, while red traffic lights often had no cars waiting. Anastacia found it interesting how people, some of whom hadn't ridden bikes in years, adapted. Many rode three-wheeled bikes and pulled carts behind.

People scrambled to get gardens planted now that the sun was shining. Unfortunately, windstorms picked up, and sudden hail returned, but a diligent gardener could cope. Jamail transplanted the vegetables he had brought indoors into the back yard. His Plexiglas covers came in handy again.

Mr. Ferguson stood beside Jamail and studied the makeshift greenhouse. He slapped the smaller man on the back, sending him into a stumble. "I'm gonna make one of these."

One evening, the wind gusts shook the trees like an angry nanny as Anastacia walked home from her new job. She worked for the city repairing roads and bridges. At first, she was given a Stop/Go sign to hold, but her boss soon discovered she could do manual labor as well as any man on his work crew.

She was tired and filthy. Citizens had to boil their drinking water as the city reservoir was unable to keep up with the latest onslaught from Mother Nature. But at least they had more of it now and she could have a bath when she got home. There may or may not be power to heat the water, but she didn't care. Clean was clean.

The sky darkened, and the wind whipped leaves and sticks toward her. It howled down the street, wildly rattling the parking signs. Anastacia swatted away a trash can lid about to hit her shoulder. The trees creaked, and the wind moaned like a banshee. A poplar tree on the left side of the road groaned and then cracked, snapping in half. Lightning lit up the darkened sky.

Anastacia launched into a run. Ten minutes later, she reached home. Jamail was nailing plywood over the front windows.

"Now what?" Anastacia rushed to Jamail's side to hold the ladder steady against the howling wind.

"Tornadoes," said Jamail. "To the south and west. We can't be sure they'll stay there."

Anastacia let out a string of curses, but the wind carried her voice away. After hammering home the last nail, they brought the ladder into the house.

"Why didn't you use screws?" asked Anastacia.

"No electricity," explained Jamail as he shut the door behind them. The entryway was dark as night. "My drill batteries are dead."

Anastacia picked up a flashlight that Jamail had placed by the front door in case of emergency.

"Great," she muttered. "Let's head downstairs."

Anastacia and Jamail huddled in the basement until morning. Then Anastacia cranked the emergency radio and searched for a broadcasting station. They learned the worst damage had struck east and south. Four doors down, the maple tree on the front lawn had fallen, crushing the family's car like a giant octopus. A section of the airport roof had torn off and landed in the long-term parking lot. Very few planes were flying anyway. Plummeting trees had taken down power lines, making it even more difficult for the local utility companies to meet basic needs for electricity. An entire row of streetlights on Strand Avenue had gone down as well as traffic lights throughout the city. Several metal sheds had disintegrated or been blown into a neighbor's yard. And, worst of all, four of the wind turbines on the Nor'wester Mountain escarpment had been torn into giant splinters reducing available electricity even more.

A rainbow appeared the next day. Weather became uncharacteristically pleasant. It felt like a normal June—if you ignored the boarded-up windows and downed street lights.

One Saturday, Anastacia was surprised to learn the Empowerment Ventures Center had reopened. Two flashlights lit the multipurpose room. Petal pounded away on the piano under Sally's encouraging smile. Anastacia waved as she headed for the kitchen to talk with Max. Two lanterns cast a flickering glow on Max while he searched through the cupboards.

"Well, kids," he said. "It looks like sardines and crackers."

"Nooo," moaned Chester. He sat at the table playing checkers with Gabriel.

"That's okay," said Gabriel.

"It's that or nothing," said Max as he set the tin on the counter.

Chester sighed heavily.

"How about you, Anastacia?" asked Max. "Fancy some sardines and crackers?"

"No, thank you. I already ate."

"What did you have?" asked Gabriel, his eyes wide.

Anastacia realized the sardines were probably the first food the boys had all day. "Oh, sardines and crackers, and they were yummy."

Max smiled gratefully.

At the end of the day, Max told the children that Empowerment Ventures would have to close until he could get more food.

"No!" said Petal. "We don't have to eat. We can just come and play."

"But we always give lunch," said Max. "We can't have you here all day on Saturday and not have any food to give you. And no evening snacks during the week."

Petal burst into tears. "But if I don't got piano, I got nothing."

Sally gathered her into her arms and spoke to Max over her shoulder. "Maybe we could just open for an hour or two in the afternoon."

"Yes." Petal was sobbing. "Please do that."

"All right," said Max. "We'll stay open for shorter time periods. I'll put the schedule up tomorrow."

Petal wiped her nose on the sleeve of her grubby, fluorescent pink shirt and nodded.

After they said goodbye, Max turned to Sally and Anastacia. "Do either of you have gasoline?"

"Why?" Sally asked.

"I think I know where I can get some food. But I need gas for the car. I'll share whatever we get, but most will go to the kids."

"Of course," said Sally. "But I can't help you with the gas."

"I think I can," said Anastacia.

She remembered the stockpiled jerry cans in Mr. Ferguson's shed. He might be willing to trade food for fuel. If she had to, she'd ask her stepfather for some more of the generator fuel. With the power off so often, the generator had been burning through the reserves to keep the freezer running — but there wasn't much food left inside it.

As they drove out of the city, Anastacia realized the roads were worse than expected. Orange paint and the occasional pylon marked the many washouts. The highway was down to one lane in several places. Water still sat in fields and flowed high and fast in ditches. They saw no one else on the road until they rounded a corner and met a red Jetta coming straight at them. Max yanked the wheel to the right. The jeep's tires gripped the slanting roadway, gravel churning beneath them. The driver of the Jetta was not as lucky.

The Jetta jerked to the other side of the lane, hit a washout, and flipped upside down into a gulley of deep muck between the road and the tree line. Quickly, the car sank until the mud completely buried the windows.

Max parked the jeep. He pulled out his cell phone and swore. No signal. He and Anastacia rushed to the Jetta, sinking in heavy mud up to their thighs as they climbed into the ditch. Max went back to his jeep, took out a small shovel, and tried to dig away the thick brown sludge encasing the car, but, as fast as he pushed the ooze away, it filled in again. Anastacia used her hands to scoop and throw the muck. Max dug until he found the driver's door handle, but it wouldn't budge.

Locked. They heard no sounds from within the vehicle. The interior must be filling with water and sludge.

"We're going to need help," said Max.

"Can't you pull it out with your jeep?" Anastacia slogged through the muck, trying to find another access point to the car.

"Not the way it's positioned. Dragging it upside down back on to the pavement would crush the roof." Max banged on the bottom of the car. "Can you hear me in there? Unbuckle your seatbelt and stand on the roof. There will be air at the top."

They both listened in silence for a few seconds. No response.

"What if they're unconscious? They'll drown," said Anastacia.

"I'm going to head back down the road," said Max. "I saw a house back there. Maybe they can help or they have a working phone. At least they can offer more hands to dig and a crowbar."

Anastacia nodded. "Go."

"Maybe you should go," said Max as he struggled out of the mud. "You run faster than me."

"No, you go. I'll keep digging." She took the shovel from his hands.

As soon as Max was out of sight, she left the ditch. Standing far back on the road, Anastacia shook the mud off her sleeve, pushed it up, wiped the bracelet, and held her hand over it.

"Back on the road," she said. Closing her eyes, she visualized the car out of the muck and sitting safely on the pavement.

The Jetta's metal screeched as the car shook and bent.

"Careful!" Anastacia said.

With a loud sucking sound, the car pulled free of the mud, rolled back in the direction it had come, and settled on the pavement with a wiggle like a cat digging in its claws. Its exterior was encased in muck. Dark, dank water oozed down all its sides.

Anastacia ran to the other three doors and pulled. All locked. She jumped on the hood and wiped the windshield with her arm. A balding man sat in the driver's seat. His head flopped forward.

Anastacia went to the passenger-side back window and kicked. Bang. The glass spider-webbed and buckled inward. She kicked again, remembering to aim for the corner. Crunch. The window tore free from the bottom and one side. She reached in, unlocked the back door, and pulled it open. Water poured out. After she climbed part way in, she unlocked the front door beside the driver.

Then she ran around the car and opened the door on his side. More muck and water trickled out. The driver was soaked in muddy water. Buttons flew when she ripped open his blue-plaid shirt and put her head on his chest. *Thump, thump.* His heart was working, but he wasn't breathing. Quickly, she unbuckled his seatbelt, dragged him from the car, and laid him out on the pavement. On her knees, Anastacia wiped the guck from his face, opened his mouth to check for blockage, squeezed his nostrils downward to clean out any mud, tilted his head, pinched his nose, and blew into his mouth. After several minutes of rescue breathing, the man coughed up muddy water and then started breathing on his own. Anastacia rolled him onto his side in the help position and stood up. Whatever he had inhaled into his lungs could be dangerous. He would need medical care, and soon.

As nausea surged through her guts, she clutched her stomach. She fell to her knees and vomited. Her whole body shook with exhaustion. Streams of pain threaded through her. The nausea was even worse than the last time she had used the bracelet. She spewed out another jet of vomit. Wiping her mouth with the back of her sleeve, she flopped into a sitting position.

A shifting shadow by the tree line caught her attention. When her eyes met another person's, she gave a small, startled scream. Faces watched her from the woods. She stumbled to her feet. One of the figures stepped out from the tree line, just far enough to for her to see while avoiding sinking in the muck. She recognized Daniel Moonwind, the elder drummer. He gave an approving smile, raised his hand in salute, and disappeared back into the trees. The other faces faded away.

A few minutes later, Max returned with three shovels, a blanket, a teenage boy, and a man in his forties. They were stunned to see the car back on the road and the driver lying nearby.

"He's okay now," Anastacia said. "But I'm glad you brought a blanket. He must be freezing."

Max shook out the wool blanket, laid it over the man, and tucked it around his shoulders, legs, and feet. He held his hand above the driver's mouth, confirming that he was breathing regularly.

"Ambulance and fire truck are on the way," said the middle-aged man.

The rescue personnel were flabbergasted when Anastacia told them a group of Anishinaabek people had worked together to put the car back on the road. The fire fighter kept shaking his head and frowning.

"I don't see how that's possible," he said.

Anastacia shrugged.

"There's boot prints along the trees," called another firefighter. "A whole bunch of different ones."

"Huh," said the head firefighter. "I guess that confirms your story, though I've never seen the like. You can go now. Try to stay off the roads as much as possible."

Max was waiting in his jeep.

"I found out my lead for food was false," he told Anastacia. "The place burned to the ground last week. We did all this for nothing. I'm going to have to close the Ventures Center."

Anastacia nodded and watched the paramedics load the driver onto a stretcher as Max backed up the jeep. How was she going to tell Mr. Ferguson they had crapped out and wasted his precious gasoline? She would have to replace it from her stepfather's stash or give him food as payment from their basement stockpile.

Chapter Fourteen - The Last Crumb

Jamail was listening to the news on the radio when Anastasia came home. He muttered a prayer of thanks as he hugged her tightly.

"What is it? What's wrong?" asked Anastacia.

"Everything."

The music programming on the radio station resumed, and Jamail switched it off.

"Rioting everywhere, and all out wars in Europe, Asia, and South America," Jamail told her. "Emergency relief organizations are exhausted. Emergency measures are failing. Country after country is experiencing economic collapse. The American dollar is falling fast. The Canadian will follow. Money isn't worth much anymore. The only commodities of any value are food and water. Our little oasis won't be safe forever. This is just the beginning of chaos."

He stopped when Anastacia covered her face with her hands.

"What about Julie?" Anastacia clutched her stepfather's arm. "What's happening in Switzerland?"

Her stepfather shook his head. "I don't know. I don't even know what's happening in Minneapolis. I know there are riots there, too. I should have bought a ham radio. I should have been better prepared. Ali could be—"

"Oh, God." Anastacia pressed her fingers over her lips.

Was her stepbrother safe? She thought about Ali's gentle smile, his dark eyes, his thick, dark hair flipped up in front like George Clooney's. He had seen so much horror in Iraq as a child. What was he seeing now?

She took her stepfather's hand and squeezed it as tears filled her eyes. They had hoarded supplies. Had Ali? Their garden vegetables were half the size they should be by now. Would Ali even have a garden? Would grocery stores be able to restock? What would happen now that no one knew the value of the money? She had to find out what was going on.

She wiped her eyes. "I'm going out, Dad."

His whole body jerked to attention. "No! I forbid it!"

They both stared at each other in shock. Jamail had never spoken to her like that in her life. She noticed how much grayer his formerly dark brown hair had become, how the lines around his eyes had deepened, and how his usually round cheeks had thinned.

Anastacia didn't know whether to laugh or cry. She patted his shoulder. "Good try, Dad. But I'm going out to get us groceries before there is nothing left in the city."

"You don't understand," he said. "This changes everything. There will be riots here, too. Laws will mean nothing. People will kill for food for their families."

"I won't," said Anastacia. "But no one is going to stop me."

"No, no, I will go. I am the man. The father. How can I let a girl do this?"

"Dad." She took a deep breath. "Daddy, listen, please. You know I'm unstoppable when I want something. I'm as tough as any man out there and faster. A way lot faster and stronger than you. I could kick your ass any day . . . . Not that I would, of course."

His eyes pleaded with her. "They will have weapons. Knives.

Even guns. You are not superwoman. You can be killed."

"I'll be careful. I promise." She squeezed his hand. "Please, trust me. I'll bring a weapon. I know what I'm doing. Please."

Jamail sighed and nodded. "I will keep trying the telephone lines and the computer. I will keep trying to contact Julie and Ali."

Anastacia kissed his cheek. "I'll be fine. Honest."

"Go with God," Jamail whispered.

Anastacia took a rolling stewardess suitcase and slipped on the largest overnight hiking packsack she had. Fortunately, her stepfather had been steadily taking cash out of their accounts for months and hiding it around the house. She had money to pay for provisions — if she could find some food for sale. How much would a loaf of bread cost? Ten dollars? A hundred dollars? She hadn't been to Safeway for over a week, and the shelves had already been pretty bare then. Many of the freezers had been empty, with frozen food crowded together willy-nilly into the few units still running on generators. Things would be worse today.

For a moment, she contemplated dressing in full hockey gear, just in case she encountered rioting, but the bulk would just slow her down. Instead, she wore her helmet and brought along a bottle of water. She considered taking her bow and arrow, but she settled for her hunting knife, hiding it discreetly down a pant leg. No use scaring anyone. People became dangerous when they felt threatened. She jogged to the grocery store.

The line of customers snaked down the sidewalk, across the empty parking lot, and down Strand Avenue. The crowd had brought carts, wagons, and packsacks. Someone had even brought an emptied golf bag. Entire families stood together. Children played listlessly by their parents' feet, babies cried, and a white-haired, old man slumped in a wheelchair. He didn't move at all. People seemed anxious, but, so far, they remained under control. In line, shoppers informed each other of stores that had closed their doors permanently, or at least until more food supplies arrived in the city.

The store manager had boarded up all the windows, and allowed only one entrance and exit to be used. A vandal had smashed the white-circle sign with the stretched red; a chunk was missing from the bottom. The manager permitted new customers in only when customers inside the store left. Rumor had it that he was rationing the number of items shoppers could purchase according to family size.

Anastacia thought everyone would behave as long as people kept coming out with food.

More customers lined up behind her. After two hours in the heat, she took out her water. Parched faces turned in her direction as she drank half of it down.

"Anastacia," said a young voice.

She turned. Twelve people back stood Kyle Brewbaker and his mother. One of Kyle's mother's eyes was swollen shut, and her lip was split open. Even now as the world fell apart, her husband beat her. Anastacia wondered if he had run out of booze.

"The Center is boarded up," said Kyle.

Anastacia nodded. "Just until things get better. It'll open up again."

Kyle's mother smiled gratefully, wincing when her split lip bled.

When Anastacia's turn came, she discovered only the manager and the assistant inside. They had been allowing three families at a time into the building, but this time they had called only Anastacia from the line. The freezers had stopped working and now contained nothing but a few limp packages of pizza and partially thawed vegetables. She saw shelf after shelf, empty of food.

"Who are you buying for?" asked the manager.

"My dad and myself," said Anastacia.

The manager nodded. He knew both Anastacia and Jamail.

"I've been keeping a list to be fair," said the manager. "I've allowed only one trip a day to each family." He tossed the clipboard onto an empty shelf. "Guess I don't need it anymore."

"So, I can come tomorrow?"

"We'll be closed," he said.

"Are the new prices listed on the shelves?" she asked.

"There are no new prices," said the manager. "Everything is priced the way it was when I bought it from the suppliers."

Anastacia nodded, smiling. "You could have asked any price, and people would have paid."

"Those who had money, yeah." He straightened his tie. "My parents came to Canada with nothing. Without help, I never would have made it this far. I'm not going to take advantage of my community. But, I'm sorry to say, I don't have much left to sell. You'll probably be my last customer."

Anastacia looked around the store and realized the food would run out before the line of customers did. The produce and dairy areas were empty. The selections were meager. She took three pizzas, seven bags of vegetables, a box of Coco Puffs, two bags of basmati rice, a can of pimentos, a leaking bag of flour, a badly dented can of cranberry juice, two bags of dried peas, several packages of flavorings and spices, two partially unwrapped chocolate bars, and sixteen packages of garden vegetable seeds. Anastacia's packsack was full, but she still had plenty of room in the suitcase. She looked down one aisle and the next. She had taken everything left on the shelves.

All sales were cash or check only. Anastacia wondered if the checks would be worthless. As she walked toward the door, she heard the manager tell his assistant to leave out the back. "Lock the door when you go." The manager stepped out the front with her and locked the door behind them.

"May I have your attention please," he shouted. Then he whispered to Anastacia, "Get out of here as fast as you can. It's going to get ugly."

She hesitated, then nodded and started walking. Her stepfather would be anxiously waiting. Kyle Brewbaker's eyes met hers as she passed. She reached out and grabbed his mother's hand, pulling her out of line.

"No, I'll lose my spot! What—"

The manager's words, "Nothing left," hit the crowd like a thunderclap. The line in front of the store exploded in protests, shouts of anger, tears.

"Quick, come with me." Anastacia pulled Kyle out of line as well.

Kyle followed as they scurried down Strand Avenue.

The shouts behind them intensified. Customers screamed for the manager to unlock the door or they would kick it down.

Anastacia reached into her pack and pulled out the box of Coco Puffs, a bag of rice, the can of juice, and two bags of vegetables. "Hide these, or someone will take them away from you."

"Coco Puffs!" cried Kyle. "Awesome."

"Thank you," said Kyle's mother as she stuffed the items into her bag.

Anastacia heard screams from the direction of the grocery store, followed by the sound of a gunshot.

"Get off the street," Anastacia said.

Kyle's mother grabbed her son's hand and ran. Anastacia watched until the woman and child were safely away.

As she raced home, Anastacia decided to give the food to Mr. Ferguson in return for the gasoline they had wasted. She wondered if he had stored anything in his basement. A large family like his would go through supplies in no time. How many people were already facing bare cupboards?

Chapter Fifteen - Missing

The next day, Kyle's mother appeared on Anastacia's doorstep. She cringed, expecting the woman to ask for more food.

Instead, she asked, "Have you seen Kyle?"

"Kyle. No? Why? What's wrong?"

"He wanted to go to the Ventures Center this morning to see if it was open." She nervously licked her split lip. "I told him no, that it wouldn't reopen until things got back to normal. I fell back to sleep, and, when I woke up, he was gone. I've looked everywhere."

"So, you checked the Center?"

Kyle's mother nodded. "I thought he might have come here."

Anastacia slowly shook her head. "I doubt he knows where I live."

Mrs. Brewbaker's face crumpled.

"Come in for a bit, and I'll see what I can think of," said Anastacia.

"No, no," whispered Kyle's mother. "I have to get back. My husband will want dinner. We're having rice with the rest of the vegetables you gave us. But I won't let him have the Coco Puffs. Those are for Kyle when he comes home."

Anastacia's stomach clenched. Was that all the food they had? She realized families who existed from check to check wouldn't have been able to buy extra to store the way she and Jamail had. How would the poor endure? She had read that during the more than two-year-long siege of Leningrad, some of the most ruthless and immoral people had resorted to murder and cannibalism to survive. Would things get that bad here?

As she shut the door, she thought how frustrated she had felt when Kyle cut up her hoodie. He must have been sending out a cry for help. She had ignored it. How many cries would she have to ignore now? And where was Kyle?

The weather was close to normal for the rest of June and all of July. It felt as though Mother Earth had dragged them to the edge of a precipice and then stepped away. Jamail set up an alarm system around the backyard. He was more than willing to teach others how to plant and care for their own gardens, but he would not allow anyone to steal his hard-earned produce. Local farms brought truckloads of early vegetables into the town and sold them for either insanely inflated prices or items of trade. A pickup would arrive filled with lettuce, radishes, cabbage, and zucchini and leave loaded with furniture, bags of jewelry, collectables, tools, and anything else people could spare in exchange for produce. Very little food arrived from outside the city.

Obviously, other shipments were getting blocked as well. The emergency room at Thunder Bay Regional Medical Center was flooded with addicts of all kinds going through withdrawal. Some of the more desperate tried substituting whatever they could find. Accidental deaths from poisoning rose.

Electricity had returned, although fitfully, and city water was safe to drink again. Several stores opened for shortened hours. Most businesses stayed closed as no one knew what the real value of a dollar was anymore. Gas stations seldom had fuel, and people mainly bought by jerry can — waiting in line with a vehicle burned too much gasoline to make it worthwhile. Anastacia still carried her hunting knife every time she left the house. Impending violence hung constantly in the air, and she did not want to be caught unprepared.

Deer became bolder. Like the moose, they were willing to attack humans to get at their vegetable plots. Plants in the wild were small and sparse. Several deer had to be shot to prevent them from destroying gardens. A new emergency city by-law had been passed to allow this. A specially created task force had to be called to kill the deer to prevent inexperienced hunters from shooting through their neighbors' homes. Some people disobeyed the by-law. Shots would be fired, and, by the time the police arrived, any trace of the deer would be gone. Neighbors learned to keep their mouths shut in return for a cut of the meat.

Parts of Europe and Asia were still at war, but rioting in most larger Canadian and American cities had stopped, and people were rebuilding. Northerners tried to prepare for a winter without food shipments from the south, just in case.

Although Jamail was unable to reach Ali by telephone, Anastacia received a long email the day internet service resumed. She shrieked with happiness when she read that both he and Lucinda were safe. They were considering coming north and wondered how the situation was in Thunder Bay.

"Tell him to come," said Jamail. "Tell him everything is wonderful."

"That's not exactly true, Dad."

"There are robberies, yes, some looting, but nothing like the large cities. He will be much safer here. Tell him."

"I'll tell him everything, and he can decide," said Anastacia.

"Yes, fine," said Jamail. "But tell him I want him to come and bring his fiancée. Tell him my cherry tomatoes are ripe."

Anastacia laughed. "If that doesn't get him here, nothing will."

Neither of them mentioned that border crossings were becoming more and more difficult. A Canadian citizen, who was born in Iraq and who had been living and working in the United States, might not find it so easy to return home. Life was far from normal.

Still, life seemed to be improving. Even Empowerment Ventures reopened half days. Instead of lunch, the children received a small mid-afternoon snack. Anastacia taught the children everything her stepfather had told her about growing and preserving fruits and vegetables. Everyone whose family prepared a garden received some vegetable seeds. She hoped they would see enough weeks of good weather for the plants to mature before frost arrived.

Chester did not return. Anastacia assumed he had joined the other Anishinaabek wherever they were headed. Gabriel came twice, but never again. Then Petal stopped coming as well.

"I was going to teach her a duet this week," said Sally as they cleaned up the kitchen and activity room at the end of the day. Her face creased with worry. "I can't imagine what would keep her away. She lives for her piano lessons. I hope she isn't ill."

"How about I check on her family?" said Anastacia.

Max nodded. "It's not something we would usually do, but these are unusual circumstances. I'll get her address from the files."

Sally thanked Anastacia and left. A few minutes later, Max

returned from his office, his face pale.

"We've been burgled," he said.

"Really? What did they take?" asked Anastacia.

"Files." Max flopped down into a kitchen chair and rubbed his auburn beard.

"Files?"

"I went to get Petal's address, and her information pages were gone. I noticed the files seemed leaner than usual, so I checked a few others."

"And there were more gone?" asked Anastacia.

Max nodded. "Chester. Petal. Gabriel. Rupert."

"Except for Rupert, those are all children who have stopped coming." Anastacia felt a fist of fear in her chest. "What does it mean?"

"It means we had better find out if any of these children are missing."

Chapter Sixteen - The Beast

After extensive research, Bedad concluded that the killer virus was a form of the measles, common in the Outworld but never seen before in Dawn's End. He created an inoculation to protect the remaining inhabitants.

Trying to combine elements from both the Outworld and Dawn's End was like trying to mix gas and oil. By adding ingredients one at a time, and magically binding them with the power of the bracelet, Bedad eventually got the results he wanted. He had a safe, effective vaccine. Distribution and administration of the vaccine went well. No new cases of the disease occurred.

Bedad had lost weight, and he walked with an old man's shuffle. Once he had succeeded in delivering the vaccine, Lissa forced him to bed and pumped him full of healthy broths and food. Bedad did not have the heart, or the energy, to resist. Lissa needed to feel she could help at least one of her children.

Within a few weeks, Bedad's strength had largely returned. He then began his second project. He did not tell Lissa and Ellsworth, or even Durward, the truth about what he was doing. The experiment was questionable, at best.

He had seen the devastation in Anastacia's world. After entering the Outworld, he had learned that every country was besieged. Droughts and floods ravaged much of the planet causing starvation, riots, and wars. Wildfires still raged in some places, and tornadoes threatened constantly. Thunder Bay, isolated by geography, high on the Canadian Shield, had sustained the least damage, but summer was almost over. Would the inhabitants be able to survive five or six months of winter with depleted food and fuel stores? Due to transportation issues and limited supplies, they would receive little or no help from the south. He had to convince Anastacia to return to her true home, Dawn's End, so she could live a life of safety and peace.

One morning, he packed his travel bag and said goodbye to his parents.

Lissa clung to him, her gray curls pressed against his cheek. "I don't think you're strong enough to go to the Outworld. It's such a dangerous place."

"That's why I have to go now. The longer Anastacia remains there, the greater the risk."

"Just a few more days of rest."

Gently, Ellsworth pulled her away. "We have to let him do this. The sooner he goes, the sooner he returns."

"I couldn't bear to lose him, too." Lissa buried her face in her husband's shoulder.

Ellsworth held her close. "He's a smart young man. He'll be all right."

"I'll be back as soon as I can." Bedad leaned in and kissed Lissa's cheek.

Ellsworth clapped him on the shoulder. "Travel in safety."

The sky over the Sleeping Giant was smoky as Bedad stepped through the door once again. Forest fires from the surrounding area turned the sun blood-orange. Bedad did not have a ride to the city, not that anyone could have driven on the devastated road anyway. He paused to adjust his huge pack as he passed by the Sleeping Giant campground. In front of the elaborate wood and metal campground sign stood a simple, hand-painted one reading "Closed." The store and restaurant at Pass Lake were closed as well; the lake itself had shrunken to a muddy slough.

When Highway 17 came into sight, he heard a crash in the bush to his left. An enormous, dark shape lumbered toward him. When it reached the graveled edge of the pavement, it reared up onto its back legs and woofed. The black bear's fur was clumped, and his left haunch oozed with pus.

"I guess you've been fighting for your life, too," said Bedad as he placed one hand over his bracelet. "What do predators eat when there is no prey left?"

The bear roared, and Bedad shuddered. "I guess they eat other predators."

The bear wagged its head left and right as it dropped back onto all fours. It took one step, then two, toward Bedad.

"Don't be stupid." Bedad's heart pounded as the bear pulled back its lips and bared its immense teeth. "I might look puny compared to you, but I'll win."

The bear paused. It woofed again, sniffed the air, stood back on its hind legs, and sniffed again. Suddenly, the beast whirled around, dropped down, and raced back into the woods.

Bedad let out a long, slow breath. "I guess I don't smell right."

He tried to walk at a calm and steady pace, even though adrenaline now flooded his body. The highway was quiet and empty. Bedad walked for a full fifteen minutes before the first vehicle, a supply truck, passed him. Ten minutes later, a militia truck rumbled by; the armed men occupying it stared at him suspiciously. No one offered a ride into Thunder Bay.

The city streets were similarly deserted. Several abandoned cars and trucks had smashed windows and flat tires.

Fortunately, Bedad found a deserted warehouse suitable for conducting his experiments. It was located in the east end, one of the oldest parts of the city. Several smaller businesses had closed over the last year and been sold to outside investors. After the sold signs went up, potential buyers ignored most of the buildings due to the global crisis. The warehouse Bedad found, with corrugated metal over the doors and windows, was empty but in good repair. He created a living space, work area, and storage room, stocking it with food and supplies he had brought from Dawn's End. There, Bedad continued his work. His research was essential to the survival of both worlds.

The neighborhood surrounding the warehouse felt as though it was under siege. Residents had boarded up their windows, parents kept their children indoors, automobiles gathered dust, and few people ventured forth. Those that did come out into the open moved quickly and seldom spoke to anyone. No one bothered Bedad. It was the perfect environment for his clandestine research activities.

When the weather began to cool and the city still showed only limited recovery, Bedad decided it was time to approach Anastacia. He walked with a bounce in his step as he headed toward her neighborhood. He took in her boarded-up picture window and the locked gate with a frown. He should have come sooner.

Bedad knocked loudly on the front door.

Jamail's voice called, "Who is it?"

An eye stared through a newly created peephole.

"Bedad."

The door jerked open.

"How did you get here?" Jamail ushered Bedad inside. "Where have you been? Are you all right?" He slammed and locked the door behind them.

"Dad, let the guy answer the first question before you give him a dozen more," said Anastacia.

She stood in the hallway, her full lips in a wide smile and her arms held out for a hug. Bedad dropped his bag and rushed into them. She smelled like lemons. He held her close until she coughed discreetly, and then he stepped back.

"I was worried about you," he said.

"Well, I was worried about you," said Jamail as the three of them went into the kitchen. "Anastacia kept telling me you could take care of yourself" — he plugged in the kettle — "but you young people all say that. I worry about Anastacia every time she walks outside. I worry about my son. He's about your age, I think. Just because you're young doesn't mean you're invincible. Taking chances that shouldn't be taken—"

Anastacia sat at the table. "Dad, Dad, take a breath."

Bedad looked back and forth from Anastacia to her stepfather. Clearly, Jamail was stressed. Bedad wondered if he was actually directing most of that tirade at Anastacia. Something twisted around his legs, and he heard a meow.

"Stumpy," said Bedad. "I'm glad you're all right."

He bent down to pet the cat.

"I had to let him out to hunt," Anastacia said. "There wasn't any meat to spare when we ran out of cat food. None in the stores either, and I don't even want to consider why. He seemed to manage on his own. Some of us can."

Jamail gave her a "don't press your luck" look.

"I thought someone might cook him up for dinner. But he's a survivor. Like us." Jamail set out three mugs. "After all, Stumpy somehow managed to regrow his tail. I've never seen that before."

"Hey," said Bedad. "What's happened to him now?"

Stumpy's left ear was gone, replaced by a ragged scar.

"We don't know," said Anastacia. "I guess it was the price of survival."

Bedad laughed. "At least he suits his name again."

The kitchen blinds rattled loudly.

"Wind's up again," said Anastacia. "I'll close the window. We've taken the boards off the kitchen and bathroom windows. It was like living in a stuffy cave."

"What's been happening?" asked Bedad. "It looks like some green things have returned."

"No drought, no floods," said Jamail. "The water level is still really low. But, with the cooler evenings, we're getting wild winds again. Lightning has started several forest fires, and the wind spreads them. Tornadoes have become common in the Thunder Bay area. They are everywhere now."

The house shook as the wind tore by. The kettle whistled a shrill, puny challenge.

"Let's drink our tea in the basement, just in case," said Jamail.

They headed for the family room.

That night, after the wind had calmed, the three of them sat around the kitchen table and listened to the windup radio. The Nor'wester Hotel and sports complex, on the city fringe, had been hit by a small tornado. Several buildings were destroyed, including the nearby gas station. Eighteen people had been killed and twenty-two wounded.

Jamail turned off the radio.

"Jamail," said Bedad. "If I could take you and Anastacia some place safe, with no food or water problems, great weather, and no wars or rioting, would you come?"

"Of course," said Jamail. "But Thunder Bay seems to be one of the safer places right now."

"Not if the tornadoes continue." Bedad leaned forward. "Drought will return. Besides, how soon until freezing nights put a stop to your gardening?"

Jamail nodded. "Frost could come in the next two or three weeks. I have ways to protect the plants for a while, as long as it doesn't go below freezing for too long."

"And then?" said Bedad. "Will you harvest enough to get you through the winter?"

"Not from my little garden," said Jamail. "I have stored a lot of food, but I'm hoping my son will bring his fiancée here. We'll double in number. Then I'll need a lot more."

"I saw many stores boarded up and almost no traffic on the highway," said Bedad. "I don't think you can count on food coming in from other places over the winter."

Jamail wrung his hands and nodded. "How can we get to this place you speak of? We have no gasoline for the car."

"It's a hundred-kilometer walk," said Bedad.

Jamail thumped the table with his hand, making the tea cups jump. "What are you talking about? Nothing within a hundred kilometers is any better than here."

Bedad looked at Anastacia. "Don't you think it's time you told him?"

"Yes, I think it is." She sighed and turned to her stepfather. "I'm sorry, Dad, but I've kept some things from you. I even lied about what happened in Lucerne when I was sixteen. You know the bracelet Mom gave me . . . . "

Chapter Seventeen - The Reveal

Jamail had seen some crazy things in his life, and shocking him was difficult. This revelation, however, was a stunner. He seemed hurt that Nicole, Anastacia's mother, had never confided in him.

"Would you have believed her without any proof?" asked Anastacia.

"I don't know. Maybe." Jamail looked from Anastacia to Bedad. "I don't really have any proof now," he said.

Bedad rolled up his sleeve to reveal his panther bracelet with the triple stone.

"That doesn't mean anything," Jamail said.

Anastacia rolled up her sleeve. "Remember when my bracelet was copper-colored? Now it's gold."

Jamail shrugged. "It could just be a different bracelet."

Bedad sighed and stood. He pulled out the fourth kitchen chair where Stumpy was sleeping.

"Unless Anastacia has an issue with the cat not suiting his name again . . . ?"

Bedad looked questioningly at Anastacia. She nodded.

The cat stretched and looked up at Bedad. Bedad placed one hand over the bracelet and concentrated. Light arched from his bracelet and poured over the cat. Jamail jumped to his feet. The kitchen chair tipped and crashed behind him. Bedad removed his hand from the bracelet and the light stopped. The cat shook his head, sat, licked his paw, and started cleaning his new ear.

"Excuse me." Bedad staggered down the hall to the washroom.

Sounds of vomiting reached the kitchen.

Jamail's mouth fell open. He went to the cat, knelt beside him, and touched both ears. "It's real."

Anastacia stood up, righted her stepfather's chair, and patted him on the shoulder. "Have a seat, Dad. There's more you need to know."

After an astonished but hopeful Jamail went to bed, Anastacia and Bedad sat around a candle and talked. Bedad knew he had to make Anastacia face reality.

"We need to go to Dawn's End before things worsen," Bedad said.

"Dad won't leave without Ali," said Anastacia. "Ali won't leave without his fiancée, Lucinda, and I won't leave without Dad."

"So, basically, your stepbrother has to somehow get to Thunder Bay before you'll return to Dawn's End," said Bedad. Her loyalty was admirable, but it complicated things.

"That's about it," said Anastacia. "And I'm not sure we want to all jump ship then either. I haven't given up hope that things will improve."

"You certainly don't make it easy," said Bedad. How could he make her see?

"Make what easy?" asked Anastacia.

"Loving you," he whispered.

The silence covered them like a heavy blanket. Anastacia looked from Bedad to Stumpy, asleep on the chair, and back to Bedad.

"It's okay," he said. "I know you have feelings for Max."

"Max!" said Anastacia. "We can't leave Max behind."

"Will he leave his family?"

"What? I don't know? Can't they come?" She clutched his sleeve.

Was it just her nature to try to save everyone?

Bedad's voice sounded frustrated. "Brothers and sisters? Their wives and fiancées? Their children? Parents? Grandparents? Cousins?"

"Julie! We can't leave Julie. And her family." Anastacia dug her fingers into his arm. "And Mr. Ferguson and his family. If he hadn't taught me to hunt, we'd be in real trouble."

"It's impossible," said Bedad. "Dawn's End has strict laws against bringing in people from the Outworld. They'll be forcibly expelled, and we'll be punished for bringing them. Probably lose our bracelets. You can't save the whole world."

"Couldn't we?" Anastacia squeezed his arm harder.

Bedad pulled his arm away. "What?"

"Save the whole world." Her voice rose. "My mother saved Dawn's End, your whole world. You'd all probably be dead now if it wasn't for her and my father. You owe us. I want restitution. Save my world."

"How do I do that?" asked Bedad. "We don't have enough crystals to fix all the problems. Your world is massive, with massive numbers of people causing massive difficulties. Even if we brought every bracelet in Dawn's End here, do you think it would really make any difference?"

"I don't know." Anastacia glanced down at her arm. "We have two bracelets. We can use them. It's worth a try."

"Have you used your bracelet yet?" asked Bedad.

Anastacia nodded. "I had to. A moose attacked me."

"A moose?"

"It's a huge animal with antlers—"

Bedad grinned. "I know what a moose is. I was just surprised."

"Oh, okay. Anyway, I tried to make him leave. He was going to destroy the garden. And, well, I killed it."

"Is that where the moose burgers came from?"

Anastacia nodded. "I didn't mean to kill it."

"Controlling the bracelets in your world is difficult."

"But, another time, I turned a car right side up that had flipped over into a gully—"

"Oh, boy." Bedad ran his fingers through his now shoulder-length hair.

"The driver would have died." She glared defiantly at him. "Anyway I saved a man's life."

"How did you feel after?'

"I . . . I threw up. I felt weak for the rest of the day."

"The bracelet pulls the power through you from the earth. You pay a cost every time you use it. I don't even know what the long-term effects of using it in the Outworld are. Its power is not to be used lightly. I told you that."

"I see," said Anastacia. "So, you're saying we can't control them very well, and using the bracelets weakens us, maybe sickens us." She traced the figure of the embossed panther with her fingernail.

He nodded. "Yes."

"That's a risk I'm willing to take if I can save my world." She held her head high.

"It's a foolish risk. Several bracelets could cause as much damage as good if we couldn't control them properly. Besides, you might be able to divert a tornado away from a building, but you can't stop it from forming. You can't control the weather with any safety. There are more disasters happening in this world than you could fix even if you worked on one a day. Which you couldn't. The bracelet would most probably kill you."

Anastacia's eyes filled with tears. "What do we do then?"

Bedad held firm. He mustn't let her see how difficult he found it to face her tears and know more would come. "We let the earth heal herself in her own time, her own way."

"By destroying everyone?"

"I read that there were always some species that survived when the earth experienced its mass extinctions. I researched it after you told me about them. If you stay here, though, I can't guarantee you or the people you love will survive." He pleaded. "The ship is sinking. It's time to get into the lifeboat."

Anastacia crossed her arms. "I won't leave without my brother. I'm not saying I'll leave even then."

"Okay, we some have time, unless Mother Nature throws

something new in the mix. But I can't be with you every minute. I have a place of my own with a laboratory. Could you just try to stay safe and not take any unnecessary risks until it is time to leave?"

"I want to go to the Center tomorrow. See the kids."

"And Max." Bedad traced a design with his finger on the tabletop.

"I didn't know you loved me, Bedad. I'm sorry. I just don't think of you that way."

He gave a lopsided smile. "I've loved you ever since you told me to go scrub in the river."

Anastacia smiled. "I think that's how I see still you. A lost, grubby, little boy."

"I'm twenty-five, the same age as Max, sort of." Why couldn't she see that?

"I know. But . . . I'm sorry."

He nodded. He wasn't going to argue, but he wasn't giving up either. He could be stubborn too.

She continued. "While we're waiting for my brother, maybe you could help with something else."

"If I can."

"Something is going on with the kids at the Center." Anastacia leaned forward. "We found some files missing, and, when we went to their homes, we found the kids were missing, too. All except Rupert. Thank goodness. It would tear my heart out if he disappeared."

"I'm not sure I can do anything, except keep an eye out for them."

"All right." Anastacia sat back. "That's something anyway."

Bedad glanced away, too uncomfortable to look her in the eyes.

Chapter Eighteen - Medicine

Deceiving Anastacia had been difficult, but Bedad didn't want her to worry. She carried too much responsibility. They had disagreed over her desire to wait for her brother. He did not want to argue any more.

Bedad made sure no one saw him go into the abandoned warehouse. Some people would be desperate enough to attack him for a bag of food. And, if they knew he was storing food, they would follow him. Then what would he do? He was also storing something much more precious. If anyone discovered what was in the warehouse, things would get complicated. He would be forced to move before the experiment was complete.

Gangs now inhabited several warehouses throughout the city. The members ranged in age from eleven to twenty, young people whose families had died or deserted them. In the way of the vulnerable, they had found strength in numbers. Bedad hoped they would never show an interest in his building.

He set the canned peaches, snap peas, bread, and peanut butter on the table. Not the best meal, but filling and nourishing, probably better than what his guests were used to anyway. He made four sandwiches and portioned the peaches and peas out into four little bowls.

He had fastened the door to the inner room with a spell. He did not want some gang coming across a suspicious lock; they would then be all the more determined to open it. The spell held the door shut for everyone except Bedad, who could come and go as he pleased. But, to all others, the door appeared to be part of the wall; it was basically invisible.

When he entered the room with the tray, two of the boys were playing checkers while the third watched. Petal was practicing on an electric keyboard with no sound. She said she could hear the music in her head, and, besides, it was better than nothing.

Bedad had taken Gabriel first. The little boy screamed and cried and would not stop trying to escape, regardless what Bedad promised him. Bedad realized that, no matter how poor his family was, no matter how much his parents struggled financially, they loved and cared for their son. Although Gabriel's father worked double-shifts as a cabbie, he budgeted his money wisely and managed to provide his son with what he needed. The love his parents gave was returned. Gabriel worried about his wheelchair-bound mother. Who would help her now when his father was at work?

"But she was alone when you went to school," Bedad said.

"Yes, but she knew I was coming home," replied Gabriel.

Bedad then had his best idea. "But she wants you to be here. She loves you so much, so she wants you to be safe. She agreed this was the best way. The adults will join us later."

"No," said Gabriel. "When we left Poland, Mama never let us be apart. She said the family had to stay together, no matter what."

"But you know families where the father came ahead to Canada to get work and sent for the wife and children later. Sometimes you have to be apart for a little while."

"But why didn't my Mama tell me?"

"There was a tornado coming. We had to move fast. Now, listen, Gabriel. Your parents would want you to eat, get strong, and be ready to travel when they join you."

"Why can't they be with us now?" said Gabriel. "There's lots of room in this big building."

"Because this is a safe place for children only. More children will be coming. There isn't as much room as you think. If I bring your parents, that means other children will be left in danger. I won't have room for them."

"I don't care. I want my Mama!"

"What about Petal?" asked Bedad.

"Petal?"

"Yes, I told her mother I would take care of her. But if there is no room, I won't be able to. You know her mother is having trouble feeding her. Petal often goes for a day or two with nothing but what she gets at the Ventures Center. If she comes here, she will get good food every day. I promised her mother I would take her. Do you want me to take your parents instead?"

"Yes."

"I don't think they would want to take a spot away from a little girl."

"Oh." Gabriel chewed his finger.

"What would your Mama want you to do? Keep crying for her, or help me take care of more hungry children? What would she think was the right thing to do?"

Gabriel gave a large sigh, tilted his head back, and flopped his arms at his sides. Then he looked Bedad in the eyes and nodded resignedly.

The other children were easier to convince. First, he had Gabriel on his side. Second, they were used to spending long periods away from their parents, often watched over by strangers. Third, they knew Bedad and trusted him. Fourth, the warehouse was warm, quiet, safe, and had food. No one hit them, or passed out on the floor, or shot up with needles.

Bedad was relieved. Perhaps he shouldn't have chosen Gabriel. Even after the other children arrived, the boy was still anxious.

The children cheered when Bedad carried in the large tray. Night had fallen. It had taken longer than expected to find food; the children must be hungry.

"Wash your hands first," he said.

"But they're clean," said Chester. "We weren't playing outside."

"You were picking your nose," said Kyle.

"Shut up!" snapped Chester.

Kyle stuck his tongue out at Chester as he absentmindedly reached for a sandwich, took a bite, and coughed, spitting his mouthful out on the floor.

"Kyle, if you don't like peanut butter, just say so," said Bedad.

"Peanut butter!" shrieked Petal. "He's allergic."

Kyle continued to spit and then wiped the inside of his mouth with his shirt.

"Is it that bad?" asked Bedad.

Petal nodded, her eyes wide with fright. "He could die."

All the children stared at Kyle, waiting to see what would happen.

Kyle's eyes filled with tears.

"What should I do?" asked Bedad.

"I have an epi pen in my bag." Kyle whispered as tears rolled down his face.

Petal dug through the bag and passed the boxed pen to Bedad. He read the instructions.

"Are you having trouble breathing?" Bedad asked.

Kyle nodded as he wheezed.

"You gotta call an ambulance," said Chester. "But they don't come very often 'cos there's no gas."

"Yeah," said Gabriel. "That's why my dad can't drive the taxi anymore."

"I'm going to take you to the hospital," said Bedad. "Can you walk?"

"My throat hurts." Kyle clutched his belly and moaned. "My stomach too."

"He musta swallowed some," said Petal. "You'd better hurry."

"By the crystal," said Bedad. "I'm sorry. I didn't know. I forgot to get your information sheet." He scooped Kyle up his arms. Thankfully, the boy was small for eleven, but, still, it was a long way to the hospital.

Kyle's lips were swelling as they exited through the charmed door.

Outside the children's room, Bedad laid Kyle down on the floor and quickly reviewed the epi pen instructions. He pulled off the blue cap and jabbed the orange tip against Kyle's right thigh holding him down with his other hand. The needle clicked. He counted off ten seconds for the adrenaline to flow into the muscle and then removed the needle, tossing it aside. He picked the boy up in his arms.

"Try to be calm, Kyle. Everything is going to be okay."

The box said the dosage could be repeated every five to fifteen minutes as needed. Bedad stumbled into the street, carrying Kyle, and started to jog. They would never make it. It would take at least forty-five minutes to get to the hospital.

When they were three blocks from the warehouse, a motorcycle cop pulled up beside them. Since gasoline was scarce, the Thunder Bay Police Force used motorcycles and bicycles as much as possible. Fortunately, this motorcycle had a sidecar.

"What's the problem?' said the officer.

"Hospital!" shouted Bedad. "Fast!"

"Get in," said the officer.

Bedad climbed into the side car and sat Kyle on its hood. He wrapped his arms around the boy. Kyle's legs stuck out in front.

"He had an allergic reaction to peanut butter," said Bedad. "I gave him an epi pen shot, but he only had one."

The officer radioed the information ahead as he hit the gas.

Fortunately, the police officer was focused on dodging the ever-increasing potholes and did not see Bedad roll up his sleeve and cover the bracelet on his left arm with his right hand. He considered trying to heal the child but, without research, was unsure what was involved. He placed his left hand on Kyle and whispered, "Forget." A light pulsed down his arm and encircled the boy's head.

"What was that?" asked the officer.

"What was what?"

The doctors were waiting at the emergency entrance. They whisked Kyle away.

"You'll have to fill out a few forms. This way," said a nurse.

"One moment," said Bedad. He walked over to a wall, placed his hand on it, and vomited into the dead grass.

"Hell of a scare," said the cop as he dismounted and approached Bedad. "But the doctors know what they're doing. I think he'll be okay."

Bedad sank to his knees. The cop placed a comforting hand on Bedad's shoulder. Bedad clamped his on top and weakly said, "Forget." Light flowed up Bedad's arm, up the cop's arm to his head, where it whirled for a few seconds. The officer staggered away and remounted his motorcycle. He sat there staring into space while Bedad heaved into the grass until he had nothing left to vomit.

Bedad wiped his lips on his sleeve, glanced toward the emergency doors, and reeled down the hill toward the exit to the hospital grounds. A few seconds later, he heard the motorcycle start, and the officer rode off in the opposite direction.

Bedad had to get back to the children. They'd be frightened. They'd want to know how Kyle was doing. He glanced back over his shoulder at the hospital's gleaming squares of light. How was Kyle doing? What if he had killed the boy? Anastacia must never know. Never.

He stumbled and fell hard on his right knee, tearing his pants. He knelt there, in the black night. Most of the streetlights no longer worked. The university was closed, all the buildings shrouded in darkness. He heard no cars, no voices, no crickets, nothing but silence. He felt invisible. Lost. He stumbled toward one of the few working street lamps, leaned against the pole, and sank to the ground. Sweat poured down his face. He couldn't do this alone. He was tired. Sore. Sick. Worn down to a river-washed pebble.

"Problem, buddy?" said a voice in the darkness.

Bedad leapt to his feet.

"Relax," said the man. "I just thought you might need some help."

"I'm sick," said Bedad.

"Then you're going in the wrong direction. The hospital's behind you."

"I can't go there," said Bedad. "They can't help me with this kind of sickness."

"Ah, I hear you. I might have something that can." Franz Hahn stepped into the light beside him. "Do you have anything valuable to trade?"

"Gold coins," said Bedad. "But I don't think you can help me."

"You want the pain to go away?"

Bedad nodded.

"You want to feel powerful, energized, unstoppable?" asked Franz.

"Yes," whispered Bedad.

"Then come with me," said Franz. "You are so lucky to have run into me. I can make everything better."

"Thank you."

Bedad straightened up and followed Franz into the darkness.

Chapter Nineteen - Memories

After the disaster with Kyle, Bedad decided to ensure the children were in perfect health before he proceeded any further with his plan. Using magic, he scanned their bodies for any anomalies. If he found malformations or anything else that could potentially cause medical problems, he researched it extensively and then fixed it as best he could. He even straightened Chester's teeth. To do this without inflicting pain on the children, he called deeper and deeper upon the power of the bracelet.

He was shocked to find a small tumor growing at the base of Petal's spine. He knew it might not have been discovered until the girl was in great danger, and, with the overloaded demands on the hospital, he could not imagine how long she would have waited for help. Perhaps she never would have received it.

The substance the man on the street had given him flowed through his veins like electricity. Physically, he felt supercharged. He felt more confident than ever. Periodically, he returned to Dawn's End through the portal by the pond, which was now operational. He rejuvenated the band and crystals and replenished supplies. While there, however, he contacted no one. He left the children with enough food to tide them over during his absence, but the fear of what could happen to them if he was delayed scratched at the back of his mind.

Still, the risk of leaving them alone was worth it. He could change the lives of these children for good and, in return, they would change the lives of others. He tried not to think of their parents. Tried not to think how the children's families might be searching and grieving, especially Gabriel's. Bedad had seen posters of Gabriel, pleading for information on the boy's whereabouts, hanging all over town. Bedad told himself that, if his parents knew the truth, they would understand. They would bless Bedad for what he was doing — he was giving their son perfect health and a brilliant future they could never provide for him.

Now all he had to do was work on the children's minds. Once he had altered their memories, especially Gabriel's, the tears would stop. He had lied to them, but they would never know.

Chapter Twenty - A New Kind of Crystal

"Why don't you stay with us?" Anastacia walked Bedad to her front door. "It doesn't make sense for you to be living somewhere else."

"I don't keep very social hours," said Bedad. "I get ideas in the middle of the night and jump up and start experimenting."

She stopped in front of the coat closet. "On the water purification system?"

"Yeah, sure. Other stuff, too."

"You could set up a lab in the garage." Anastacia reached for his gray jacket. "Although Dad keeps adding to our woodpile and we had to move the car out, I'm sure we could make space."

"I'd rather not expose your father, and you, to questionable fumes." Bedad chewed on his thumbnail.

"I don't think it's good for you either." She examined his face. "Your eyes are super blood shot, your face is flushed and" — she leaned in closer — "even your pupils are dilated."

Bedad shrugged. "I'm fine."

"I noticed you're kinda twitchy. You're more hyper than usual, too. Maybe I shouldn't have introduced you to caffeine."

Anastacia took the jacket off the hanger and held it out to Bedad. Stumpy raced in and twisted around her feet, meowing. He climbed her leg, sinking in his claws.

"Ouch, bad cat."

Anastacia dropped the jacket just as Bedad reached for it. A small bottle fell out of the pocket.

"Oh, sorry." Anastacia looked at the container. "What's that?

"Don't worry about it." Bedad bent to retrieve the bottle.

"I got it." She snatched it up. "Wait a minute. Is this what I think it is?" She stared at the bottle of white crystals.

Bedad took it from her hand, picked up his jacket, and slipped it back into the pocket.

"Is that cocaine?" asked Anastacia. "The police come to the Center every year and give us a workshop on what to watch for. I'm pretty sure that's coke."

Bedad avoided her eyes as he slipped on the jacket.

"It is, isn't it? What the hell are you doing with cocaine? Who gave this to you?" She clenched the fabric on his sleeve and shook his arm.

He twisted away. "Someone named Franz. It helps me with my work."

"Bedad! Are you kidding me? You know this is the same kind of thing we fought against in Dawn's End?" Anastacia spoke loudly and quickly. "Wait. Did you say Franz?"

He nodded.

Her eyes narrowed in fury. "Was his hair mixed brown and gray? Blue eyes? Dimple in his chin? Long face? Perfect teeth?"

"Yeah."

Anastacia uttered a long string of curses.

"I just need it for a while. Then I'll stop." Bedad stepped away from her.

"You'll stop right now. You don't understand what this is doing to you." She held out her hand. "Give it to me, and I'll flush it down the toilet."

"No." Bedad quickly opened the door.

"Bedad! If you don't give that to me, you won't be allowed back at the Ventures Center. We don't allow coke-heads around the children."

"You don't understand. I'm doing it for them . . . . "

She put her hands on her hips and leaned toward him, eyes flashing angrily. "What? For who?"

He shut the door.

Anastacia considered running after him and knocking him to the ground. She could take him in a fair fight; she knew she could. He'd lost weight and looked burned out. But, if he used magic, she wouldn't stand a chance.

"Damn it!" She slapped her hand against the closed door.

Chapter Twenty-One - Banned

Anastacia had no choice but to tell Max and Sally about the drugs she found in Bedad's pocket. She knew Bedad would never deliberately harm the children, but what if one of them discovered the cocaine accidentally like she had? Besides, the Center allowed no dealers or users on the premises. That was a die-hard rule. No exceptions.

Anastacia brought Sally into Max's office before the children arrived.

"I can't believe I'm telling you this," she said, avoiding their eyes. "Bedad came over to my place yesterday. I found cocaine in his jacket pocket. He admitted he's using and refused to give it up."

"Bedad?" said Sally. "I can't believe he's an addict. He seems so sweet."

"He is," said Anastacia. "He just thinks he can do anything and be all right. He's pushing himself too hard. That might be partly my fault. I don't think he understands what this will do to him."

"But why?" asked Sally.

"It doesn't matter why. At least not as far as Empowerment Ventures goes. He's banned," said Max. "I'm sorry, Anastacia. I know he's your friend."

She nodded.

"Did he have a tough childhood?" asked Sally.

"Very," said Anastacia as she remembered the scar on his temple, given to him as a boy by his alcoholic mother. "But he was adopted by good parents when he was twelve."

Sally nodded, her eyes filled with sadness. "The programs for addicts have collapsed. I don't even know how we can help him."

"My job is to help these kids," said Max. "And keep them safe while they're here."

Anastacia knew the small salary Max received had stopped months ago. Donations had stopped as well. Like her, he was doing this out of love. She felt shame at having brought a drug addict into the Center. Bedad had been behaving strangely lately, but she had never imagined this.

"Of course, we can't let him come back here," said Sally. "But maybe we can do some kind of intervention at Anastacia's. Let him know we care."

Max hugged Sally's shoulder. "Our big-hearted lady," he said.

He gave her a warm smile. Sally beamed at the attention.

Awkwardly, Anastacia muttered, "I'll think about that."

She left the room trying not to look upset. Nothing seemed to be going her way.

She unlocked the front door. Two teenagers and little Rupert were waiting outside.

"Where's your Auntie Faith?" she asked Rupert.

"She left him with us," said the taller teenager. "She'll be back to pick him up though."

Anastacia tried not to frown. Normally, the parents and guardians of children this young were supposed to hand them over personally to a supervisor. But nothing was normal anymore. She managed to greet them with a smile, ruffling

Rupert's hair as he entered.

Only one other child, a fourteen-year-old girl named Kari, who seldom came, showed up that day. Time dragged. Sally played the piano as usual, but no one was interested in taking lessons or joining a sing-along. It was obvious how much Sally missed Petal's enthusiastic absorption.

Just when everyone was cleaning up before closing, Bedad walked through the door.

Anastacia rushed over. "I told you, you can't come here anymore."

"I just came to tell you I'm returning to Dawn's End for a while. You're going to have to decide soon if you're coming, you and your father. I had a vision. This is just the calm before the storm. Things are not going to get better."

Max approached, his expression stern. "You are no longer welcome here."

Bedad looked from Max to Anastacia. "You told him?"

"I had to."

Anastacia chewed her lip as she watched Bedad's expression crumple.

"Bedad." Rupert ran to Bedad and wrapped himself around his waist. "Can you do the egg trick? I'm hungry."

"Bedad has to leave." Max peeled the boy off Bedad.

"Why?" cried Rupert. "I want him to stay."

"Bedad won't be coming to the Center anymore," said Max. "He's here to say goodbye."

"That's right," said Bedad. "I'm going home for a while. But I'll be back. Everything is going to get better."

Max glared at him. Anastacia remembered the lonely, brave boy she had met in Dawn's End. What was he doing? Why did he tell her things were going to get worse and then tell Rupert the opposite? What was wrong with him? She watched him walk away, looking beaten and alone.

As he left, Anastacia called after him. "Bedad, come to my house before you leave. Please."

After all the children were gone and they had locked up, Anastacia saw that Sally was crying. Max silently passed Sally a tissue.

"I'm sorry," she said. "I just think if all these awful things weren't happening, Bedad wouldn't have . . . you know." She gave a little sob.

"I'll walk you home," said Max. "You look like you need to talk."

They all stepped outside. Max clicked the door shut and turned the key in the lock.

Anastacia watched the pair pick their way carefully down the cracked and heaved sidewalk. She could use someone to talk to. She could use a strong shoulder to lean on.

Max saw her as a tower of strength. He was five years older than she was, but, at their age, that shouldn't make a difference. Sally was several years older than he was. Anastacia had no doubt Max liked to feel strong and needed. Mousy little Sally with her round, girlish face and her wispy hair probably made him feel like a giant. Anastacia suspected kicking his ass at almost every sport they played and being taller, stronger, and faster than he was put her at a disadvantage. But she was who she was, and she wouldn't pretend otherwise. In Dawn's End, she would find others like her, others even more powerful than she was. Perhaps she would fit in there. But what was she thinking? *This* was home. Why would she leave everyone and everything she knew?

She would never leave without Ali and his fiancée. And, since the world seemed to be in a slow, painful recovery, perhaps neither of them would want to leave. Bedad would have to return on his own, and she would never see him again. The thought depressed her. She wished she hadn't become so fond of him in the time since he had shown up with the antidote. He had destroyed the poison in her body, but now he was poisoning his own. What would his time in the Outworld cost him in the end?

Chapter Twenty-Two - Kidnapped

When Bedad came to see Anastacia, she pulled him into the kitchen and pushed him into a chair.

"I've been thinking," she said. "This drug abuse, it's my fault."

Bedad looked up at her and shook his head.

"Yes, yes, it is. I kept pressuring you to solve our problems. To pay my family back for what we did for Dawn's End. Restitution and all that. But there are so many things wrong. One person can't fix it. Not even the most powerful wizard I know. You aren't responsible for our bad decisions."

"I was making progress on purifying the water," said Bedad. "But I can only do a little at a time. It takes so much out of me, using the bracelets in the Outworld. I can't keep vomiting up everything I eat."

"Oh, Bedad." Anastacia crouched beside him. "I'm sorry. I used the bracelet to stop the moose, and I was weak for the rest of the day. I threw up, too. I can't imagine what it must be like for you using it day after day."

He cupped his hands toward her, leaned forward, and looked into her eyes. "It's all right, Anastacia. I'd do anything for you."

She clasped each of his hands. "Would you? Would you really?"

He nodded.

"Then give me the cocaine, I'm—"

He sat back in the chair. "No, I need it, I—"

"No, stop the water experiments. Stop it all. Go home. Get better." She shook his hands. "Go back to being Bedad, not some strung-out, haunted creature."

He gave her a sweet smile. "Okay, I just have a little more work here. Then I'll throw the cocaine away."

"No more work. No more cocaine."

Anastacia released his hands, shoved her right hand into his jacket pocket and pulled out a piece of paper, which fell to the floor. "Where is it? Where's the bottle?" She tried to search his left pocket, but he pushed her hand away.

"Stop it!" He jumped to his feet.

"Bedad—"

His voice was firm. "I'm leaving. I don't know when I'll be back, but when I do come back, it will be for the last time. You will have to come with me then, along with whatever family you choose to bring, or not come at all. I'm warning you. I can't hold your world together. You have to come or—"

"Bedad, I can't leave. I—"

He held up his hand. "You don't know what's coming. I've had visions. They aren't as clear as the ones I have in Dawn's End, but I can tell you it isn't good. I'm talking mass extinction. Millions will die, and I can't stop it. I can't bring hordes of people through the portal either. After the disaster with the imports from your world, a law was passed. No adult Outworlders will be allowed to enter. After the disease, they made the rules even tighter. Only children or family members of the Esteemed Nicole and Alaric Morrel and family members of their daughter, you, Anastacia the Bold, may enter. But time is running out. If you don't come now, you may not ever be able to come."

Anastacia crossed her arms, pursed her lips, and shook her head.

He groaned, then walked quickly down the hall and left.

As the sound of a slammed door faded, Anastacia picked up the paper that had fallen to the floor. She unfolded the page and saw a child's drawing, a boy, a father, and a mother in a wheelchair. *I miss you. Love, Gabriel,* she read.

Her heart seized. She grabbed the back of the chair to steady herself before falling into the seat. She set the picture on the table and stared at it. How could Bedad have a letter from Gabriel to his parents? Bedad had Gabriel. That was the only explanation. Did he have other children as well? The kids from the Center? What was he doing with them? His behavior was bizarre . . . drugs, and now this. She would have to tell the authorities.

Suddenly, the door flew open, and Bedad strode into the kitchen. He snapped up the picture from the table.

"You're a kidnapper," she whispered. "Why? What are you doing to those children?"

"I'm saving them, you idiot, what do you think I'm doing?" Bedad's face was flushed and angry.

"How? How are—"

"I'm taking them to Dawn's End. To safety. They don't have a chance here."

Her eyes widened. "What do you mean? Things are getting better."

"Things are getting worse. I can see things you can't. If the children remain, they will die along with almost everyone else."

"You're exaggerating. You have no right to take these children from their families."

"Families! Gabriel is the only one with a real family, and I know they would want him to survive."

She covered her mouth, horrified. "The kids must be terrified. They must miss their parents."

"Actually, Gabriel is the only one who hasn't adjusted. That's why I asked him to make the picture for his parents. But don't worry. Soon, his sadness will be over."

She dropped her hand. "What do you mean?"

"I'm erasing their memories, little by little. When we go through the door to Dawn's End, they won't remember anything of the Outworld. They'll become one of us. They'll be deeply loved by parents who have lost their own children."

She leapt to her feet. "That's what you're doing. Stealing children for Dawn's End?"

"You think the kids will be better off here?" Bedad waved his arm. "Watching everything they've known and loved get destroyed?"

Anastacia poked him in the chest with a finger. "What about their families, their culture? You're destroying who they are."

"No, your world is destroying all that. Do you think they'll have a culture left when they are digging through trash cans and eating rats in order to survive?" His voice was cold, filled with disgust. "Maybe being the last ones alive in their family. Facing the apocalypse alone."

Anastacia blanched. "It won't come to that. Things are—"

"Things are going to hell, Anastacia," Bedad shouted. "I'm

making sure these kids don't go there as well."

He whirled around and hurried down the hall. Anastacia followed.

"I'll call the cops. They'll stop you."

"Good luck with that," said Bedad.

Chapter Twenty-Three - Three Arrows

"Don't count your chickens before they hatch," Anastacia's mother used to say. She had done just that. To Anastacia's relief, Julie had emailed to say her family was getting by in Switzerland.

Because farms were succeeding locally and some items were arriving from outside the Thunder Bay District, Anastacia had thought things were improving and would keep on improving. Then shipments of food stopped.

Growers sold food grown in the south to nearby cities, but it wasn't nearly enough. The hungry rioted for food in the north and south. The federal government enacted martial law. Anastacia could not get used to the sight of military vehicles and armed soldiers in the street. Careful to avoid them, she carried her bow and arrows with her everywhere.

In town, squirrels, crows, pigeons, and sea gulls fell victim to her skill. Three years ago, Anastacia had purchased her own bow, splurging on a custom-designed Buffalo Recurve with handmade Flemish string and other special features. Mr. Ferguson had recommended a compound bow. The clever pulley system could be drawn by beginners and women, but Anastacia thought it too easy. Crossbows, also, did not provide enough challenge. The romantic history of the long bow was attractive, but she achieved more accuracy with a recurve. Although heavier in weight, the recurve was also shorter and faster. It seemed more important to have clean kills than to imitate the English bowman of medieval times. She didn't want to risk causing an animal unnecessary suffering. The dealer had measured her draw length twice, surprised by her height.

Mr. Ferguson crafted his own bows and arrows. "Something

to do outside of hunting season," he said.

Anastacia was not that much of a purist. Mr. Ferguson gave her three of his handmade arrows with cedar shafts and turkey-feather fletching. The others, which she purchased herself, were aluminum.

"Why use them when you got my beauties?" Mr. Ferguson asked. "Don't you think they'll fly straight?"

"Of course, I do. I'm saving them for something special."

Those three wooden arrows still remained in her quiver, waiting for that singular moment. She developed a routine: choose an aluminum arrow, use it over and over until it no longer flew true, and then choose the next. Once she spotted it, no animal escaped her keen precision. As well, her height, confidence, strength, and her imposing weapon prevented anyone from bothering her, muggers and gangs included.

Not everyone had weapons or skill. Without food shipments, more people would starve. Hunters competed for even the smallest prey, using baseball bats, rocks, anything they could find to make the kill. Anastacia kept Stumpy inside, afraid he would become someone's meal.

What would happen to all the children who had frequented the Ventures Center? Did they have anyone who could hunt for them? Were they starving? Maybe Bedad was right to take the children. No. Not without asking the parents. He should have given them a choice.

And what of the disease in Dawn's End? Bedad said he had created an inoculation against it. Would that work on children from the Outworld, or was he taking them there to die? Would this new disease wipe out any survivors he brought with him?

As Anastacia dumped her latest quarry on the kitchen counter, she wiped her eyes, remembering. Nine-year-old Petal with her thin face and grimy, black hair. Did they have pianos in Dawn's End? Would Petal forget how to play a keyboard? Would it be better if she did? Eleven-year-old Kyle, with his sad, hazel eyes and a heart filled with pain. Would erasing his memory have fixed that? Kyle had turned up at the hospital in anaphylactic shock. He had no memory of how he got there. Was that Bedad's work? Ten-year-old Chester never knew his birth father. His mother and stepfather were both alcoholics. A quiet boy with an explosive temper. Would he be better off without his memories? Gabriel wouldn't. Gabriel had a courageous family and a home filled with love. Who was Bedad to take that away from him? No. It was wrong. Wasn't it?

Anastacia ran her fingers through her hair in frustration. What should she do? No one would be able to stop Bedad, even if they could find him. She didn't know what to think. Maybe this was something she could discuss with her stepfather. If anyone knew about losing a family, he did.

Chapter Twenty-Four - Ripe Cherry Tomatoes

Her stepfather listened patiently as Anastacia explained what had happened.

"He was wrong to take the children without telling their parents," said Jamail. "But he was not wrong to take them to safety. The problem, it seems to me, is that he doesn't trust the parents. He believed they would stop him."

"Wouldn't they?" Anastacia nervously twirled a strand of her long, black hair around her finger.

Jamail stared at the ceiling, thinking. "No. I don't think they would. When I lost my wife and children, Ali was all I had left. My precious son. He was my whole world."

Anastacia nodded, sorry to be reawakening her stepfather's painful memories.

"Keeping him safe and getting him out of Iraq alive was all that kept me going. But, if someone had come to me and said, 'Jamail, I can save your son. I can bring him to Canada where a childless family will love him as if he was their own. If he stays here, he will surely die,' I would have said, 'Take him. Never let him forget that I loved him enough to let him go.' I would miss him every minute, but I would not regret giving him a chance at a real life."

"But Dad. They won't remember their parents. Bedad is erasing their memories."

"That is very wrong," said Jamail. "It will change who they are. Why would he do this thing?"

"I think because his own memories haunt him," said Anastacia. "I think he wishes he didn't have them. He probably thinks it's a kindness."

"Then you will have to help him see otherwise," said Jamail. "But gently, with compassion."

Anastacia nodded thoughtfully and then jumped when the door flew open.

"Bedad?" she called.

"No," said a familiar voice. "Weren't you expecting me?"

"Ali!" she shrieked. She ran to him and threw her arms around him. "You made it!"

"Yes, yes," Ali said. "We made it. Of course, we made it. I was told there were ripe cherry tomatoes waiting for me."

She gave his arm a soft punch, laughing. Then Anastacia realized his fiancée was standing behind him.

"Lucinda!" Tears ran down Anastacia's cheeks as she hugged Lucinda.

"She is usually tougher than this," Ali said to Lucinda when his sister released her.

Jamail approached and drew him in for a hug.

The young woman laughed as Anastacia shut the door.

They spent the day catching up and trading stories about what was happening around the world. The farther south, the worse the violence and hunger became. Anastacia was surprised until she considered how many people lived in the southern cities.

"I didn't think we could get across the border," said Ali . "Thankfully, they allowed a Canadian citizen to bring his wife home with him."

"Wife?" said Jamail.

"It seemed like a good idea," said Ali. "Sorry you couldn't be there."

More excitement and tears followed.

"So, Anastacia said there may be a safe place we can go until things get better," Jamail said. "But, I have to say, I don't have much hope for improvement."

"What if we had to stay away?" Anastacia asked. "What if you had to leave everyone and everything behind? Not come back?"

"Been there, done that," said Ali. "At least I know what to expect."

Anastacia did not respond. In this case, he would have no idea. She looked at Ali's new wife. "What about you? Can you leave everyone and everything behind?"

Lucinda's eyes filled with tears. "My family did not survive the last riot. There is no one to leave behind. Ali is all I have."

Anastacia nodded, swallowing hard. She just hoped Bedad would return in time. If he returned. Their parting had been pretty nasty. If she had to, could she get everyone to the Sleeping Giant and find the portal? Her ability to do so might be their only hope for survival.

"I'd better tell you where we're going," Anastacia said. "You may find it hard to believe. When I say leave everything, I mean everything."

Chapter Twenty-Five - Slaughtered

Anastacia went to the Ventures Center the next day. Only Rupert, looking as thin as a twig, and Kari, more listless than before, attended. Sally tried to interest the girl in making a treasure box, but the teen kept staring off into space and sighing. Anastacia wondered what Kari might have witnessed these last weeks. She herself had come across more than one emaciated body propped against a wall or lying on the grass. All she could do was close their eyes.

Max was helping Rupert build a city out of Legos and Connex. For the first time, Rupert had all the materials to himself.

"Look what I'm making," he said to Anastacia. "Here's the day care, where there's lots of food. Here's the bus that's going to bring Mom home from Toronto. Here's Auntie Faith's house. Here's the store where they give kids clothes for free."

Anastacia nodded and smiled as Rupert described his wonderful city.

"I'm outta here," said Kari, suddenly.

Sally followed her out the door, talking softly.

"Kyle doesn't have a dad anymore," said Rupert.

"What do you mean?" asked Anastacia. She hoped he hadn't been killed in the street brawls over supplies.

"His mommy threw him out. He was a bad daddy."

"Was he?" asked Max.

"He hit Kyle's mother lotsa time. Then he beat Kyle."

"Why?"

"He took some crackers."

"Oh, Lord," said Anastacia.

Rupert nodded. "He gave Kyle a black eye, so goodbye." He slapped his hands together as though he was removing dust.

Anastacia laughed uncomfortably.

"I think it's a good thing Kyle's daddy is gone," said Max. "Daddies are supposed to protect their children, not hurt them."

"Yep, it's a good thing." Rupert grimaced as he tried to snap two difficult pieces together. "Kyle said the crackers are all gone now. But I haven't seen Kyle for a long time."

Sally reappeared, wiping her eyes.

"I feel so helpless," she said. "I just didn't know what to say to Kari. I can't even promise things will get better."

Max stood up and gave Sally a hug. He walked away with her, whispering words of consolation. Then Anastacia turned and smiled at Rupert.

"Do you have any pets in your Lego city?" she asked.

"Nope," said Rupert. "Everybody ate the pets."

The next day was the first day of September. Instead of autumn rain, falling ash greeted Anastacia. Everything was covered in gray. Forest fires had resumed, but the burning cities were even worse. Wind from the south had carried the ash high over Lake Superior and dumped it on Thunder Bay. It piled on the roofs, abandoned vehicles, and fences like dirty snow. It fell and fell and fell.

A snow plow was used to clear the major streets around the hospital. Those who had the strength cleared walkways. Again, stores closed, their doors and windows boarded up, as supplies were exhausted. Nothing arrived by vehicle or boat.

Jamail frantically tried to protect his garden. He repeatedly cleared the ashes away. The Plexiglas covers kept the tops of the plants clean, but ash kept blowing in from the sides. Ash also blocked the sunshine, depriving the plants.

All across the north, frantic farmers and gardeners tried to save their crops knowing their harvest was all they had. Gardens were destroyed by fire or ash all across Ontario, Minnesota, Manitoba, Quebec, and Michigan.

Driven by hunger, people slaughtered the few animals left in zoos and wildlife preserves and murdered any caretaker who tried to protect them. Starving people killed and harvested both domesticated and wild animals on sight. Only a few riding horses escaped the butchery. People used horses for transportation, although feeding them was a huge challenge.

Thousands of dead fish washed up on shore, suffocated by the ash in the water. People collected them in buckets, garbage bags, packsacks, anything they could find. A smothered fish was better than no fish.

More children disappeared. Anastacia hoped Bedad was responsible. That was the best of all the possibilities.

When governments decided to release prisoners because the prisons could not provide food for them, the *Seven Billion* group assembled a mob to wait outside the prisons. The community did not have enough food to share with criminals, and, besides, once armed, these lawbreakers would do anything to get what they needed. Better to stop them before they could become a menace to the honest people who were trying to survive. The guards locked the doors and watched through the windows as the crowd attacked and butchered the inmates.

"They might as well be good for something," one attacker shouted as he hacked meat from the thighs of a dead criminal.

Then the rain arrived, falling in torrents. The fires fizzled out. The moisture saved the remaining crops. North America heaved a sigh of relief.

Max told Anastacia that the police had found Rupert's Aunt Faith in the street. Dead.

"Who's taking care of Rupert?" asked Anastacia, her voice tight.

"I don't know." Max stroked his long, red beard. "I went to his house. No one was there."

Chapter Twenty-Six - Scavaging

As September crept over the calendar, rumors of bombings in the larger cities circulated. Refugees tried to flee to smaller towns. The borders closed. Isolated communities barricaded the roads going in and out of town. Thunder Bay initiated a curfew. Southerners headed north.

"We don't have enough to feed ourselves," the residents shouted at the new arrivals, as they drove them off with gunshots. One hundred kilometers from Thunder Bay, Nipigon Residents bombed the Nipigon Bridge, stopping any vehicles from the east or south from using the Trans-Canada highway.

"That's idiotic," said Jamail. "How will we get supplies?"

"There are no supplies to bring in, Dad," said Ali. "We're actually better off than the southern cities. There's just not enough food for all the people there."

"My God," said Anastacia. "It's that much worse in other places?"

Ali nodded and gently squeezed his wife's hand as she whimpered.

Anastacia realized they would go through their provisions twice as fast now that they had four mouths to feed.

Every day Anastacia searched for Rupert. Armed with her bow and arrow, she strode through creepy alleyways and outside empty buildings other people avoided. The authorities couldn't help. They were overwhelmed trying to keep order in the streets. Many people had died or disappeared. The police added Rupert's name to a list of hundreds of other missing people.

October brought nuclear explosions. The Candu reactor in New Brunswick was first. Scientists blamed the rise in sea level. Peach Bottom, Pennsylvania exploded next, followed by a plant in Salem, New Jersey. Radioactive fallout spread across the North America.

Knowing they couldn't count on a natural gas supply through the coming long winter, Anastacia and her family began to stockpile more wood in the garage. There was a wood fireplace in the basement family room and main floor living room. They cut down the green space behind their home. No one bothered to enforce city by-laws anymore.

As the cold intensified, families moved in together, sharing the challenge of providing warmth. The temperature hovered around freezing at night and not much higher during the day. Furniture was chopped for fuel, but little of it was safe to burn since most was composed of toxic substances. Burning it caused more accidental deaths.

People were murdered for food, fuel, and other supplies. Jamail built alarms and booby traps around the house to keep out intruders. No one would steal a single log from his attached garage while he lived to protect it.

Scavenging for fuel became the best way to survive. One afternoon, when Anastacia was cruising for wooden pallets to break up and take home, a large figure stepped into the alley behind her. She whirled and whipped an arrow from her quiver, notching it as she turned.

"If I wanted to kill you," said a deep voice, "you'd already be dead."

"Mr. Ferguson!" She watched him lower his rifle and gave a sigh of relief.

"I know you're bloody good with that bow and arrow, but you

might want to trade it in for a gun. There's people here about who would kill you for a bread crumb, and a gun don't take so long to reload." He wore camouflage pants and jacket and work boots. His ever-present toothpick waggled between his lips.

Behind Mr. Ferguson was his oldest son, Tanner, about seventeen. He was tall, but not as wide or large-footed as his father. Mr. Ferguson had two other teenage boys at home, a wife, and a little girl. That was a lot of mouths to feed.

"Thanks, Mr. Ferguson," she answered. "But I feel more confident with my bow. I can use it without thinking twice, and it doesn't make a sound."

"I'll teach you, if you change your mind and can get hold of a rifle." Behind Tanner sat a red plastic Lil' Tykes wagon filled with wood scraps and a dead groundhog.

"Thanks, I'll think about it," she replied. "Good idea with the wagon. That's smarter than carrying it in a packsack like me."

"It's also good to have someone with you. Watch your back," he said.

He nodded to his son who turned the wagon around, heading in the opposite direction.

Anastacia expected rats as she made her way through the alley, but she saw none. Either they'd starved, been killed by hungry cats, or been eaten by people. She shivered at the thought.

The next alley over, she found a broken, wooden, green bench. It slouched to one side, the left legs bent. She wrapped her bow over one shoulder, picked the bench up under one arm. One leg fell to the ground with a soft thud. She picked up the leg with her other arm. She really would have to get a wagon or something. With both arms occupied, she was defenseless.

Two blocks from home, she heard the sound of gunfire. Militia? But then she realized she had not seen any soldiers all week, and only one police officer lived in the neighborhood. She ducked behind a BFI bin and waited. A few moments later, she heard running feet and cursing. She peeked around the giant trash bin and saw three teenagers run past, armed to the hilt. A moment later, another one ran by, clutching a bleeding upper arm, struggling to catch up. She ran in the opposite direction and found Mr. Ferguson watching over Tanner as he refilled the wagon.

"Little bastards tried to ambush us," he said.

"Are you okay?" she asked.

Mr. Ferguson nodded. "They'll think twice before coming after us again. Right, son?"

Tanner nodded, his face pale.

"Seriously, girl, get someone to hunt with you. I know you can handle yourself, but you shouldn't be alone."

"You're probably right," she said.

She gave a small wave and headed back to the alley to get the bench.

At home, she broke apart the bench, pulled out the nails, and threw it in the pile of "use only if desperate" wood, trying not to think about Mr. Ferguson's near escape. The pile contained wood that had been painted or treated some way. The fumes might be deadly. All the wood they gathered would barely get them through a normal winter. No telling what might be coming. Bedad's prophetic comments were unnerving.

She saw no point in telling her father what happened. She

wondered if Max knew what was going on in the streets. The Ventures Center was closed, so she went to his home address on Egan Street. He rented an upstairs apartment in an older home. The elderly landlady lived on the main floor below him.

Sally, dressed in a heavy sweater and knitted ski cap, answered the knock on the door. Sharp cheekbones accented her usually round face. Anastacia's heart sank.

"Anastacia's here!" Sally called over her shoulder. Her breath hung in the cold air. "Come in, come in."

The living room was filled with stacks of chopped pallets and other wood scraps.

"There's a little fireplace in the basement," explained Sally as they entered the kitchen. "We only use it if it goes below freezing."

"Hey," said Max. "Have a seat. We'll make tea."

"No, no," said Anastacia. "I'm good."

Max had also lost weight. His autumn beard and mustache had grown thicker. Dark, sunken circles shadowed his eyes.

"That's a new look for you." She pointed to his whiskers.

He laughed. "Keeps my face warm."

"I need to know something." Anastacia looked from Max to Sally and back again. "If you could escape somewhere safe, but not be able to come back, would you do it?"

"Is there some place safe?" Sally said.

"What about food?" asked Max. "And fuel?"

"No problem. But it would be rustic in some ways and

different from any place you've ever been. It would be a pretty intense culture shock."

Sally smiled. "How intriguing."

"We can't bring everyone," said Anastacia. "A mob would not be welcomed. We can't bring your landlady. I know you're fond of her."

"She died two weeks ago. Some kind of bronchial infection," said Max.

"Max had been taking care of her." Sally rubbed his arm.

Anastacia noticed that, behind his ruddy beard, Max was pale and thin. His arms and hands looked old; the skin sagged over bone.

Sally and Max looked at each other. He took her hand and squeezed it.

"So just the two of us then?" he asked.

"My stepdad, my stepbrother, and his wife, too."

Sally nodded at Max. "When do we go?"

"Well, as soon as I figure out the . . . exit strategy. And I want to look for Rupert a little more. I haven't given up."

Sally pressed her lips tightly together and looked away.

Max nodded. "What do we bring?"

"Pack like you're going on an extended hike. Make sure you have good walking boots. Be prepared to leave at any time."

Sally hugged her goodbye, and Anastacia tried to be pleased for the two of them. Max deserved to be happy. He spent all his time and energy trying to help others. If Sally was what he needed, Anastacia would not interfere. She wondered, however, if they could hang on long enough. Max was resourceful and determined, but he looked about two missed meals away from starvation.

Chapter Twenty-Seven - Shot

Somewhere on the Sibley Peninsula, in or near Sleeping Giant Provincial Park, there was a magic door. That was how Bedad had traveled from one world to the other. Anastacia wondered if Bedad had checked on the old portal, the one her mother had found near Centennial Park, not far from a small pond. It was worth a look. The pond, where her mother, Nicole, had entered Dawn's End, would take an hour to reach on foot. She would search for the portal until an hour before dark. Hopefully, the bracelet would give her some indication when she was near. She should have asked Bedad more questions about the doors, how to find them, and how often they worked.

Once she left the residential area, she saw no one. She paused to examine some tracks in the mud. Either a weasel or badger had made them. She was amazed at how many wild creatures had survived the onslaught of Mother Nature, especially the ravenous larger predators, not to mention the humans. Life always found a way.

Some of the leaves were turning color, a few were still green, and other trees were bare. She would have to watch for hunters since everyone was out looking for food. The Ministry of Natural Resources no longer bothered to issue licenses or enforce seasonal hunting. Anyone who could get their hands on a weapon was eager to use it on anything that could be eaten. She had heard of accidents in the woods, hunters shooting other hunters. At least Anastacia hoped they were accidents.

An unexpected sound drew her attention. Young, excited voices giggling and chatting with exuberance. Intrigued, Anastacia sought out the source. Through the trees, she glimpsed flashes of color. Stepping quietly, she crept through the underbrush and watched. She saw a line of children, boys and girls, ages five to ten, making their way through the forest. She needed a minute to figure out what else was unusual about the children. They looked well-fed and happy!

After the last child passed, she followed, staying far enough to avoid being spotted. After five or six minutes, her bracelet tingled, a familiar feeling. She had felt the same sensation in Lucerne, just before she accidentally opened the door to Dawn's End. She hurried forward, catching up with the last child.

The path opened up to a clearing where about twenty children gathered together. She heard a familiar male voice say, "When the door opens, hurry through. There are people waiting on the other side. They will be your new families. They are excited that you are coming."

"How do we know which family is ours?" asked a child.

"They will be holding signs with your names. Does everyone know how to read their names?"

The children greeted this remark with laughs and groans. "Of course. We're not babies."

She pushed forward and stepped into the clearing. Bedad looked up, recoiled, and then placed his hand over the bracelet. A bright arch appeared.

"Hurry, children, hurry, someone has come to try to stop you from leaving."

"No," said Anastacia.

A little girl turned and looked at her.

"Petal!" cried Anastacia.

"Run!" shouted Bedad.

The children bumped and pushed, trying to rush through the arch.

"Wait!" she called.

Bedad gave her a quick glance and then stepped through himself. "I won't let you stop us."

"But—"

Anastacia jumped at the sound of a gunshot. The bullet impacted Bedad's shoulder. Children screamed. Still, Bedad held his bracelet as blood flowed from the wound. He kept the portal open as the last child raced through.

Anastacia twisted. Franz Hahn stood at the tree line with a gun in his hand. She didn't have time to latch and pull an arrow. Instead, she put her right hand over her bracelet and shouted, "Drop the gun!"

Franz cursed as the gun flew from his hand. He turned and crashed through the woods.

Rotating back toward where the children had fled, she tried to force the fading door open. A painful jolt traveled up her arm. She saw a faint glimmer where the arch had been and then nothing. She tried again. More pain. The forest tilted. She fell down on her knees, sick to her stomach.

Somehow, Bedad must have blocked her, or else he knew the door was about to disappear. Either way, she could not get to Dawn's End through this portal.

As she stumbled to her feet, she shouted. "Bedad! Listen to me. I wasn't going to stop you. I want to leave, too, with my family. Bedad! Bedad!"

But they were gone, like the children of Hamlin following the Pied Piper. She was left behind, just like the little lame boy.

It was not the happy arrival the foster parents had been expecting. As the children raced through the door into Dawn's End, screaming with fear, the adults froze, unsure what was happening. Several dropped their signs, which bore carefully printed names.

Many of the children ran past them, searching for a place to hide. Two collapsed on the grass and cried. The rest huddled behind the adults, looking fearfully back toward the arch.

Bedad stepped through, closed the arch, and muttered a few arcane words. A red crackle filled the air, followed by a loud boom. The children screamed again, covering their ears.

Bedad turned to the shocked adults. "Sorry about that."

At least the pain from his bracelet had stopped. Its power had been wavering for days. He took two steps, fell to his knees, vomited, and then collapsed; his wound bled profusely. This launched more wails and cries.

Misty stepped forward. "I'll take care of Bedad. Lissa, see if you can get the children calmed and sorted."

"Good thing I brought cookies," said Lissa as she spotted a whimpering Gabriel wetting his pants. "And spare clothes."

Chapter Twenty-Eight - Nanabijou

In and around Thunder Bay, the winds increased and tornadoes became common. Anastacia walked to the Marina, wondering if she could find a way to get to the Sibley Peninsula by water. Between the sudden downpours and the increasing winds, Lake Superior surged with the power of an ocean. Gray waves crashed against the breakwater, rode over it in a wild white froth, and continued into the harbor. The white surf rose over the large, gray armor stones placed to prevent erosion and up onto the wooden walkway, park benches, and pavement.

Day after day, she walked to Prince Arthur's Landing, staring out over the frigid, wild water to the Sleeping Giant. He lay on his back, arms folded on his chest, and thick necklace on his throat. Shrouded in gray mist, surrounded by dark water, staring up at a hazy sky, Nanabijou seemed as dejected as Anastacia. Lake Superior was as angry as a bee-stung wolverine. Did the Anishinaabek feel abandoned by the Great Water Spirit? She brought her binoculars up to study the ancient landform, hoping for some clue to the location of the portal. Somehow, she would have to get her family onto the Sibley Peninsula and find the hidden door.

But what if that door no longer worked? One hundred kilometers was a terribly long way to go, especially for the hungry.

The water receded and settled as the wind died. To her right, a colorful shape departed one of the docks. Then another and another. Canoes! Were they insane? Canoeing on Lake Superior was a risky business the best of times. No one ever canoed in November. Capsized, any canoeist would succumb to hypothermia in minutes. She trained her binoculars on the lead canoe. In the front sat a small man with a gray braid down his back. He turned, looked straight toward Anastacia, and raised his hand. Daniel Moonwind! The elder turned away and resumed paddling. Nine canoes followed his, each holding two adults and one or two children.

What were they doing? The canoes threaded their way through the small gap in the break wall, out past the lighthouse, and into cold Gitchigumi, The Great Water. She watched their progress, steady as a clicking clock, heading toward the Sibley Peninsula. Her breath tightened in her throat. If the wind picked up—

A tall, growing shape on the left horizon drew her attention. Anastacia tensed. She refocused her binoculars. A twister, far out in the middle of the deep water, was heading toward the Sibley Peninsula. Its long, cone-shaped body dipped down toward the lake, pulling the water up into its funnel. It was moving quickly!

She focused back on the travelers. Their canoes would be flipped; they would all drown. None wore life jackets. Not that it would make any difference. The cold autumn water would shut down their muscles and organs one at a time, paralyzing even the best swimmers.

The twister danced across the water, churning the lake like beaters in a bowl of cake mix. The spout sucked up more water. She could hear the swoosh and rumble from the shore. The sky blackened. For a moment, she considered taking cover, but she could not pull her eyes away from the canoes. Daniel Moonwind raised his arm as though signaling. The canoeists paused, watching the twister, not retreating, not panicking, simply waiting.

The twister hit the peninsula, ripping up conifers and deciduous trees as if they were pixie sticks, shredding the

Sleeping Giant. A mass of green, gray, and brown rose into the sky. The blur was hard to focus on with her binoculars, so she lowered the glasses.

Anastacia gasped. Above the peninsula a shape formed in the dark debris. First a chest, then a head, then a right arm and a left. The arms stretched out on either side as though offering an embrace.

Horrified, Anastacia realized the canoes were moving again, straight toward the twister. Her bracelet tingled. As the wind rose, water splashed up and over the bench, drenching her. She jumped up, took several steps back, wiped her face, and turned to watch the canoes. The tingle stopped. The canoeists were gone. So was the dark, giant figure of a man. The twister headed out into open water and disappeared from sight.

Chapter Twenty-Nine - Tricks

Even though the cookies helped, Durward actually relaxed the children the most by presenting his silly magic tricks. He had never been well-coordinated, but had learned to enjoy acting like a happy bumbler. When Petal asked him to pull a hard-boiled egg from her ear, he pulled out a baby chick instead. When Chester asked him to pull a rabbit out of his hat, Durward presented a comical routine of chasing his hat. When he put it on his head, two rabbit ears grew out of the sides. Before long, the children were laughing and begging for more.

Bedad lay on the grass, watching Durward perform while Misty attended to his injury. The wound would take a while to heal, no doubt about it. But what would take longer was the realization Anastacia distrusted him so much she had shot him. No doubt, she only meant to wound him. He knew, if she had meant to kill him, Misty would be closing his eyes right now. Did she consider what he was doing so wrong that she would risk causing him permanent harm? That she would terrify the children with gunfire?

The adults set up camp by the disabled door. Bedad had magicked it shut. No one from the Outworld would be able to open it unless he freed it first. Exhausted, he was the first to fall asleep, his last waking thoughts of Anastacia. Did he dare to go back for her at a later time? Would she ever see things his way? Would she try to kill him the next time she saw him?

No. He wouldn't believe that. He couldn't. Anastacia was his soul mate. He had known it since she told him to scrub behind his ears. She just didn't know it yet.

Chapter Thirty - Frozen

Even though she had no idea what had happened to the canoes, the boldness of the Anishinaabek inspired Anastacia. Trying to get her friends and family through forty-four kilometers of highway and twenty-seven kilometers of side road seemed impossible, but, by water, they would need to travel only half the distance. If they could find a boat and the fuel to power it, they would only have to walk a few kilometers when they got onto the Sleeping Giant.

Part of the Sibley Peninsula had been destroyed by the twister. The trails would be gone and the forest would be full of widow makers — trees or large branches that had fallen and hung precariously in the branches of another tree. That section of the journey would be brutal. Anastacia planned to leave her family by the shore and search for the door alone. She knew her father and brother would argue with her about that.

Could the portal be buried under dirt and uprooted trees? If so, would it still work? She knew so little about how it operated.

Max was the first person she asked about getting a boat. He was friends with many outdoors people. In exchange, they could give them what was left of their wood and food. Getting a boat would be complicated and crossing the bay would be risky.

Max, however, just shook his head. None of his friends had a working boat in the harbor. Many had them at their camps, or cottages, at smaller lakes. Those who had larger boats berthed at the marina had lost them during the repeated storms. Getting gas was impossible anyway.

"What about a sailboat?" asked Anastacia.

Max shook his head. He looked pale, ragged, and frailer than she had ever seen him. Even though her family's food supply was stretched to the limit, Anastacia could not leave Max and Sally in their cold apartment with their meager supplies.

"You and Sally need to come and live with me and my family," she said. "More body heat and less fuel. Bring whatever you think could be useful."

The snow arrived soon after they moved in, and, as with all first snowfalls, it was beautiful. At first, the flakes drifted lazily down, seesawing through the air, sitting on the tips of the dead grass. Then they came faster and heavier, clumping together, filling the spaces between, perching like scoops of ice cream on the trees along the boulevards. Everything became bright and white and clean. But behind that beauty lay death. Without natural gas or electricity, people without fireplaces struggled in the cold. Their water pipes froze and burst. Frost formed inside their homes.

Even generators were useless with no gas left to run them. Before long, people felled all the trees on the boulevards, and in city parks, playgrounds, schools, and backyards for fuel. The city was a graveyard of stumps.

Anastacia thought of all the children who used to come to the Empowerment Ventures Center. How many would make it through the winter? How many had already succumbed to cold and hunger? Only those who had gone with Bedad were truly safe.

Anastacia continued to hunt for food further and further from home. Somehow, wildlife still survived around Boulevard Lake, in Centennial Park, and along Lake Superior's waterfront. She also hunted in the wooded area between Lakeshore Drive and the Trans-Canada Highway. Pickings were slim, and everyone had the same idea. She fled whenever she heard the sound of voices or the crack of broken bush.

The few soldiers and police officers who still patrolled sometimes responded to the sound of gunshots. They often demanded a portion of the meat in return for their protection in helping people get their kill safely home. Anastacia suspected they were neither being fed nor paid, so it was a fair exchange. She, however, did not need protection. One of the advantages of bow and arrow was the silence.

Bodies appeared more often in the streets and parks. Most had frozen or starved, but others were the victims of foul play. Jamail and Ali insisted they should be the family providers and she should stay inside the safety of their home. When Anastacia pointed out her superior speed, her ability with a bow and arrow, and what she could do with her bracelet, they begrudgingly acquiesced.

"You'll put me in more danger if I have to go out to find you," she told them.

As brave as she sounded, she dreaded leaving each morning. Looking into the faces of the dead, especially the little ones, horrified her. What if she recognized a neighbor or a child from the Ventures Center? Maybe, because of her, Bedad had taken fewer children. Maybe, because of her, more children would die.

On her way down Chamberlain Street, she spotted the body of a small woman partly buried in snow. Her blonde hair was frozen in clumps. Because of a sense of familiarity, Anastacia could not pull her eyes away. She brushed the snow off the woman's blue, hollow-cheeked face. Blue eyes stared up at the sky. Anastacia shuddered—it was Tammy Hahn.

Did Franz know his wife lay dead in the snow? Had he played a part in the tiny woman's death? Without her makeup and her "My life is perfect" smile, Anastacia had barely recognized Tammy. The woman had always been thin, but now the skin stretched over sharp bones and sank deep below her eyes. Being so skinny to start with would not have helped Tammy when starvation began.

Tammy and Franz had two children, a boy and girl. Where were they? Anastacia looked around, but she saw no other bodies. She took that as a good sign. She placed her fingertips on Tammy's eyelids, but they would not shut—she was frozen solid. Anastacia knew the ravens would find Tammy. She shivered, realizing that, eventually, she would be hunting those ravens. The cycle of life could be vicious.

Her take for the day was a large seagull—why the bird was out in the snow she didn't know—and a Canada jay. Her family still had plenty of packaged food left, but they had had to empty the freezer when the gas for the generator ran out.

As she walked up the front steps, Anastacia noticed a piece of paper sticking out of the mailbox. They hadn't received mail in ages. What could it be?

She set the birds down on the step and took out the paper.

My Brave Anastacia,

I know you never want to see me again. Even though you attacked me, I cannot stop worrying about you. After talking with Lissa, I can see where I made mistakes and lost your respect and trust. I cannot make you come to Dawn's End but, in spite of the shooting, you would still be welcomed, as would your family.

I want you to know the children I took are loved, safe, and well-fed. Before we left, I reconsidered what you said about their memories and have left them intact, returned those memories I have taken, and given every child the choice to come or stay behind after talking with their parents. However, most of them no longer have parents, or their parents are missing.

I have left you a gift. In spite of your strength and courage, survival must be difficult. In the backyard you will find a cache of food. Jamail has installed some pretty tricky alarms and traps, but I managed to not set them off. I wish you a long, healthy life, but I fear, in my deepest heart, that this may not be possible.

You do realize that your bracelet will drain eventually. Use it sparingly.

Always,

Bedad

Anastacia fought back tears. He had risked his own safety to bring her food, even when he believed she had shot him.

Food!

After unlocking the front door, she threw the dead birds on the kitchen counter, ignoring her father's bewildered expression, and then ran out through the back door. She saw it there, sitting on the deck—an enormous bag. She shrieked with excitement and dragged it indoors.

Jamail, Ali and Lucinda, Sally and Max approached.

"Bedad brought us food," Anastacia said in wonder.

They made a circle around the bag. Max put his arm around Sally's shoulder and waited expectantly. Anastacia unknotted the drawstring and pulled open the top. Everyone leaned forward with all the excitement of children peering into Santa's sack.

Chapter Thirty-One - Orphaned

Beyond Thunder Bay, the frequency and severity of disasters escalated. Inevitably, without proper maintenance, the Alaskan pipeline burst in several places. Perhaps melting glaciers caused the breech. Or perhaps one of the eleven pump stations stopped working. Perhaps all the maintenance crew had died or disappeared. Or perhaps some idiot shot at it with a rifle again.

Seven hundred thousand gallons of oil a day spilled into bogs, streams, forest, and tundra. Oil choked the Yukon River. Consequently, a fire beyond all fires ignited. The few remaining caribou and musk ox tried to flee but could not outrun the inferno. The city of Fairbanks burned down in three hours. No one was available to deal with this catastrophe of monumental proportions.

In Thunder Bay, as in most places on the planet, the power stayed off for good. The radio stations no longer broadcast. The internet remained down. Telephones didn't work. Every community became isolated from every other.

In the faint hope Bedad might return again, Anastacia left a note encased in a freezer zip lock bag for him on the deck. His name was printed in large letters on the outside. She checked every day to be sure it hadn't blown away or succumbed to the elements.

She saw fewer and fewer people on her excursions. She knew the stream of refugees now flowed in the opposite direction. Many people chose to head south toward a milder, shorter winter. It was a foolhardy quest. The journey to Toronto used to take two days by car. On foot, it was impossible. Besides, Toronto would be under snow as well, and the Americans, facing their own struggles, would not welcome lines of Canadians bringing nothing but hunger.

Most homes in her neighborhood were dark and silent. Very few had smoke rising from the chimneys. How many families had given up and climbed into bed together, choosing the final sleep rather than one more day of struggle? She was relieved to see Mr. Ferguson's huge footprints, accompanied by one or two smaller pairs, leading out of and into his house. That was one family that would fight to the bitter end. However, she could understand the people who had given up. Freezing together, in their own homes, seemed more civilized than collapsing on the highway, one by one. But she could never see herself climbing into bed and surrendering. Like Mr. Ferguson, she would make death struggle for her soul.

Although she cleaned and repaired any damage to her aluminum arrows so that they could be reused, one by one they became too twisted and dented to be trusted. She checked the stores in town that carried arrows, only to find everyone had been cleaned out. She should have gone sooner.

Returning home empty-handed from her hunt, Anastacia spotted two figures sitting on their front steps. Someone had seen the smoke from their chimney and hoped to gain shelter. Sharing the space would be tough, but the real difficulty was food. It would disappear rapidly if they opened their doors to everyone. She cringed when she saw one of the figures was a child. A small suitcase sat on the top step.

The adult stood and turned to face Anastacia when she reached the yard. Quick as the flick of a hummingbird's wing, Anastacia notched her last metal arrow and aimed at his head. Franz Hahn!

His eyes appeared dark and haunted above the scarf wrapped around his hood.

"Don't shoot. I'm unarmed." He raised his hands in submission. His mittens were bright red with a pattern of white maple leaves, an incongruent image of better times.

"What do you want? Why are you here?" demanded Anastacia.

"My wife is dead," he answered.

The child sitting behind him hunched over on the step. Anastacia nodded, resisting the urge to ask why Tammy had been left in the street.

"So is my son." He licked his lips. "I can't take care of my daughter. I have a vault full of money, and coins, and jewels, and no one wants them. I couldn't buy a single bag of rice with everything I own."

"People can't eat jewels," said Anastacia.

He nodded. "I brought the best of what I have anyway." He unzipped his parka and reached inside.

Anastacia motioned with her bow — a warning.

Cautiously, Franz removed a metal box from inside his parka and set it on the step.

"This is for you."

"You're not coming inside. I know what kind of person you are, and I'll be damned if I put less food in my family's mouths in order to help you. You'd probably kill us in our sleep."

He gave a single nod. "I understand. I'm not asking for me. I'm asking for Oprah. Please, take her. We haven't eaten in three days. I saw you hunting."

"Why don't you hunt for her yourself?" asked Anastacia.

Franz stepped closer and lowered his scarf. His lips were cracked and pale, his eyes yellowed, and his skin tinged with gray.

"I've been spitting up blood for the last month," he said. "There's no one at the hospital anymore. No one alive anyway. I don't think I can last much longer. What will happen to Oprah? She's only five, for God's sake. You can't let her die."

The little girl pressed her red-mittened hands against her ears, trying to block out her father's voice.

Anastacia thought of the children Bedad had saved. If she had helped him, perhaps he could have saved more. Surely, she could help one little girl.

"I can't let you in," repeated Anastacia.

"I know. I don't want her to see . . . . It's for the better if I leave her here."

Oprah rocked back and forth, humming *Itsy Bitsy Spider*.

Franz gave a weak smile. "She's a terrific singer and dancer, though she doesn't have the energy anymore. She's sweet, like her mother. Even though I've spoiled her, she's still a good kid. I brought her Junior Kindergarten report card. All her social skills are marked 'Excellent.'"

He reached inside his jacket again.

"Keep it," said Anastacia.

Franz nodded and withdrew his hand. "Try not to hold her father against her," he said, his eyes filling with tears.

Anastacia lowered her bow. She nodded.

Franz went to his daughter and sat beside her on the step. "I have to go now, honey."

"No, no!" She threw her arms around him.

"We talked about this. You have to stay with Anastacia."

"But I don't want to. I'd rather be with you."

He whispered into her ear. She sobbed and clung to him. He kissed her wet cheek and stood.

"No, Daddy, no!"

"Don't let her follow me," he said to Anastacia as he stumbled away.

Oprah jumped up and staggered through the snow after him. Anastacia clasped her arm. The girl struggled and fought. Anastacia dragged her up the steps and unlocked the door. She pushed Oprah inside and slammed the door closed.

Ali entered the hallway, a concerned expression on his face.

"Please keep everyone out for now," said Anastacia.

He retreated.

Oprah collapsed onto the floor, sobbing. Anastacia sat beside her and waited until the cries turned into hiccups. Then, approaching Oprah as carefully as she would a nervous fawn, she unwrapped the girl's blue scarf and pulled off her boots. Bit by bit, she got the heaviest winter clothing off. She dug through the suitcase and found a pair of running shoes. Oprah sat limply as Anastacia shoved her feet in and tied the laces.

"Come into the living room," said Anastacia. "There's a lovely warm fireplace, and I think my brother has made beans for supper."

"I'm not hungry," said Oprah.

"That's okay. Just take a taste. My brother is trying to learn to cook, and we don't want to hurt his feelings. Just a bit, all right?"

"'Kay," said Oprah. She looked up at Anastacia, reached out, and took her hand.

Someday, Anastacia might tell Oprah about her own parents, Nicole and Morrel. It might help the child to know others had some idea how she felt.

Together, they walked into the living room.

Chapter Thirty-Two - Not a Creature was Stirring

Nightly, Oprah screamed out, as if her dreams filled with unspeakable memories. She often stood in the hall, staring at the front door, as if willing her father to open it. Gradually, as the days passed, she warmed to the others, although her eyes were still fearful, and she jumped at the slightest sound.

It was the strangest Christmas season any of them had ever lived through. Originally, they were going to let December 25th go by without any notice. Sally, however, insisted that this was not the time for a kindergarten child to lose her faith in Santa Claus. She helped Oprah with her letter to jolly old St. Nick. She reminded Oprah that Santa, too, would find it difficult this year and encouraged her not to ask for too much.

Oprah nodded. "Can I ask for a puppy?"

"No," said Sally. "We don't have enough food for a puppy."

"I can share my food," said Oprah with a hopeful expression.

"Puppies need special food and care, and a lot of things we can't give them right now."

Oprah nodded. "How about a toy puppy? One that barks."

"Maybe," said Sally. She looked over Oprah's shoulder to where Anastacia sat, trying reading in the dim firelight.

Anastacia shrugged. The stores had been abandoned. While survival supplies, blankets, and other similar items had been stripped, there were plenty of toys. She was sure she could find a toy dog of some kind. She wondered if there would be other people in the same situation. How many families still survived?

After Oprah had gone to bed, everyone discussed what they should do for Christmas. Jamail insisted they should get the artificial tree from the basement on Christmas Eve and put up the decorations.

"But, Dad," said Ali. "It's going to look pretty sad without lights."

"She's five years old," said Jamail. "She'll love whatever we do."

They agreed. Other than for Oprah, they would conduct no exchange of gifts. A new leather belt was not worth dying for; it was still dangerous outside. Fewer people roamed the streets, but those that did were tough survivors and not to be taken lightly.

"I don't much like the idea of you shopping for toys," said Jamail.

"It's okay, Dad. I'll be in and out as fast as a fox in a rabbit hole. I hunt every day anyway."

On Christmas Eve, when Anastacia returned with a packsack full of goodies, everyone distracted Oprah while Anastacia hid the loot in the hall closet. She did not tell them she had used her last metal arrow against a feral dog. It had gone through his throat and struck the metal dumpster behind, flattening the head and bending the shaft beyond repair. She looked at the carcass but decided dog meat for Christmas was just too depressing.

They lit the basement fireplace and made a bed for Oprah downstairs.

"If Santa sees you upstairs, he might not come," said Sally.

"I don't want to be down here alone," said Oprah.

Ali and Lucinda volunteered to stay with her and keep the fire going.

Once she was asleep, Anastacia and Max carried the tree and boxes of decorations upstairs, creeping like burglars in the night. Jamail kept the upstairs fireplace going as Max, and Sally assembled and decorated the tree. Underneath, Anastacia placed the plush stuffed dog (barking ones required batteries which they couldn't waste), a Candyland game, Duplo building blocks, a Sesame Street coloring book and crayons, beads and strings, and several books.

"I'm impressed," said Max. "You scored some awesome stuff."

"Do you think she'll be happy?" asked Anastacia.

"I think you saved Christmas," said Sally.

Max kissed Sally and smiled. Anastacia waited for the twist of jealousy, but she felt nothing.

Oprah had been told she could not go upstairs in the morning without the adults. Anastacia woke with the uncomfortable feeling of being watched. Oprah, her sleeping bag wrapped around her like a shawl, sat by Anastacia's shoulder and stared down at her, her face inches away. Anastacia suppressed a yelp and then snorted with laughter.

"Were you waiting for me to wake up?" she asked.

Oprah nodded, her eyes wide with excitement. "Forever and ever."

Anastacia pressed the light button on her watch and checked the time. "Seven. That's pretty reasonable, considering it's Christmas morning."

"Do you think Santa came?" asked Oprah.

"Yes," said Anastacia. "But he might not have been able to get you exactly what you wanted."

"That's okay," said Oprah. "Can we go see?"

"What's up?" Max moaned as he sat up in his sleeping bag.

"Oprah is." Anastacia laughed.

"Cool," said Max. He shook Sally awake. "It's Christmas!"

Soon everyone was climbing out of their sleeping bags, voices loud with excitement. Anastacia went upstairs and woke her stepfather, who had kept the fire going all night. The room was warm and cozy, and the metal baubles twinkled in the firelight.

When Oprah saw the toys under the tree, she shrieked like a winner on *Who Wants to Be a Millionaire*.

"It's a Christmas tree!" She looked at everyone. "Right?"

Anastacia nodded. Oprah would only have a faint memory of last year's tree. She didn't seem to notice the absence of lights. Everyone watched tensely as Oprah picked up the plush dog. Its fur was white, long, and silky. It had blue eyes, a black nose, a red tongue, and a diamond-studded, red collar. Oprah stared into its face. Anastacia bit her lip.

"I'm going to name you Snowy." Oprah gave the toy a fierce hug and rocked from side to side.

Everyone relaxed and exchanged looks of relief.

Candyland was a hit. They soon learned to play her one at a time, since she never seemed to tire of it. Ali loved the blocks as much as Oprah. Together they built a doghouse for Snowy. Anastacia took out the good dishes, Duchess English bone china with the violet flowers and gold trim that had belonged to her grandmother, and they sat on the floor around the tree.

"I just wish we could have given her a real Christmas dinner," whispered Sally after they finished the creamed corn, dried apricots, beans, and rice meal.

Anastacia grinned. "I can't do that, but I do have a surprise. It's from last year, so they are probably pretty stale, but I found something in storage." She giggled and hurried to the closet. She came back to the living room holding something behind her back.

"Ta da!" she said as she showed the box of white, green, and red striped candy canes.

"I remember these," said Oprah.

"Of course you do." Anastacia laughed. "Candy canes are one of the best things about Christmas."

Ali didn't like sweet candy, so they had enough canes for everyone to have two. They licked and laughed and told stories about other Christmases until their tongues were red and their fingers sticky.

"Let's sing some Christmas Carols," said Sally. "I wish I had a piano."

"If I could have fit it in my packsack, I would have," said Anastacia.

Sally laughed. "I believe you."

She started with Rudolph the Red-Nosed Reindeer. Max and Ali provided the silly responses. They thumped their way through Frosty the Snowman, Six White Boomers, We Wish You a Merry Christmas, Santa Claus is Coming to Town, Deck the Halls, and, in spite of Jamail's groans, finished with the Twelve Days of Christmas.

"I think that song was invented as a test of endurance," Jamail said.

Then they moved on to the Christian songs. Children, Go Where I Send Thee, The First Noel, Good King Wenceslas, Hark! The Herald Angels Sing, and more, ending with a sweet solo by Sally of Away in a Manger.

"It seems our little Christmas angel has fallen asleep," Max whispered.

Quietly, Sally prepared Oprah's sleeping bag. Max scooped her up, carried her downstairs, and tucked her in. Sally gave her a kiss on the forehead. Everyone said, "Merry Christmas." Then they crawled into their own sleeping bags.

Anastacia wondered if Bedad knew about Christmas. The older children would remember, but would the people in Dawn's End celebrate with them?

Were survivors all over the world gathering around trees and playing Santa? Was Julie celebrating with her husband and mother? She hoped other voices had been raised in song today, other children with surprises.

The last carol Sally had sung circled around and around in Anastacia's thoughts. It was a silent night. The pop and crackle of the wood in the fireplace, the occasional person adjusting his or her sleeping position, and Jamail's soft snoring were the only sounds. No traffic on the street. No airplanes overhead. No neighbors slamming their car doors. No horns honking. No dogs barking. Nothing. Anastacia wondered how many survived to celebrate Christmas and how many had been silenced forever.

When they woke on Boxing Day, they discovered that water no longer ran through the city pipes.

Chapter Thirty-Three - The Council

"Remember," said Ellsworth. "Only Anastacia's family will be allowed in. No one else over ten years old."

Bedad nodded. Kyle had been eleven, but Bedad knew, in his heart, that no one would have turned the child away. He wondered where Kyle was now.

Since Bedad returned the children's memories, they often spoke of their former lives and families. Their new families listened with compassionate interest. No one dismissed the children's hopes that, somehow, their parents survived.

Bedad's parents had adopted Chester. Bedad had explained the risks — the boy was full of anger; his alcoholic mother and stepfather had been inadequate to fill his needs. He had felt this child, most of all, would have benefited from amnesia. Lissa said no; she would help him work through whatever emotional scars he carried, just like she had helped Bedad.

Another family living in Harmony had adopted Petal. The mother played pipes, the father played the lute, and they both sang beautifully. Bedad felt Petal would blossom in the musical environment. She acted as though she had received a trip to Disney World.

Durward and Misty adopted Gabriel. He was having the most difficulty adjusting. He worried for his mother.

Bedad wondered how much he should tell the children about the deaths and devastation in the Outworld and when. It was highly unlikely any of their parents still survived. A woman in a wheelchair would have no chance. But, at least, she would have died knowing her child was safe and cared for. Still, it hurt Bedad to think of her. He hoped she had not died alone.

Dawn's End couldn't take everyone, but perhaps he should have fought, somehow, against the law banning adults from entering. Gabriel's parents must have been remarkable people to raise such a sweet child in such difficult circumstances.

He knew, in his heart of hearts, that Anastacia still lived. He also suspected her bracelet had only days left. He had psychic flashes of it turning copper-colored.

He and Anastacia were connected in a way he couldn't explain. From the moment he first saw her, he knew he was destined to be part of her life. He must give her one last opportunity to return to the land of her birth. Without the power of the panther bracelet, she would better understand how dangerous remaining in the Outworld would be. Perhaps he could appeal to her stepfather.

He loaded his pack on his back and went to the kitchen to say goodbye to Ellsworth, Lissa, and Chester. They were interrupted by a knock on the door. Lissa answered.

"Beora! How wonderful to see you. Welcome."

As Beora entered, Bedad marveled at how well she looked. Beora had been horribly burned in a house fire. An evil wizrd had enslaved Beora with a pain-numbing potion and given her the curse of burning anyone or anything on contact. Beora's skin was rough with small scars but much improved. She still wore the long, red, hooded cloak, but her hands were bare. She now had complete control over her ability to create fire.

Although she was a small woman, she had a powerful presence. Under her long sleeves, she also wore a panther bracelet. The evil feared and the virtuous respected Beora the Bright, for good reason. She was the most renowned Enforcer of the Law in Dawn's End, now using her power of fire, and her bracelet, for righteousness.

Strangely, she did not hug Lissa in greeting as she entered. Nor did she smile at Ellsworth. She barely glanced at Chester. Her eyes settled on Bedad. She frowned. "Unfortunately, I am not here as a friend. I am here to"—she pulled her small figure erect and took a deep breath—"I am here to arrest Bedad Ellsworthson."

"What?" cried Lissa.

"What for?" said Ellsworth.

Chester, eyes narrowed and lips pressed together, ran into the hall and peeked around the doorway.

"He is charged with bringing unsanctioned Outworlders into Dawn's End," said Beora.

Bedad's forehead furrowed as he removed his packsack. "I don't understand. Everyone was approved by the Council."

"Everyone you showed them," said Beora. "But not those you hid."

"I didn't hide anyone," he said.

"You must come with me. All will be explained at your trial."

"Don't go," Chester shouted. "Use your bracelet. Make her go away."

"I have a bracelet too." Beora raised her arm and pulled back her sleeve.

"You can beat her," said Chester.

"Probably," said Beora. "But it would not be easy."

"They didn't send you because you're powerful," said Bedad. "They sent you because you're my friend, and I would never harm you."

Chagrined, Beora lowered her arm. "I will give you time to pack a few things. This may take time to resolve."

Bedad looked at Beora with grief in his eyes. "Time is the last thing I have. Promise me you will do everything you can to expedite this. Anastacia's life may depend on it."

"Anastacia." A flash of shame crossed Beora's face. "Yes, of course."

Bedad was stunned when they read the charges. He had no idea what they were talking about.

Four Council Elders sat on heavy wooden chairs on a raised dais. Bedad stood below. Two muscular guards, armed with swords, guarded the exit. Beora sat on a chair against the wall on Bedad's left. The tiny windows were barred. A small table to Bedad's right, and a long thin one in front of the Council, held jugs of water and glasses.

Bedad faced four Councilors. He looked directly into Vessa's pea-green eyes. Lissa had told him women liked his dimpled grin, so he flashed his most disarming smile. She ran her hand through her spiky hair and frowned distrustfully. Two of the Councilors were not fully human. Charn, a male, had a flat, black nose, elongated whiskers, and excessive body hair. The other, Thisbe, a female, had maroon and rose-colored feathers instead of eyebrows and hair, holes instead of ears, and talons for fingers. They looked down at Bedad with a mixture of concern, dismay, anger, and fear.

The Eldest Councilor, Markis, a human male with white hair and hands gnarled by arthritis, explained the charges. About thirty people, with light brown skin, had landed in Dawn's

End on the river behind Durward and Misty's home. They arrived in canoes and had paddled south. They stopped to talk to no one and disappeared into the unsettled forest.

"But I didn't bring them in," Bedad replied.

"Who else would it have been?" said the Eldest.

"Anyone with a bracelet could have done it."

Vessa looked at Beora. Her green eyes narrowed. Beora crossed her arms and stared her down.

"There are few who know how to even find a door to the Outworld much less open it," said the Eldest. "Who else could have done it?"

"Anastacia the Bold could. Perhaps she let them in," said Bedad. "She does not know our laws."

The Councilors whispered amongst themselves.

"Impossible," said the Eldest as he stood. "She has been outside our world for too long. Her bracelet would be powerless."

Bedad didn't tell them he had found a way to reactivate it. For a while at least. A while that was rapidly running out. If he didn't get to her soon, all Anastacia would have only her wits and strength left to rely on.

"I vow on the Great Crystal, on the Golden Bringer of Light and Life, and on the lives of all my family and friends, I did not bring these strangers into Dawn's End," said Bedad.

The Council considered his words in silence.

Beora stepped forward. "May I speak?"

"Of course, Beora the Bright," said the Eldest. He gave a small bow and sat down.

"I trust Bedad with my life," Beora said. "If he says he did not bring these people, then it is the truth. If you would punish him without proof, then you will have to go through me."

The Councilors gasped.

"You have always been the voice of justice," said The Eldest.

"As I am now," said Beora.

The Councilors whispered again.

"Very well," said the Eldest. "However, if he is truly innocent, then he should be willing to protect Dawn's End from the invasion of Outworlders."

"Invasion seems a harsh word for refugees," said Bedad. "You do not understand what is happening in the Outworld."

"Isn't it something they have brought upon themselves?" asked the Eldest.

Bedad resisted rolling his eyes. "Did the people of Dawn's End not bring our own troubles to our world as well? A growing darkness that could have become permanent were it not for the help of Outworld women?"

"Can a single person from our world solve all their problems?"

Bedad did not respond.

"I thought so. Therefore, we ask you . . . no, we command you to find these interlopers, these refugees as you call them, and send them back to the Outworld. Do whatever you have to do but remove them. Even if you have to kill them to do so."

Beora interrupted. "But you said there were children in the group."

"I will not kill children," said Bedad. "In fact, I will not kill anyone. The panther bracelets are not weapons of slaughter. I am accountable to the Alaric line for how my band of power is used. They have given the sacrifice. They must approve."

"Very well," said the Councilor. "We will send for an Elder from Alaric Place to attend this trial before we decide what is to be done. You will be locked away until that time."

Bedad nodded. What fools they were. There wasn't a lock or prison in existence that could hold him as long as he wore the bracelet.

The Councilor nodded to a guard who stepped forward, grasped Bedad, and covered his mouth with a damp cloth. Bedad felt as though he was falling into a long, black tunnel. His knees folded.

He woke in a cell. His head throbbed. How much time had passed? He had to escape. He pushed up his sleeve, but the panther bracelet was gone. In feeble hope, he pushed up his other sleeve. Nothing. They had taken his bracelet of power.

Chapter Thirty-Four - Death All Around

For six days, Bedad begged for release. Anastacia was running out of time. How could they risk her life? Didn't they understand what Dawn's End owed the Newmans? Why did they think the panther people named a village after them?

His pleas fell on deaf ears. He had thought to convince Beora to break him out. If she accompanied him to the Outworld, they could rescue Anastacia. But she did not visit. Bedad paced his cell, imagining the worst.

Then, Calix, the panther village elder, arrived. For three more days, the Council held court, arguing about judgment in Bedad's case. The Eldest, Markis, felt Bedad should be sent after the interlopers. Vessa agreed, but only if he was given back his panther bracelet. Otherwise, he could be killed, and Dawn's End would lose its best ally. Bedad was tempted to say that, if they held him any longer, he would no longer be their ally. The bird woman, Thisbe, felt the Council should immediately release Bedad to rescue Anastacia. Bedad promised himself he would do something special for her people. Charn felt everyone who owned a panther bracelet should be brought in for questioning.

It was the panther elder, Calix, the one summoned by the Council at Bedad's request, who decided the final outcome.

"Both Anastacia and Bedad risked their lives to save Dawn's End. If Bedad says he did not do this thing, it is my honor to believe him. If he says he did do this thing, it is also my honor to support his decision. Either way, he must be released immediately."

The Councilors continued to argue.

Again Calix spoke up. "I have nothing more to say. I will return to Newman Village tomorrow, hopefully with news of Bedad's release and Anastacia's impending rescue. If not, there are those who have power bracelets of their own. I suspect they will not hesitate to free Bedad and give him whatever he needs for his rescue mission, including their own panther bands."

"Are you threatening this Council?" demanded Markis.

"I am informing this Council of what will be." Calix bowed to Bedad, turned, and strode toward the door.

"Do not allow him to leave!" commanded Markis.

The two guards stepped in front of the door, nervously fingering their swords. They had no doubt the panther man could kill them both without elevating his heart rate. The other Councilors whispered frantically. Thisbe spoke. "We have no right to hold the Elder of Newman Village against his will. Rescind your order."

Markis gritted his teeth and waved the guards away. The guards heaved a sigh of relief and stepped aside. The one on the left opened the door for the panther man and gave a small bow as he passed through.

In the end, Bedad was released. He gave his word to find the interlopers as soon as he returned from the Outworld with Anastacia.

"We wish you a safe and easy journey," said Markis. He smiled thinly.

Bedad did not bother to respond as he snapped his bracelet into place. He raised his arm and glared at the white-haired man. The Eldest nervously plucked at his robe. Bedad's eyes narrowed.

"I will be back," he said. "You can count on that. You had best pray that I have Anastacia safely with me when I return, or this Council will be held accountable for her death."

Markis flinched but did not respond. Thisbe stroked her feathers and stared at the ceiling.

Bedad turned and marched from the room. The left guard jumped to open the door for him.

"A successful journey," he muttered as Bedad passed.

Bedad snarled at the guard. "For everyone's sake."

Because Bedad had determined the patterns of the availability of doors to the Outworld, he knew the pond entrance would still be accessible by the time he reached it. He would remove the block he had put on it to stop Anastacia from following him and the children. That door was the closest to Anastacia's home — if she was still there.

He had never felt such rage as when Vessa returned his bracelet. If Markis knew how close he had come to being turned into a pile of dust, he would have nightmares for the rest of his life. As a child, Bedad had come close to being boiled alive, but his desire for revenge at that time had been as small as an ant compared to how he now felt toward the Council. He knew of a spell which enabled the caster to kill a person, revive him, and kill him again. If Anastacia was beyond help by the time he reached her, he just might try that spell out on the Eldest.

He entered the door to the Outworld and walked through Centennial Park. People had harvested numerous trees for firewood. However, once the fuel for chainsaws ran out, they reverted to axes and crosscut saws. Many abandoned their efforts part way through because, suffering from hunger, they simply did not have the strength to complete the task. Bedad saw a felled tree with several branches removed. A saw rusted in a last, shallow cut through the trunk of another tree, which had been partially sawed into logs.

Bedad grimaced when he came across a couple in their twenties, huddled together in the snow. The woman sat in front of the man, her head turned to the right, leaning into him. His arms were wrapped around her chest, pulling her close. Her eyes were closed, but he stared off into the distance, keeping watch for danger or hoping for rescue. Snow had accumulated over most of their bodies, including their eyelashes. The animals had not found them yet.

Bedad approached to check for signs of life, wondering what he should do if he found any. They were too old to bring back to Dawn's End. He could leave them some food. Give them a little firewood. But what good would it do in the long run? He was almost relieved to find they were beyond help. Bedad wiped his damp eyes and took a shaky breath.

In the parking lot, he found a middle-aged man lying near a sled filled with logs. The man had done an admirable job but had collapsed before he could return home with the fuel. Bedad wondered who would have been waiting for him, freezing in the cold.

What horrors Anastacia must have seen. Bedad had no doubt she would come with him to Dawn's End now. If she was still alive.

Chapter Thirty-Five - The Pack

Anastacia fingered her copper bracelet. She knew the change in color from gold meant the bracelet was now powerless. Searching for a door would be pointless since she would not be able to open it. Because she did not want to have to lie to her family should they ask questions about the change in the bracelet's appearance, she kept the panther band covered at all times.

They had adequate firewood to last a couple of months, but food was running low. Jamail had stockpiled enough for the two of them. But then Ali and Lucinda had arrived. Anastacia had added Max and Sally, and then Oprah. They would not make it to spring unless she brought back a large amount of meat every day.

Hunting was becoming more and more challenging. The creatures living in and around the city had been hunted out, so Anastacia had to travel further afield. As well, many animals had migrated south or hibernated through the cold northern winters. Even so, coming home empty-handed was not an option.

Carefully picking her way through deadfall, Anastacia moved through the woods, bow ready. The only arrows left were the three cedar arrows from Mr. Ferguson. Soon enough she would find out if his fletcher's skills were adequate.

Her boots crunched in the icy snow. Then the hairs on her neck prickled. She paused and looked back. Was that a shadow behind the tree? To her right—a soft creak. Another shadow. Adrenaline surged through her body. She lowered the hood on her parka in order to see better. The hunter had become the hunted.

Then she saw the leader, a striking husky with a black forehead, except for two feather-shaped, white patches above his eyes and a white stripe that ran between them. His muzzle, chest, and throat were white. He watched her with cornflower blue eyes. He still wore a black collar with a metal license tag. What had been his master's fate?

She'd seen evidence of packs of dogs, both in the city and in the wild. She'd stumbled over the stripped carcasses of animals they'd eaten, a deer, a terrier — *dog eat dog*, she had thought — and once a human. They harbored no fear of her and no taboo against killing and eating her. She would do the same to them if she could. It was survival of the fittest, or in this case, the most well-organized.

When the husky gave a sharp bark, the pack moved in, slipping from tree to tree, a German shepherd, a part Labrador mutt, a golden retriever, and a speckled long-legged Dalmatian. No longer man's best friends. She tried to train her arrow on the husky, hoping that taking down the leader would create confusion among the others, but he was clever and evasive. Once she fired her arrows, she doubted she would have time to retrieve them before she would have to shoot again. Three arrows, five targets. Not the best odds.

As she turned one hundred-eighty degrees, she dropped to one knee, and, without thinking, took her marking, lining the string up with the tip of her nose and the corner of her lip. Mr. Ferguson's voice echoed in her memory, "A poorly aimed shot is a wasted shot." She loosed her arrow as the German shepherd growled and charged. It flew straight and true. The arrow caught him in the jaw and protruded up through his skull and out the top of his head with bits of brain attached to the arrowhead. Bright blood poured from his mouth as he fell to his side and thrashed in the white snow. She notched the second arrow and fired it into the flank of the Dalmatian who yelped, took three steps, and then flopped over on his side, whining.

The Labrador, the retriever, and the husky waited. Maybe they would let her leave, now that they had a German shepherd and Dalmatian to eat. She wondered if they might let her take some of the meat. But no. The husky was committed.

Inch by inch, they tightened the circle, closing in. The leader must have decided she was a threat to his pack, a threat that needed to be eliminated. The husky barked, and all three dogs raced toward her at the same time. Anastacia cursed and let fly her last arrow. Realizing she could hit only one, she aimed for the leader. She knew that even if she stopped the husky, the Labrador and the retriever, two gentle dogs by nature, would still try to tear out her throat.

The husky went down as her arrow entered his chest.

Quick as a cat, she pulled out her knife. The others would find the daughter of Alaric Morrel was not so easily killed.

The Labrador reached her first. Its teeth were bared, and its brown eyes bulged. Anastacia gripped the knife tightly and drove it toward the dog's throat. As the blade sank, the dog's teeth clamped onto the left side of her head, sinking through the woolen toque and into her cheek and ear. She screamed in searing pain as she jerked the knife across the animal's throat. Blood gushed over her suede mittens and the sleeve of her tan parka. The dog collapsed at her feet.

She braced for the last dog's attack as she staggered backward, refusing to be brought down. Suddenly, an enormous flash of light filled the woods. The retriever turned to ash, and its remains fluttered over her boots like a million tiny bats.

In the silence that followed, Bedad stepped from the woods, his face filled with concern. "Anastacia?"

She sank to her knees, dropping the knife in the bloodied snow. The pain in her cheek, the exhaustion, the fear, the ebbing adrenaline—it all caught up with her. She cried—loud, choking sobs.

Bedad rushed to her side. He knelt down, gently peeled off her woolen toque, and flinched. Then he turned to the right and vomited into the snow.

"That bad, huh?" said Anastacia, trying to smile.

"No, no. Just using the bracelet in the Outworld still makes me sick."

"Yeah, I know," said Anastacia. "Not that I can anymore."

Bedad wiped his mouth on his sleeve. "It's powerless then?"

"Has been for a while," said Anastacia as she regained control.

They helped each other stand. Anastacia looked around. "Help me butcher them. We can't let this meat go to waste."

Bedad frowned. "You're staying then?"

"Huh?"

"You don't want to come to Dawn's End? You don't want to leave?" he asked.

Anastacia coughed. "I want to leave more than anything. There's nothing left here. Nothing. Nothing."

She started to cry again, more softly. Even crying seemed to take too much effort.

Bedad took her in his arms and held her tightly. Feeling safe and protected, Anastacia did not want him to let go.

"It will be all right now, Anastacia. I'll take you home. To your birth home."

"What about my family?" she whimpered.

"Your family, too."

"It's grown since you've last been here," she said.

"All your family," said Bedad. "We'll take them to Dawn's End, where there's food and warmth and safety."

Anastacia nodded. She glanced around at the carnage.

"Too bad. I always liked dogs," she said.

"They probably liked you, too."

"Desperate times," she whispered.

"That looks nasty," said Bedad, pointing to her cheek.

The blood was thickening in the cold, congealing on the side of her face. She suspected her ear was split in two. She removed her mitten and fingered her torn ear. "I guess you'll have to call me 'Stumpy' now."

"I can fix it," he said. "No point in frightening your family."

"Good idea," said Anastacia. "It's not something Oprah needs to see."

"Oprah!"

"Not the media queen. Long story," she said.

"I have a special medicine, a blend of lilyvern root and faerie wing. Combined with the magic of the panther bracelet, it can heal just about anything. I don't have much, but it should do the job."

Anastacia's eyes widened. "Did you say faerie wing?"

"Yes, did you not know the fairies and the lilyvern have a shared ancestor?" said Bedad.

"No, I guess they forgot that part in history class," said Anastacia. "Do they shed their wings like snakes?"

"No," said Bedad. "That's why this is a rare and very secret ingredient you must never mention to anyone."

Anastacia grimaced. "How did you get it?"

"I didn't kill her, if that's what you are thinking. I was there when one died. I begged the queen for the wings before they interred the faerie. It was a stroke of luck."

"Kinda grim."

Bedad nodded, and then took a deep breath. Anastacia noticed the dark circles under his eyes. He seemed older than he had the last time she saw him. He could easily pass for thirty now. Surely not that much time had passed in Dawn's End.

"Are you okay, Bedad?" She touched his arm.

"Using the bracelet so much takes a lot out of me, especially in the Outworld."

"I'm sorry I'm going to make you sick again."

"No problem," said Bedad. "I'll purify the bite, close it, and let it finish healing on its own. It might leave a scar."

"Cool," said Anastacia. "It'll make a great story. I think I was the only one on my hockey team with all my teeth and no scars."

Bedad laughed. "By the Crystal, I missed you."

Chapter Thirty-Six - Fangs in the Dark

It was snowing when they left the wooded area. Bedad watched, fascinated, as Anastacia butchered the dogs.

"I know a family that would appreciate this meat," she said.

Theirs were the only footprints in the snow. Bedad was horrified by the unburied bodies lying on the streets, several partially eaten by cats, crows, rodents, and other scavengers. He had always found the Outworld streets loud and over-stimulating, but, now, he had never felt such an oppressive silence.

Street after street, they found no sound or movement other than the gently falling flakes. Anastacia stopped on the way home to pound on Mr. Ferguson's door. When no one answered, she shouted his name. A moment later, the door flew open.

"Get off the street, girl," Mr. Ferguson said as he pulled her inside.

He eyed Bedad suspiciously but then nodded. Bedad entered.

Anastacia held out the large gunnysack. Blood dripped through the bottom onto the floor.

"Oops, sorry about that," she said. "I brought you some meat." She leaned in to whisper to him. "It's dogs. They didn't give me much choice."

"Are you all right?" Mr. Ferguson stared at her bloody face as he took the bag.

"Just a scratch," she said. "Dad will take care of it."

"Well, I'm glad you took my advice and went hunting with a

partner this time, but why are you giving me this?" He held up the sack. "I know you have mouths to feed."

"We're heading south," said Anastacia. "There's too much to carry. I figured you could use it. Actually, you can have what we can't carry. There's still a little food in my father's crazy pantry."

Mr. Ferguson shifted his toothpick to the other side of his mouth and leaned in to give her a hug. "I hope that works out for you. We're staying. Here, I know how to provide and protect my family. On the road . . . not for me."

"Good luck, Mr. Ferguson," said Anastacia as she opened the door.

"Good luck to you, girl," he replied.

When Anastacia slipped her key into her front door lock, she wondered why she bothered. No other living soul seemed to be around. Their home and Mr. Ferguson's were the only ones she had seen with smoke rising from the chimneys.

Jamail greeted them in the entrance. He hugged Bedad fiercely and thanked him over and over for the food he had left and for coming back for them.

He blanched at the blood on Anastacia and again thanked Bedad for protecting her and closing the wound. They hung the bloody clothes in the closest, and Jamail fetched water and a cloth to clean her face.

Bedad was surprised to see Max and Sally. Oprah, petting Stumpy, watched him cautiously as he shook hands with Ali and Lucinda. Oprah ducked her head and buried her face in Stumpy's fur when he approached.

"Stumpy," said Bedad. "Aren't you going to say hi to an old friend?"

As though he understood, Stumpy meowed. Oprah giggled.

Anastacia explained to the group that Bedad had come to take them to Dawn's End.

"Dawn's End?" said Oprah. "I don't want to go."

"Why not?" asked Jamail. "Anastacia said there's lots of food there, and it only snows in the mountains. It's so warm you can swim in the lakes."

"But how will my Daddy find me?" she asked.

The adults exchanged glances.

"We'll leave a note," said Sally. "Just like Anastacia left for Bedad. And Bedad can draw a map of how to find it."

"Sure," said Bedad. "I can do that."

"We have to get going," said Max. "It will be dark in a couple of hours."

Jamail brought paper. Anastacia wrote a note, and Bedad sketched a quick map, taking care to avoid everyone's eyes, especially Oprah's. He hated deceiving the child, but, without this pretense, she would resist leaving and make the journey even more difficult for everyone. They all bundled up and stuffed their pockets with the little food they had left that could be easily carried.

"What's it like in Dawn's End?" asked Oprah.

"It's magical," said Bedad. "There are wonderful creatures that can do marvelous things. Some of the animals talk. And, if you are very lucky, you may even see a faerie."

Max snorted.

"No, really," said Bedad as their eyes met.

Max blinked rapidly and looked at Anastacia, who smiled and said, "All true."

Jamail, Max, and Ali carried the remaining food over to Mr. Ferguson's. His sons came for the rest of the wood. They were reluctant to take it all, worried Anastacia's family might change their minds and return.

She reassured them. "Not gonna happen. You can take anything you want from the house. Strip it if you have to."

The boys expressed their gratitude and continued moving the wood as Anastacia and her family prepared for departure.

Anastacia shouldered a pack and picked up Stumpy from the floor where he was circling round Oprah's legs.

"I want to carry him," said Oprah.

"Not while we're walking," said Anastacia. "He'll get heavy, and we have a long way to go. Besides, I'm going to slip him inside my jacket to keep warm, and yours is too small. I'll keep him safe."

Oprah stuck out her lips in a pout. Anastacia ignored her, slipped the cat inside her jacket, and zippered it up with his head peeking out under her chin. As her stepfather shut the door behind them, Anastacia realized she would never again see their home, the place her mother had chosen and decorated and loved. She slipped the photograph of herself and her mother at the Olympics into her pack. If only she had time to get the Norval Morrisseau painting from Franz's office. What about all the art, books, music, theatre, and sports memorabilia that would disappear? The Stanley Cup!

She swallowed the lump in her throat and took up the rear. Bedad took the lead.

Anastacia's family and friends stared in shock at the ravaged and silent city. She had been the only one outside for weeks. Jamail waited until she fell in beside him.

"I am so sorry, Anastacia," Jamail said. "You have been facing this alone. It is like Iraq."

"It's okay, Dad," she said. "We'll soon be out of here. I'm sorry you have to go through this again."

"Strange to think I am going to your mysterious birthplace," said her stepfather.

Anastacia wondered how her birth father's descendants would react to his presence.

They followed the road to Centennial Park, saddened by the devastation of all the green spaces. So many trees brought down by wind or axe.

Stumpy squirmed, his claws digging into Anastacia's abdomen.

"Be still, you little monster," she said.

The cat hissed and scrambled out of the coat, racing past Max and Sally and into the dark woods.

"I'll get him," said Max.

Oprah wrapped herself around Anastacia's legs. "You said you would keep him safe," she cried.

Anastacia pried the girl off and passed her to Sally. She followed Max into the woods. Darkness closed around her. The tree tops were outlined against the dusk. She had to carefully pick her way through the stumps and fallen branches.

Like a Halloween display, Stumpy sat on a dark branch silhouetted in the dimming light. His eyes gleamed yellow as he arched his back.

"Well, at least he didn't go far," said Max as he stood at the bottom, his fists on his hips.

"I'll get him," said Anastacia. "He'll probably rip your face off. He's having some kind of hissy fit."

She removed her packsack, her bow, and quiver, and set them in the snow beside Max.

Stumpy yowled.

"What has gotten into you?" asked Anastacia as she reached up for the first branch.

A chilling roar sounded behind Anastacia.

"Look out!" shouted Max as he knocked her to the ground.

Anastacia's arm bent awkwardly under her as he landed on top. Then another creature thudded on top of him, and Max screamed in her ear. She twisted and looked up as he was dragged away. Bright yellow eyes, but four times the size of Stumpy's—cougar!

"Bedad!" she screamed. "Bedad, help!"

She scrambled for her bow and arrows, knowing it might already be too late.

A flash of light filled the woods. The cougar howled. It crashed through the woods, yowling as it fled. She searched for Max by following the moans. At least those cries meant he was alive. She could hear Bedad retching and groaning in the dark.

A flame appeared. Bedad carefully made his way toward them, a small ball of light floating above his hand.

"Here he is," said Bedad.

Cautiously, they sat Max up.

"Where are you hurt?" asked Misty.

"My leg," he gasped.

Bedad's fireball cast enough light to examine the wound. Max's snow pants and jeans had been partially torn away. Blood soaked the snow. Bedad peeled back a flap of fabric to reveal ripped muscles and exposed bone.

Anastacia felt her stomach churn. "Can you fix it?"

Bedad didn't answer.

"You can fix it, right?"

"Yes, but not completely," said Bedad. "I already used the bracelet to heal your wound from the dogs and just now to fight the cougar. I'm going to have to hold the door open long enough for us all to pass through, and I'm not feeling very strong. I can't risk weakening myself or the bracelet. Besides, I don't have any of the medicine left. I used it all on you."

"He'll bleed to death," said Anastacia as she crouched beside Max.

"I saw your father pack emergency medical supplies," said Bedad. "We'll have to use that to keep him going until we get through the door. Then I can fix him for good."

"I don't think he can even stand, much less walk."

"He has to, for about a half hour," said Bedad.

Bedad and Anastacia dragged Max back to the path. He cried out in pain, and Anastacia felt his warm blood soaking through her mittens. If he kept bleeding, nothing would save him.

Anastacia explained the situation to her father while Sally took Oprah aside and sang songs with her.

Jamail sprang into action. Anastacia cranked up the portable flashlight and held it while her stepfather quickly and tenderly pressed the torn bits of muscle and skin back into place and wrapped a tight bandage over the wound. He put on a second layer. "It's tight, so he won't bleed to death in the next little while, but it can't be left like that for long. I've restricted the circulation."

With Ali on one side and Anastacia on the other, they hefted Max into a standing position. He screamed out in pain and lost consciousness.

"That's a blessing," said Bedad. "Now, we have to get him to the gate as fast as possible."

He did not tell Anastacia that he was suffering from his own pain. The warning signal from his bracelet had become almost unbearable. His severe headache made it difficult to concentrate. The bracelet's power was nearly drained. He had been overusing it, on both sides of the door, not giving it time to recover between uses. If they didn't hurry, he would be trapped in the crumbling Outworld with them. Forever.

Chapter Thirty-Seven- Judged

Originally, the thought of returning to Dawn's End had horrified Anastacia. She had almost died the last time she visited. She had no memory of her happy toddler years, except for the images of her father that had flashed through her head while dancing with the Anishinaabek. By age three, she had left with her mother, Nicole, for the Outworld. Now, she couldn't wait to get to Dawn's End. When Bedad opened the door, she felt water form in her eyes from relief.

As she and Ali stumbled through the gate and carefully lowered Max onto the grass, Anastacia instinctively crouched, knife in hand, ready for anything. Next came Sally and Oprah, then Lucinda, and Jamail holding Stumpy, and finally Bedad. The door faded with a sizzle.

"Wow," said Sally. "It really is magic."

Out from the trees stepped Durward, Misty, Kaie, Beora, and Daniel Moonwind. Anastacia stared at Daniel. Everyone began talking at once.

"People!" shouted Jamail.

Anastacia jumped. She had never heard her stepfather raise his voice like that.

"This man is dying." He bent over Max with concern. "We need help."

Kaie took charge. She, Durward, and Beora combined the power of their bracelets. Misty played her healing pipes, even though Max was fully human. It couldn't hurt. At the very least, the music would soothe everyone's nerves. Off to the side, Daniel chanted. The grove surged with power. The air felt electric, the grass trembled, and the wind howled around them.

The Outworlders removed their winter clothes and sat back to watch.

When the healers joined them, exhausted by their effort, Jamail moved forward and gently unwound the bandages. The wound was closed.

"Under the skin, is everything as it should be?" he asked Misty as she carefully washed the blood away with water from a canteen and examined the wound.

"Yes," she said. "All the muscles, veins, and arteries seem to be back in place and functioning. He may be stiff and sore for a while, but I believe he will regain mobility completely."

"Thank you," said Anastacia. "It should have been me the cougar got. Max pushed me out of the way and took the hit himself. He saved me."

Durward and Bedad exchanged glances.

Durward smiled. "That may be what saves him in the end."

As they made camp, everyone got to know each other. Beora explained to Bedad that she had gone in search of the interlopers, hoping one of them would clarify to the Council how they had arrived at Dawn's End. Daniel Moonwind had agreed to come with her to enlighten them. When they arrived, they learned Bedad had been released and had departed to get Anastacia. Beora thought it best to wait by the gate for him in case he needed assistance. Daniel volunteered to join her. He was curious as to how others opened the gate.

"Others?" said Bedad.

"He opened the gate for his people," said Beora. "Through something called the Nanabijou, the Sleeping Giant. He's a Shaman. His people say *Jĕs´sakkîd*."

"Oh," said Anastacia. "I'm so relieved. I thought they were all killed."

"I waved to you," said Daniel. "Did you think I would lead my people to their deaths and pause to say goodbye?"

Anastacia shrugged. "It's been a pretty crazy year."

The other Outworlders laughed loudly.

One of the blue jay people had alerted Misty and Durward that Bedad had been arrested and then released temporarily. They arrived before Beora and Daniel Moonwind. When they reached the door, Durward, putting his faith in Bedad, decided to wait a reasonable time before opening it himself. Bedad showed up with days to spare.

Oprah asked question after question about fairies, the door, Beora's cloak, magic, and more.

"She reminds me of someone," said Anastacia. "Someone with an insatiable hunger for food and knowledge."

She winked at Bedad, who beamed a huge smile in return.

Beora started the campfire with a touch of her finger.

"Can you teach me that?" asked Oprah.

"Sorry, no," said Beora. "It's something only I can do."

"Oh." Oprah pouted. "You're lucky."

Beora blinked twice and then said, "Yes, I guess I am."

The Outworlders laid out their meager supplies, and the others added their bounties. Misty and Durward gave vegetables and bread. Beora offered dried fruit, and Daniel provided dried venison. Kaie added frothy milk.

The people from Dawn's End tried not to notice how much food the Outworlders ate. Their pale, gaunt faces confirmed that they had been living with hunger for quite some time.

The Councilors, eager to portray themselves as defenders of Dawn's End, challenged the presence of Max, Sally, Jamail, Ali, and Lucinda. The hearing had to be held outside in the village courtyard, as the townspeople insisted on attending.

Oprah, as a child of five, was instantly accepted. Within a day, she had been given more gifts than she could carry. Her grubby winter clothes were replaced with a silk dress and velveteen shoes. Her hair was festooned with satin ribbons. She sat with the Outworlders playing with an elegant faerie doll and Snowy, the stuffed toy dog.

Everyone had bathed, received new clothes, and been given haircuts, and the men had shaved. Although thin, the Outworlders looked much better after a good night's sleep and a hearty breakfast than when they had come through the door. Bedad had thought they might arouse more sympathy if they stayed ragged, dirty, and tired, but Beora said, "You do not need sympathy. You need respect."

She addressed the Council first. "You have always said the family of Nicole Newman is welcome here, have you not?" Beora had appointed herself spokesperson for the group, as the one most knowledgeable about the law.

"Of course," said Markis. "But look at these people. They can't all be family."

Beora drew Jamail forward. "This man," she said, "was second husband to the Esteemed Nicole, stepfather to Alaric Morrel's only child. Is that not family?"

"Of course," said the Eldest, as the crowd agreed with Beora.

She gestured for Ali to step forward. "This is Anastacia's stepbrother, son to Ali. The only sibling she has ever known. Her elder brother who has loved and protected her as an elder brother should."

Ali and Anastacia exchanged smirks. She had never liked to think of her stepbrother "protecting" her.

"Family! Family!" chanted the crowd.

"Yes, yes." Markis waved his hand impatiently.

Beora nodded to Lucinda who stepped forward and took Ali's hand.

"His wife, Lucinda. Would you separate a married couple?"

The crowd booed.

"No, of course not," said Markis. "Welcome, Lucinda. But what of these other two?"

Bedad exchanged a look with Durward. She gestured again. Max limped forward and stood, favoring one leg.

"I neither exaggerate nor sensationalize when I say that without this young man" — she paused to look at the faces of the crowd — "Anastacia, daughter of the Esteemed Nicole and Alaric Morrel, Anastacia the Bold" — she paused again — "would be dead."

The crowd gasped and then whispered amongst themselves.

"Quiet!" ordered Markis. "You claim blood debt for her, then? Explain."

"This man, Max Marshall, pushed Anastacia out of the way of a leaping cougar, a golden leopard of the Outworld, and took the attack himself. If not for the unprecedented combined healing powers of myself and the others, he would have died. His leg was torn down to the bone, shredded by the cougar's fierce teeth."

The crowd cringed. A young woman covered her mouth and leaned into a young man's chest. Men looked at Max with admiration. Max, unaccustomed to such attention, slowly turned red.

Beora's voice rang through the courtyard. "He is a hero of the purest kind, and, yes, we claim blood debt."

The audience applauded. Markis looked around, nervously plucking at his robe.

"And the other woman?" he asked. But his heart was not in the challenge anymore.

This was the tricky part. With Misty and Durward as witnesses, Beora had quickly performed the ceremony herself this morning.

"Sally Marshall is his wife," she said.

Anastacia blinked. She had not been told, but she smiled with true joy. They were perfect for each other, and she loved them both as dear, dear friends.

"Well, then, it seems we have been blessed with more additions from the Newman family," said Markis with forced joviality.

"More?" Anastacia whispered to Bedad.

He put his finger to his lip and winked at her.

"So, I am glad that is settled, and we will not have to worry about anyone challenging the right of Anastacia, and her family, to live in Dawn's End," said the Eldest, as though he had never doubted it. "The only thing left to do is execute the leader of the interlopers. Seize him!" He pointed to Daniel Moonwind, who sat on the grass beside Oprah.

Two guards jumped forward and pulled Daniel to his feet. Taken by surprise, he stumbled. The taller guard punched him in the stomach. Oprah began to cry.

Chapter Thirty-Eight - Thunderbird

The crowd erupted. Even though they didn't know who Daniel Moonwind was, he seemed part of Anastacia's group, and that was enough for them. They shouted, hissed, and booed.

"Brutes, beating an Elder—for shame."

A young man tore up a clump of grass and threw it at Markis. "We're sick of you and your judgments."

Suddenly, clumps, sticks, rocks, and even sandals were thrown at the Councilors. The first guard still held Daniel Moonwind; the second drew his sword and threatened the agitators. The Councilors lifted the hems of their robes and ran.

The sword-wielder was struck in the forehead by a particularly large rock and fell backward, out cold. The other guard was surrounded by villagers screaming for Daniel Moonwind's release. He stared around at the angry faces, released Daniel's arm, and ran after the Councilors.

Daniel slumped, still in pain from the blow.

"He's hurt!" cried a woman.

Misty was brought to tend to the Shaman, as he sat back down on the grass.

"I'm sorry," he said. "I didn't mean to cause a riot."

"It's been a long time coming," said Misty. "They've been abusing their powers ever since Anastacia left." She dug through her bag for a small vial of lavender powder. "I need a mug or glass," she called out.

"I'll get it," said a brown-haired village woman.

Misty continued. "The Council is supposed to represent the voice of the villagers. Keep a rein on the magicians. But they are the ones out of control."

Daniel nodded. The woman returned with a mug. Misty poured a tiny amount of the lavender crystals into the top, and then filled it with water from her canteen. The villagers split into small groups, and loudly discussed their next course of action.

"Stop!" said Bedad as he approached Misty. "It may not be safe for him to eat or drink anything in Dawn's End. I haven't administered the antidote to him yet."

"A little late for that," said Daniel Moonwind. "We've been here for weeks." He drank the mixture. They studied his expression. Slowly, Daniel got to his feet. He rubbed his stomach.

"How do you feel?" asked Misty.

"Better. Thank you."

"Let's find a place for you to rest while we sort things out," said Bedad.

Calix, the panther Elder from Newman Village, returned to supervise the hearing. Markis withdrew from the Council. The remaining three Councilors appeared nervous sitting on the dais. Each had his or her own bodyguard, and two more bodyguards sat down in front. Faster and more powerful than any guard, even at his advanced age, Calix declined the protection.

Daniel Moonwind explained that he had a vision of Nanabijou telling him to bring his people to safety. He described, in horrifying detail, the death of millions in the Outworld. He spoke of finding a child crying in the streets, her parents dead or missing. He spoke of the pain of Mother Earth. Some of the villagers wiped their eyes. Others appeared ill or angry. They had heard stories from the children Bedad had brought to Dawn's End, but they did not understand the scope of the destruction.

Then Daniel told them how his people had lived in harmony with nature for centuries before the arrival of the Europeans. He explained the cultural and spiritual devastation of residential schools. He explained how his people had been struggling to find their way back to their traditions and values and how his small drumming group had helped. When the vision was sent to him in the middle of a drumming ceremony, he told the people in attendance; he had invited those attending to join him in his quest for a safe, new world. Not everyone followed, but twenty adults and teenagers with twelve children accompanied him. They set up camp in the unclaimed forest, and, since their arrival, they had seldom seen any of Dawn's End's inhabitants.

"They are south of The Meeting Place," said Beora. "In the wild lands."

"Those lands are important," said Calix. "Although no humans live there, many precious animals call that area their home. There are plants that grow nowhere else. We would not want it destroyed."

"Neither would we," said Daniel. "We wish to live in harmony with our world and with all the tribes that inhabit it. We may not even stay in the unclaimed woods. We will explore further south until we can find a place to call home."

"Why should we break our law against allowing any adult Outworlders to come here?" asked Thisbe. "What is to prevent our land from being overrun by refugees?"

"I do not think there are many who could gain entry on their own," said Daniel. He turned to Anastacia. "Do you agree?"

"I'm shocked that you were able to get here," she answered.

"Thunder Bird led me. He has guided me since Animiki, the thunder god, gave me my gift as a young man. He would not lead me astray. Very few are given this power. I have only met one other in my life, but I think he is gone."

Thisbe frowned. "Could there not be someone you haven't met?"

"But, even if there were other Shamans," Anastacia said, "there may not even be anyone left alive to bring here. When Bedad came for me, very few people still survived. I don't know how much longer they will last."

The crowd whispered.

Calix nodded somberly. "I am sorry to hear this, Anastacia the Bold. We are blessed that Bedad was able to save you and yours."

"I am grateful for that," said Anastacia. "We all are."

"But I also think we cannot round up thirty-two of Daniel Moonwind's people and question each one. How could we pick and choose to whom to provide sanctuary and whom to send to their deaths? How can we split families apart?" Calix smiled. "This decision is too large for one man, one Council, or even one village to decide. We must call upon the land itself."

The villagers' voices rose in anticipation.

"Daniel Moonwind will represent his people. What is decided for him is decided for all," announced Calix.

"What does this mean?" Anastacia asked Bedad.

"He is going to have to appeal to Dawn's End for his life and the lives of his people," said Bedad. "I have no idea how it will end."

Chapter Thirty-Nine - The Drummers

It took a week for Daniel Moonwind's large drum to be carried from the unclaimed forest. Three of his people walked with it the whole way, not allowing anyone else to touch it. The other Anishinaabek were ordered by the Enforcers of the Law to stay behind. The Councilors did not want another riot, this time of Outworlders.

Anastacia recognized the men as those who had drummed for the Ventures Center. Again, Daniel asked the crowd to form a circle around them. Anastacia noticed new decorations on the drum. Perhaps the Anishinaabek had found the bright feathers and shells in Dawn's End.

A woman in a jingle dress would not lead the steps this time; Anastacia knew that was not the type of dance they needed.

"How does it work?" she asked Bedad.

"You'll see," he said. "If you don't see, then it didn't, and the drummers will die, and their people will be hunted and driven out."

"You'll kill them!"

"No," said Bedad. "Not me. Shh. Just watch."

Kaie sprinkled a white substance in a circle around the drummers. She stepped back into the crowd of villagers. Beora touched the circle with her fingertip. Fire sputtered around the circle and then blazed up in swirls of color. When the fire died out, the drummers began.

The drum may have been the heartbeat of Mother Earth, but it connected to Dawn's End as well.

"Hi, yah, hi, yah" the Anishinaabek chanted.

Anastacia found her body rocking in rhythm with the chanting. The beat pounded through the clearing, entering the hearts of the villagers, trembling the blades of grass, speaking to the trees and the soil.

Periodically, the rhythm changed to louder single thumps, like exclamation points. On and on they went. The drummers' foreheads glistened with sweat. Every so often, one of the drummers took a sip of water from a canteen Misty had provided for each of them. The chanting paused periodically, but the drumming never stopped.

The wind picked up. Villagers came and went for their meals, but no one talked in the presence of the drumming. Something sacred and hopeful hung in the air. During one of their meal times, Anastacia asked Bedad how the Councilors would know when it was over.

"Because it ends," he said with a frown.

Anastacia made an exasperated sound. "But how does it end?"

"Oh, I see what you don't get," he replied. "The drummers drum until they can't anymore. If Dawn's End has not embraced them by that point, then they will collapse and not recover. If she has, then we celebrate."

"How do we know if she has?" asked Anastacia.

"We'll know. It's different every time. But we'll know."

"I'm afraid for them," said Anastacia.

Bedad gave her a gentle hug. "Don't be afraid. I'm not."

He smelled of forest and soap. He felt warm and solid against her. She wanted to pull him tighter.

As he pulled away, Anastacia wondered if his feelings for her had faded. He had been treating her the same as he treated everyone else since rescuing her from the wild dogs. She felt a pang of disappointment.

They drummed through the night. Anastacia listened to the steady rhythm as she fell asleep, a guest of the village baker. The smell of baked dough, the warm room, and the pounding drum seemed foreign but welcoming. She had become accustomed to hunger, cold, and silence.

When the sun rose, Anastacia quickly ate breakfast and returned to the village square. She saw that the Anishinaabek were tiring. Their voices were raw and strained, their backs slightly hunched. Daniel, the oldest, seemed to be enduring the best.

As the day progressed, the drummers sipped water more often. Sweat trickled off the braids of the youngest Anishinaabe. How long could a human bladder hold it? But, then, perhaps most of the water they drank was released in sweat.

By midday, the three younger drummers were faltering. They glanced at Daniel, who continued as regular as a metronome, his voice still strong, and his arm still steady. More and more of the villagers returned to the circle. An air of expectancy grew as the day wore on. Anastacia felt as though the drumming was echoing in her brain. She breathed in rhythm, walked in rhythm, even thought in rhythm.

A figure appeared inside the inner circle. Anastacia sat up straighter. No one but the drummers was allowed to cross the burn mark. Who had dared to break the rule? What would happen?

It was a bear. Huge, black, and shaggy, it sniffed the air and then moved to the drum beat, its powerful head swaying left and right with each step. The drummers sat up straighter, rejuvenated. Anastacia saw nods and smiles spread through the villagers. What did it mean?

A little later, a blue jay appeared. It stretched its head forward and back and then strutted behind the bear, who ignored it. One by one, others appeared—a delicate long-necked deer, a sleek, black panther, and a graceful woman with green skin and fluffy, white hair who seemed to be floating. A long, undulating, white snake followed a large lizard with human eyes and a flickering tongue. A coral-colored, dolphin-like creature swam through the air. Silver fish shimmered in the sun, and a pink creature waved its tentacles like an East Indian dancer. Anastacia gasped when the next arrival glittered and flitted above the group—a faerie.

The crowd rocked in rhythm to the drumming, which had taken on a joyful tone. The creatures wove around and through each other, around and over the drummers in a spectacular display of wings, claws, fins, and tails. The very air was electric. Daniel Moonwind raised his hand. The four drummers struck together, loud solid thumps, once, twice, three times. They stopped, the last beat reverberating in the silence. The beings turned toward them, bowed, shimmered, and disappeared.

Tears ran down Anastacia's face. She understood. Dawn's End had accepted Daniel Moonwind and his people. They were safe.

After the Anishinaabek left, the spectators went their separate ways. Bedad and Anastacia sat together on a bench under a broad-leafed tree, enjoying the warm breeze.

"Do you want your family and friends to stay together?" Bedad said. "If so, they will have to decide where they want to live. Personally, I think you would like my village of Harmony. Lissa and Ellsworth would love to help you become part of the community, and I have a surprise waiting for you there."

"A surprise," said Anastacia. "What kind?"

"The best kind," he said with a grin.

"After that, I think you need a holiday," Anastacia said. "Every time I see you, you've aged more."

He shrugged.

"At first I thought it was the time difference, but you've aged faster than anyone I met here before. Since you've spent time in my world, shouldn't you actually have aged less?"

Bedad looked away and bit his lip.

"I know that look," said Anastacia. "You're not telling me something."

"When I brought the children here, I was terrified they might catch some disease from our people," he said. "I worked a lot of magic to increase their immune systems. I also cured and fixed any medical problems they had. I didn't want some parent to adopt them and then lose them to a spinal tumor."

"Spinal tumor! Who had that?"

"Petal."

"I saw her go through the door." Anastacia clapped her hands like a little girl. "We have to tell Sally. She'll be so happy."

Bedad smiled. "You and Sally, you're friends now?"

"Absolutely."

"And Max?"

"A friend."

Anastacia swallowed and stared into his aquamarine eyes, which were haunted but hopeful.

"Just a friend," Anastacia repeated. "And I'm happy with that."

Bedad's smile widened.

"Wait a minute," said Anastacia. "Are you saying the magic aged you?"

"Certain spells and excessive use of the bracelet can drain life from the user, yes. Nothing you have to worry about, though. I would have warned you."

"I am worried." Her brow furrowed. "Not about me. I don't want you turning into an old man before your time."

Bedad shrugged.

"Never mind shrugging. I mean it." Her voice was scolding. "I want you around for a long, long while."

"You do? Why?"

Anastacia squirmed. "Well, I find I'm . . . ."

"Taken with me?" He leaned in toward her. "Thinking about me day and night?"

"I wouldn't go that far." She giggled.

"Oh." Bedad twisted his face in an exaggerated pout.

"I've been pretty busy during the day." She quickly kissed his pouting lips.

"Whoa. That went by too fast," said Bedad.

"I agree," said Anastacia as she leaned in again.

Bedad's soft, warm lips met hers, a feathery kiss. Like the first touch of cotton candy. Then she melted into him. His arm circled around her shoulder, pulling her into his chest. For the first time in a long, long time, Anastacia felt utterly content.

Chapter Forty -On the Way to Harmony

On the journey to Harmony, Bedad informed Anastacia and the others where each of the Ventures children had been placed. Those Anastacia had seen Bedad take through the door were all either orphans or children whose parents had asked him to take them. She and Bedad hung back from the rest and spoke in low voices. Neither wanted Oprah to hear what had happened in the Outworld.

Petal's mother had died from injecting bad heroin. Chester's mother had died from an untreated illness, and his stepfather did not want him back. Gabriel's parents had wept with gratitude when they learned that their son was safe. They wrote a long letter for Bedad to give him when he reached adulthood. Bedad couldn't find Kyle or his family.

"It was the hardest thing, leaving them behind, especially Gabriel's family," he said. "Now, I wonder if I should have brought them anyway. Maybe it would have turned out well."

"You couldn't take everyone," said Anastacia. "And, if you pushed it, we might have all been sent back. Any other kids from Ventures?"

"Just one. His Auntie died, and I really didn't think his mother would ever make it home from Toronto. She'd been missing for so long."

"Rupert?" Eyes widening, Anastacia stopped walking.

"Yes," said Bedad. "Lissa adopted him."

Anastacia burst into tears. Bedad held her as she cried. He motioned the rest of the group on ahead.

"That's the best surprise you could have given me." Anastasia sobbed.

Bedad stroked her hair and smiled to himself. He would save the best for last.

When they reached Harmony, Anastacia noticed the same scarcity of children as at the other village. Rupert would be cherished here. Lissa and Ellsworth hugged her, and welcomed everyone into their home. They had plenty of empty rooms available since the plague.

Rupert had grown, and he could now say Anastacia's name correctly. She missed the way he used to mispronounce it, but she was so happy to see him healthy, strong, and full of energy. He took Oprah by the hand and led her to his room to play.

"Sally and I will be getting a place of our own," said Max. "As soon as I figure out what I'm going to do here."

"Oh, Max," said Sally. "There isn't anything you can't do."

He gave her shoulder a squeeze.

"You might think about living next door to another young couple," said Lissa. "I know just the people. They're new to the village too. They'll be joining us for supper. I asked them to give you a little time to settle in before coming over."

Bedad smiled gratefully at his mother. She already had so many mouths to feed, but she would think nothing of adding more. He knew she loved to be surrounded by people, especially the young.

"As long as they don't mind sleep disruptions," Sally said.

Anastacia looked at Bedad, surprised by Sally's remark. Sally caught her expression and blushed.

"Oh, my goodness. Not from that. From the baby." She put her hand against her belly and smiled.

"Baby!" said Max.

Sally nodded. Max scooped her up and twirled her in a circle, laughing.

"That's worth a fist bump," said Bedad.

Max punched his fist and then hugged Sally again. Everyone congratulated them.

Lissa's eyes lit up like stars. "A baby. That's so wonderful. I'm afraid it will be terribly spoiled by us all."

Sally laughed. "I always wanted my baby to have a big family."

Anastacia quietly took Bedad's hand and squeezed it. "That baby wouldn't have had a chance to live if you hadn't come for us. For me."

Bedad squeezed her hand in return and smiled. "Or if you hadn't taken them in."

They heard a knock at the door.

"I want to get this," Bedad said, letting go of her hand.

He opened the door a tiny crack, looked out, nodded, and then flung the door open.

Anastacia clapped her hands over her mouth and screamed.

Chapter Forty-One - Reunion

Her chest exploded with emotion as tears, again, ran down her face. She really was turning into such a girl. She threw herself toward the entering guests. How was this possible? Was there nothing Bedad couldn't do? Oh, she was going to smother him with kisses for this, not let him up for air for a week.

"Their eyes are exactly the same color," said Ellsworth, trying to be heard above the squealing and screaming.

"Anastacia said they are the same blue as Nicole's," said Bedad.

"I'm so happy to see you," said Jamail as he stepped forward.

Julie held her arms open and smiled.

Anastacia was disappointed at how little time Bedad had for her. Luckily, she and Julie had much to catch up on. Bedad spent most of his days, and some of his evenings, in the laboratory. Anastacia used the time for visits to the panther villages, Newman's Refuge and Alaric Place. Many villagers treated her with a reverence that made her uncomfortable.

During one visit, she watched a young woman with tawny hair and golden eyes, more human than panther, shoot arrows at a target.

"Care to try?" the woman said to Anastacia.

"Sure."

The woman introduced herself as Brindle.

Anastacia noted the difference in weight and tension in the bow. It was of simple construction, without pulleys. Most women from the Outworld would not be able to load this weapon. The resistance was too strong. Brindle watched her with a barely suppressed grin.

Anastacia suspected the girl thought she couldn't shoot it.

The first shot went wild, over the top of the target, and into the woods beyond.

"Don't worry," said Brindle. "The area beyond is marked out of bounds. You won't accidentally impale anyone."

Anastacia nodded and adjusted her stance. The second shot hit the outer top circle.

"Well, done!" cried Brindle.

With a grin, Anastacia replied, "I have a bow and arrow with my things. Let me fetch it, and you can try mine out."

So began a glorious competition. Anastacia felt her face flush with excitement. Here was someone she could challenge fairly.

By the end of that afternoon of shooting, she would have been hard pressed to say either one was superior to the other. They cleaned up and headed back toward the village.

Then Anastacia asked, "So, do you like to run?"

"I'm so close," Bedad kept saying. "It's the only thing you've ever really asked of me."

"Please," said Anastacia. "You saved my life and the lives of my family and friends. And children I care for. You owe me nothing."

"I want to do this for you."

"I don't need any more grand gestures. You've done enough."

Occasionally, Bedad left for several weeks, consulting with other wizards about his project. He did not ask Anastacia to travel with him, and she found these times dull and slow. She kept waiting for him to pop the big question. Then she could insist on going with him.

"Why don't you just ask him?" said Julie when Anastacia complained. "I always thought you went after what you wanted. Besides, we don't even know how proposals are done in his culture."

"You're right," said Anastacia. "I will ask him as soon as he gets back from this trip."

Sally named her son after Bedad, guaranteeing the child would be spoiled for life. Every time she heard his name, Anastacia felt a pang of loneliness. She couldn't imagine existence without Bedad. He was the first person she thought about when she had a question, or something to share, or felt depressed thinking about the Outworld.

But Bedad was gone longer than usual. As weeks became months, Anastacia's emotions ran from loneliness to anger to worry. It would be difficult to ask a man to marry you when you felt like wringing his neck.

Just when she was about to organize a search party, Bedad returned. He was whistling and had a twinkle in his eye.

"What are you so happy about?" she said. "Where have you been?"

"I went to see Daniel Moonwind. I've decided to stop my experiments."

"So will you have a life outside the laboratory now?" Anastacia asked, steeling herself for the big question.

"I plan on having a wonderful life outside the laboratory," said Bedad. "If you'll share it with me as my wife."

Anastacia opened and shut her mouth. He had deked her out.

"Well?" His eyes searched her expression.

"Yes. Yes! Of course." Anastacia threw her arms around him.

The thrilled-to-her-toes kisses were almost worth the time apart.

"Before that happens, will you accompany me to the Outworld?"

Anastacia shook her head no. She couldn't bear the thought of seeing her dying world again. What would be left? Who would be left?

"I think it will help you to feel better," he said.

"Why?" Her face was creased with pain.

"I want you to help me release a tiny little micro-organism into the water system."

Anastacia's eyes widened.

"It may take centuries to purify all the pollution," he said. "But I believe, in the end, the Outworld will recover."

Anastacia pressed a hand over her mouth to suppress a sob and nodded.

They left the next morning. They used the door that opened

up beside the pond in Thunder Bay. Most of the trees near the pool were dead or dying. No cormorants or ducks swam on the thick, dark surface. The pond plants had rotted into clumps. The grass was brown, and smelled of mold. Smoke choked the air.

"Is it too late?" Anastacia searched for any sign of life.

"Keep the faith." Bedad passed her a small vial. Inside, a glowing, green liquid churned. "You release it. It's my gift to you."

Anastacia knelt beside the pond and carefully poured the vial's contents into the murky water. The liquid glimmered on the surface, then it slowly swirled in ever widening circles. She looked up at Bedad, who nodded and smiled.

As they headed back to the door, she paused at an enormous zigzag-patterned footprint in the mud. It seemed fairly fresh. A familiar boot print. Huge as a hobbit's.

"Mr. Ferguson!"

"What?" asked Bedad.

Slowly, she picked up a small wooden item. A toothpick.

"Somewhere, somehow . . . ." She blinked back tears as she slid the toothpick into her pocket.

"What did you find?"

"Hope," said Anastacia.

She took Bedad's hand and turned toward the door to Dawn's End.

The End

About the Author

Learn more about Bonnie online at **BonnieFerrante.ca** or checkout her author page on Amazon or Goodreads.

Follow her on Twitter (**Bonnie Ferrante**) or Pinterest.

Connect on Facebook

Bonnie Ferrante - Author

Bonnie Ferrante - Books for Children